To

Lian

Kill the Devil

Best wishes

Tony Macaulay

KILL THE DEVIL

A LOVE STORY FROM RWANDA

Tony Macaulay & Juvens Nsabimana

Matador
Unit E2 Airfield Business Park,
Harrison Road, Market Harborough,
Leicestershire. LE16 7UL
Tel: 0116 2792299
Email: books@troubador.co.uk
Web: www.troubador.co.uk/matador
Twitter: @matadorbooks

ISBN 978 1803136 219

British Library Cataloguing in Publication Data.
A catalogue record for this book is available from the British Library.

Printed and bound in Great Britain by 4edge Limited
Typeset in 11pt Minion Pro by Troubador Publishing Ltd, Leicester, UK

Matador is an imprint of Troubador Publishing Ltd

This book is dedicated to all those who lost loved ones in the genocide in Rwanda and live with the memories every day.

Author Biographies

Dr Tony Macaulay is an author, peacebuilder and broadcaster from Belfast, Northern Ireland (www. tonymacaulayauthor.com). He has spent the past thirty-five years working to build peace and reconciliation at home and abroad. His memoirs of growing up in Belfast during the Troubles, *Paperboy (HarperCollins, 2011)*, *Breadboy (Blackstaff Press, 2013)* and *All Growed Up (Blackstaff Press, 2014)* have been critically acclaimed bestsellers in Ireland. His autobiography *Little House on the Peace Line (Blackstaff Press, 2017, 2nd Edition, so it is, 2022)* tells the story of how he lived and worked on the peace line in Belfast in the 1980s. His debut novel *Belfast Gate (so it is, 2019)* was Book of the Week in the *Irish News*. *Paperboy* was adapted into a hit musical by Andrew Doyle & Duke Special at the Lyric Theatre in Belfast in 2018 and 2019. In the summer of 2022, the same team produced a musical adaptation of the sequel, *Breadboy*, once again to sell-out audiences at the Lyric Theatre in Belfast. Tony has been a regular broadcaster on BBC Radio for the past twenty-five years and is a regular speaker on Northern Ireland, peacebuilding and creative writing at universities and colleges in Europe and the USA. In 2019, he was awarded an Honorary Doctorate by Ulster University for services to literature and peacebuilding at home and abroad. He coaches a youth empowerment project in the slums in Kampala, Uganda and is on the steering group developing a Rwanda Peace & Reconciliation Centre. It was on a visit to Kigali in 2017 that he met his co-author, Juvens Nsabimana.

Juvens Nsabimana is an author, screenwriter and film-maker from Rwanda (www.juvensnsabimana.com). He was born in the slums of Gikondo in Kigali and has been writing and telling stories since he was a child. To escape from the slums, at an early age he spent many hours every day in the cinema halls of Kigali watching films, learning about the art of storytelling and the different genres on the screen. This experience fired the imagination in his mind. Perhaps it was inevitable that grappling with words and language would become his chosen career. As a young man, he spent many hours in the libraries of Kigali, reading and learning. In early 2013, he started writing film screenplays and throughout his twenties he developed his career as a professional writer with poetry blogs, books and screenplays. *Kill the Devil* is his first novel.

Acknowledgements

Tony Macaulay: I want to thank my friend and peacebuilder Diane Holt, who first introduced me to Christophe Mbonyingabo, a truly inspiring leader of reconciliation in Rwanda. I am grateful to Christophe for hosting me in Rwanda and for educating and inspiring me through the remarkable reconciliation work of CARSA ministries. I want to thank my wife, Lesley, who has listened to every word of this book and offered honest feedback to improve the telling of this story. Finally, I want to thank Juvens for his hard work and commitment in this unique collaboration. His talent and resilience are an inspiration and I hope the publication of this book launches his international career as a writer.

Juvens Nsabimana: I want to thank my friend Colin Flinn from Northern Ireland who first introduced me to Tony Macaulay when he came to Rwanda. I have never met Colin face to face but our long-distance conversations between Africa and Europe are like sitting in the same living room. I want to thank Tony for his collaboration on this novel, his gift of a computer to write with and everything he helped me with on our journey of writing *Kill the Devil*. I am grateful to collaborate with the retired *Paperboy*!

CHAPTER ONE

All she wanted was peace. No more pain. No more hatred. An end to the despair ripping her heart apart. As she gazed across the vastness of Lake Kivu, her long white robe fluttered in the breeze, framing her elegance. The beauty of her face contradicted the harshness of her shaven head. Alone on the shore in the darkness, she was like a tiny light teetering on the edge of eternity. She noticed the beauty of soft moonlight glistening on the tranquil black waters. As the gentle lap of waves caressed her feet, she welcomed the stillness of the night. She knew what she wanted. She'd always known. Tonight, she wanted solitude and silence to be forever.

She remembered standing on this very spot watching her father cast nets for fish. Her mouth watered at the memory of the delicious *tilapia*[1] he caught and cooked on the shore. Many years ago, she sat here feasting on fish with her father, mother and older sister, laughing at her

---

1   *Tilapia* is a freshwater fish and a popular dish in Rwanda.

baby brother throwing fishbones to the otters. She inhaled deeply and imagined the smell of fish cooking on the fire. For a moment, her girlish sense of wonder returned as she noticed the lanterns of hundreds of fishermen twinkling across the expanse, like stars in a moonless sky. The distant sound of rhythmic singing, whistling and paddling seemed closer now, suggesting the nightly toil of the fishermen was near an end.

Lost in reflection, she had no sense of time passing until she began to notice the sensation of cold, wet sand between her toes. Suddenly she was startled by a rumble of thunder. She looked up and the moon was gone, concealed by clouds. Soon, beyond the shadows of the little island nearest the shore, she spied the elegant silhouettes of three-haul fishing boats with long eucalyptus rods attached to their bows and sterns. The fishermen were returning and time was running out.

Roused from her trance, she looked around the deserted shoreline. A smile flickered across her face as she recalled walking barefoot on the silt with Bernard. She ached for that perfect family day with a picnic on the shore and little Alice asking questions about the baby growing in her tummy. All joy was gone now, but this remained her place of peace.

Suddenly a flash of light in the sky illuminated the great mountains and volcanoes on the horizon. Now she understood the swift return to shore. She could hear the approaching fishermen singing traditional songs of courage in *Amashi*[2] as they fled the threatening thunderstorm.

2   A language in Rwanda and the Democratic Republic of Congo, traditionally spoken by Lake Kivu fishermen and their families.

Alert now, the anguish of loneliness returned. She closed her eyes and tried to dismiss any doubts that might divert her from this chosen path. She was determined in her belief that there was no love in her world. In one hand she held a bottle containing her handwritten, tear-stained goodbye. Perhaps one day someone would find it and remember her.

When she opened her eyes for a final look at the moon and the stars, they remained cloaked by dark clouds. A single thin tear trickled down her soft cheek. One last time, she asked God to embrace her. After ten years of praying for answers, she feared God was not listening. God was not there in 1994. Perhaps God had never been there. Raindrops began to dimple the water and spit on her face. Eyes wide open, she steadily walked forward into the cold, dark water, releasing the bottle from her hand and letting go of everything. All she wanted was an end to desolation. No more grief. No more anger. She was seeking rest and peace in the dark waters of Lake Kivu, but a storm was beginning to rage.

Chapter Two

'The deep waters were generous tonight!' said Eugene Karasira.

He raised his gas lantern to illuminate hundreds of small, silvery *isambaza*[3] leaping in the plastic buckets on the wooden deck.

'But the sky is not so kind,' replied his older brother, Migambi.

Hassan, the youngest of the three brothers, was standing still on the deck, transfixed by the view of forked lightning in the sky above the volcanoes of Congo in the far distance.

'Keep moving, Hassan!' shouted Migambi, pulling a plastic sheet over his shoulders. 'This is a time for respecting the power of nature, not admiring it!'

Hassan ran towards the other end of the boat to retrieve the nets. As lightning flashed and heavy rain began to

---

3   *Isambaza* are minnow-size fish that are attracted by the light
     from the lanterns of fishermen on Lake Kivu.

pour down, Migambi stood tall, paddling aggressively and steering the family fishing vessel towards the shore.

'Quick, Hassan! The nets are slowing us down!' called Eugene, now drenched with rain and paddling furiously to traverse the increasingly turbulent waters.

The thunder reverberated across the wooden deck as young Hassan hopped along the long protruding eucalyptus rod, like a tightrope acrobat, to gather in the remaining nets. With the safety of their mooring point in sight, they sped past the small island closest to the shore. For a moment, Eugene's lantern spotlighted a frightened vervet monkey, frantically jumping across the branches of a tree overhanging the lake. The startled monkey stopped and stared, wide-eyed at the sight of the passing craft.

'Go to sleep, little devil,' shouted Eugene. 'The storm has no respect for the likes of us!'

Migambi laughed and threw a plastic sheet towards Eugene as the rain pelted down on the boat.

'Almost there!' he cried.

Hassan managed to drag the last bulging net of fish into the boat but as the vessel rocked from side to side in the stormy waves, the catch spilled across the deck.

'Oh man!' cried Hassan. 'Come on, Eugene, give me a hand!'

'No, little brother, we must get to shore first. The storm is too angry,' Eugene replied.

Hassan leapt towards his brothers to seize a paddle and hasten their return to safety, but suddenly he stopped and froze. His eyes fixed on the surface of the lake.

'Oh my God!' he cried.

'What is it?' said Eugene.

'Look, there's a ghost in the water!' cried the teenager.

Hassan pointed at a body shrouded in white floating in the waves beside the boat.

'What are you talking about, little brother?' said Migambi. 'We are still awake. Your nightmares can wait!'

'I'm telling you. I see it!' cried Hassan. 'We must stop!'

'We cannot stop now!' cried Migambi. 'The nets are heavy and the storm has no mercy.'

'I think it's a person!' shouted Hassan, peering at the dark waters. 'We cannot leave them here. Some family will want to bury this body.'

'Keep paddling, brother,' cried Migambi. 'We must get this catch to shore. Our families will bury all of us if we don't!'

Eugene lowered his lantern towards the side of the boat where Hassan was pointing.

'Oh brother! It is a body. I can see it!' he cried.

'Keep going!' Migambi replied.

Hassan fell back into the boat, curling into a ball, shivering and whimpering. When he was six years old, he had seen scores of bloated bodies floating on this lake. The childhood trauma remained a part of him, his fears and his nightmares.

'Look, Migambi,' called Eugene, pointing towards the water, 'it is a body! We cannot leave them. It might be a brother fisherman. Paddle closer!'

Migambi relented and steered the boat close enough to the white object so that Eugene could reach out and touch it.

'It IS a person!' shouted Eugene. 'Throw me that net, quickly, Migambi!'

Eugene lowered the net into the choppy waters and, holding on to the side of the boat with one arm, he used his other arm to hook the body into the net. Migambi clambered towards the stern to help haul the body into the boat. Eugene lay back, soaking and shivering as Migambi removed the body from the net. Hassan remained locked in a foetal position on the deck under the bow, clasping his head and crying, as Migambi and Eugene examined their human catch.

'Oh my God! It's a woman!' said Eugene, shining the lantern on her face.

'It's a dead woman,' said Migambi.

'But she was still floating,' said Eugene.

'There's no time, brother,' said Migambi. 'Get paddling again or we will all be dead!'

'She was a beautiful woman,' said Eugene.

He tenderly touched her cold cheek with the back of his hand. The woman took a sudden breath and her body jolted. It was as if this touch of compassion had ignited a final spark of life.

'Quick, brothers!' yelled Eugene. 'She's alive! We must save her!'

The lightning flashed, the thunder roared and waves crashed across the deck, scattering buckets of leaping fish.

'We must save ourselves!' cried Migambi, bounding across the deck and dragging his youngest brother to his feet.

'Pull yourself together, Hassan! This final part of the return is going to be tough! We need all hands on deck! We might not make it!'

CHAPTER THREE

When Doctor Louise Uwimana was on night duty, a telephone call in the dead of night was often the signal of a serious incident on the lake. Within minutes, she was in the emergency room, buttoning up her white coat and preparing herself for whatever trauma might be on the way. Outside the room, three soaking fishermen burst through the doors of Gisenyi Hospital carrying a near lifeless woman on an improvised stretcher made with boat paddles and fishing net. Immediately, the patient was triaged by a team of nurses and rushed to the emergency room for urgent treatment.

'Looks like another attempted suicide on the lake, female, probably in her late thirties,' explained the nurse.

The doctor began to examine the woman.

'Vitals?' she enquired.

'Lungs clear now, blood pressure low, heart rate high, stable, Doctor Louise,' reported the nurse.

'Prepare oxygen, add saline drip and monitor,' said Doctor Louise, checking the woman's body for any signs of injury.

The nurse pointed to a large scar on the left side of the woman's lower back and Doctor Louise nodded.

'Machete,' she said.

The woman tightened her left hand into a fist, as if hearing this word had re-opened the wound.

'Next of kin?'

'We've no idea,' said the nurse. 'She was brought here by fishermen who, by chance, found her in the lake. They fished her out of the water with a net. Those men saved her life. They are waiting outside. The young boy is quite upset.'

'She's a very lucky woman,' said Doctor Louise. 'Few people survive the lake, especially on a stormy night like this. Someone up above must be looking after her.'

The woman opened her eyes, squinting in the harsh light of the emergency room.

'No one… is looking after me, no one,' she said.

'Well, I'm looking after you now,' said Doctor Louise, taking her hand.

The woman attempted to get up, but exhaustion and the lines to the monitors pulled her back on the bed like a puppet flopping from its strings.

'You must stay in the bed,' said the nurse. 'You must relax now, relax, please.'

Doctor Louise smiled and stroked the forehead of her patient.

'What is your name, beautiful woman?' she asked, gently cradling her shaven head in her hand.

The woman began to cry. Doctor Louise wiped the tears with her thumb.

'My name was Patricia. Uwera Patricia.'

'Do you live in Gisenyi, Patricia?'

'I left here many years ago.'

'Rest now, Patricia,' said Doctor Louise, 'you are alive and you will be well once more.'

As the doctor turned to leave, the patient replied.

'I do not wish to live,' she said, with a flash of anger in her eyes.

'Listen to me, my sister,' said Doctor Louise. 'I promise you will live long and be happy.'

'I do not wish to live,' said Patricia. 'Leave me alone, please.'

'Your family will be worried about you. Who shall we call to come and see you?' asked the nurse.

Patricia turned away and pulled the bedclothes close to her chin.

'I have no one,' she said.

'Are you married?' asked Doctor Louise.

'All gone,' replied Patricia.

'Have you any children?' asked the nurse.

'All gone,' whispered Patricia.

'What about your parents?' asked Doctor Louise.

'All gone, all gone… all gone…' Patricia repeated until her eyes closed and she drifted off to sleep.

Gently, Doctor Louise rested Patricia's head back onto the pillow and sighed deeply. The nurse shook her head and mopped Patricia's brow. Doctor Louise patted the nurse's back and walked out of the emergency room, determined to find out more about this mysterious woman.

CHAPTER FOUR

In the hospital corridor, the three fishermen were sitting on a bench, waiting for news. Hassan could tell by his eldest brother's loud sighs that he no longer wanted to be here.

'Why are we waiting here?' asked Migambi, yawning. 'If she lives or if she dies, there is nothing more we can do for her.'

Hassan shook his head at his brother's lack of empathy for the life he had just helped to save.

'Have some heart, Migambi,' said Eugene. 'She is someone's wife, someone's daughter, someone's mother.'

'We need to go home,' said Migambi. 'My own wife, daughter and mother will be worried that something has happened to me in the storm.'

Hassan shook his head again and plunged his hands into the pockets of his coat. He felt the shape of the bottle he had found on the lake shore and took it from his pocket.

'What's that?' asked Eugene.

'For years, I dreamt of finding one of these floating on the lake,' he said, 'and tonight, of all nights, I finally found a letter in a bottle.'

Hassan had often imagined discovering a mysterious note in a bottle. In his dreams, the contents would be a map with directions to find hidden treasure that would make him the richest man in Rwanda. In the midst of the drama of securing the boat on the shore in the storm, he had stopped momentarily to pick up the curious object for later examination.

'Well, don't keep us in suspense,' said Eugene. 'What does the letter say?'

Hassan carefully removed the scroll from inside the bottle, unfurled the stone-dry paper and began to read.

'Listen, my brothers,' said Migambi. 'Forget about dreams and nonsense. It's been a hard night for us. We should go home right now, before anyone here tries to charge us for her medical fees. We need to drink some *urwagwa*[4] and get some sleep!'

The three men looked up expectantly as Doctor Louise approached.

'Is she okay?' asked Eugene.

'Yes, she's alive,' said Doctor Louise. 'You saved her life. God bless you, brothers.'

Eugene and Migambi sighed with relief and shook hands. Hassan remained fixed on the note he was reading.

'Do you want to see her?' asked Doctor Louise.

Eugene smiled, nodded and got up, but Migambi held him back.

4   *Urwagwa* is an alcoholic beverage, popular in Rwanda, made from the fermentation of mashed bananas.

'But we don't even know her, Doctor,' said Migambi. 'We are just fishermen who found a poor soul in the water. We have to go. We have work to do. We've no money to pay for her treatment and we don't want to get involved.'

'Are you going back out onto the water now? In a storm? It's almost dawn,' said Doctor Louise, not hiding her disappointment.

'We just wanted to know if she survived,' said Migambi. 'We must go now.'

'But you registered this patient,' said Doctor Louise.

'She is a stranger and we have no money to pay for her treatment,' said Migambi.

'Let's go and see her,' said Eugene, grabbing Migambi's elbow. 'I want to see her open eyes. Every night, we have to risk our lives on the lake. I want to tell this beautiful woman to have courage and to hold on to her life.'

'We are fishermen, Karasira Eugene, not doctors or social workers,' said Migambi, bowing his head and covering his mouth with one hand as he spoke. 'How many extra buckets of fish will we need to fill to feed and look after this woman? We have families of our own to care for.'

'What do you think, little brother?' Eugene said to Hassan. 'You are the one who found her.'

'I am ashamed,' said the young man, holding the tear-stained letter in his hand.

Hassan had not been listening to the conversation because he was absorbed in the contents of the letter.

'What do you mean, Hassan, you saved a life tonight?' said Eugene.

'I've just read her note,' said Hassan. 'This is her letter, Doctor. It was in the bottle I found at the shore as we carried her from the boat. It is the story of her life and I am so ashamed.'

'Who is she? Why is she here?' asked Doctor Louise.

Hassan shook his head.

'Her name is Patricia Uwera,' said Hassan. 'She is a Tutsi woman and our people did this to her. Animals. Beasts. Worse than beasts. I am ashamed.'

'What are you talking about, little brother?' asked Migambi.

Hassan handed the letter to Doctor Louise, placed the bottle back in his pocket and walked out of the hospital doors, head down, as if in a trance.

'We can't just leave her!' said Eugene.

Migambi followed Hassan, shaking his head with confusion and guilt as he walked towards the exit doors.

'I'm sorry,' said Eugene, following his brothers and leaving Doctor Louise alone in the corridor, holding the note. She opened the folded paper and began to read it:

My name was Patricia Uwera. I was thirty-four years old when I died. I was a woman like any other. I had a husband who loved me and I loved him so much. I was a mother of two beautiful children – my sweet daughter, Alice, and my precious boy, Innocent. Every single day and night with my family was like heaven on earth. As a young woman, I used to see my bright future at every sunrise. But our ancestors did not lie. God really does spend the whole day working for other nations and only comes to Rwanda at night to sleep.

One night I will never forget, when God was deep asleep, as if dead, the Hutu Interahamwe[5] came for us. I lost my husband, my daughter and my baby son. I saw their blood flowing on the ground. After killing my family, they wanted me to die too. I survived but I wish I would have gone with my family. Every single day and night, I am suffering because of the evil of Hutus. I once had Hutu friends but they abandoned me. Now I know that most Hutus are devils and deserve nothing but death.

I do not deserve to live like this anymore and tonight I decided for myself to stop my heart from beating. I do not wish to live. As I leave this dirty world, anyone who finds this note and reads it should know the cause of my death. I never forgave any Hutu in life and I blame them for my death. May God awaken and avenge for me and every Tutsi.

---

5   The Hutu paramilitary group, who were the main perpetrators of the genocide.

CHAPTER FIVE

Patricia looked up and noticed a ray of light beaming through the simple stained glass window. She felt the sunlight warm her neck and caress her face. She noticed how the sunbeam was dancing on the beads of her dress, illuminating her. Today, she was shining and she felt blessed.

'For richer, for poorer…' said Father Jean, smiling.

She glanced over her shoulder and saw her mother wipe away a tear of joy with a pure white handkerchief.

'Beautiful, Momma,' she whispered as she admired the vivid colours of her mother's *umushanana*[6].

Her mother had spent weeks sewing this garment and a matching headdress for the special occasion. Patricia noticed her father was wearing his brand-new round spectacles for the first time and clutching the handle on his walking stick, both signs that he was getting older now. Papa looked professorial and proud as he stood tall in his

---

6   An *umushanana* is a traditional Rwandan dress often worn at weddings.

white suit, but he also donned the same wide-brimmed hat which protected him from the sun when tending his cows, including the new cows Bernard's father had just presented to him as a dowry.

'In sickness and in health…'

She looked over her other shoulder towards a sea of smiles. Everyone was there; her brother Albert and sister Amina, her aunts and uncles, and of course, Isabelle and Felice, her best friends from school, wearing matching *imishanana*. She could hear Bernard's younger brothers and sisters giggling in the pews, and his old school friend Damascene was there too with his little brother Kalisa, who was already dancing in the aisle.

'Forsaking all others…'

She felt Bernard squeeze her hand with his strong grasp and she looked up into the face of the man she loved. He looked so handsome in his wedding suit, not the usual attire of a farmer. When he pulled at the tight shirt collar around his neck, she remembered the day she fell in love with him in this very place, on the Easter Sunday he sang in the church choir for the first time.

''Til death us do part.'

Suddenly she felt a piercing pain at the base of her back.

She looked up and the stained glass window was shattered. It was 1994 and the sunlight was gone. There were rough gaps in the wall and the altar was broken in two where the grenades had exploded. Patricia began to gasp. She looked up at the lines of bullet holes across the sheet metal roof of the church. She turned around and saw the horror; piles of skulls and bones and clothes scattered

17

across the pews. She was overwhelmed with nausea. She saw her mother's headdress filthy and unfurled and her handkerchief sullied with dark blood. Her father's spectacles lay broken on the mud floor. She could smell the stench of blood and rotting flesh. She spotted Isabelle's best shoes curled up and sticking out of a pile of hundreds. Then she saw Felice, poor Felice, in a coffin at the back of the church with a spike still impaling her skeleton from the day of her murderous rape.

'Patricia,' said a kind voice in the distance. 'Can you hear me?'

Patricia spun around to see who had spoken but all around her was death. The church of her childhood, the place she met Bernard, her wedding day, the family and friends who died here and the Hutu devils that betrayed her.

'The fishermen have abandoned her. She's on her own now,' said another voice.

Patricia felt dizzy and nauseous, spinning around and around; with every turn, revisiting the screams, the blood, the bones, the skulls, the pain.

'I think she's coming round,' said the kind, distant voice.

Suddenly Patricia stopped moving and looked up. At the front of the church, Father Jean stood tall, blood dripping from his hands as he stood at the broken altar, laughing with delight and repeating, "Til death us do part.'

'Hutu devil!' she screamed, spitting in the face of the genocidal priest who had opened the doors of his sanctuary to the attacking militia.

'Kill the devil! Kill the devil!' she screamed.

She woke up and vomited across the bedsheets.

'Patricia, look at me. It's Doctor Louise,' said the kind voice.

Patricia wept and writhed on the bed for several minutes until she began to realise that she had been dreaming.

'You've had a nightmare, sister,' said the nurse.

Patricia took a deep breath and spoke calmly.

'No. I did not have a nightmare,' she said. 'I had a dream of my truth. My memories are worse than a nightmare.'

Doctor Louise held Patricia's hand and chose not to speak. This was not a time for words. Finally, Patricia broke the silence.

'I want to leave this place.'

'That's not possible,' said the nurse. 'It's the middle of the night.'

'I do not wish to be here.'

'She needs sedating,' said the nurse.

'I do not want your medicines,' said Patricia. 'I do not wish to live.'

'Patricia, you need some help and you will be all right,' said Doctor Louise. 'You are safe now and I promise you, everything will be okay. I will make sure of it.'

'Do not be kind to me,' said Patricia, weeping. 'Please, do not be kind to me.'

Doctor Louise leant forward and embraced Patricia, like a mother holding her distraught child. She rocked her back and forth and stroked her cheek, the same way she nursed her own children to sleep after a bad dream. In fact, it was the way she used to comfort her own husband when the trauma of his army days resurfaced in his nightmares.

'You are going to be okay, Patricia Uwera,' said Doctor Louise, 'I promise you. You are going to be okay.'

As Patricia drifted back to sleep, for a moment, she felt a tinge of something familiar but long forgotten. A feeling from the beginning of her dreams that always turned to nightmares. Perhaps it was kindness.

CHAPTER SIX

Louise Uwimana stared out through the grubby, steamed-up window. She never tired of the beauty of this landscape. She loved her land, with hill after hill after hill, each with a unique, colourful patchwork of plantations of bean, wheat, coffee and banana. Rwanda was known as the land of a thousand hills. Sometimes, she passed the time on this bus journey trying to count the number of hills between Lake Kivu and Kigali, but she never quite reached one thousand. She tensed when the driver accelerated to overtake ageing, heavy-laden trucks on the hairpin bends, but she smiled when the bus brushed past groups of children in clean, bright uniforms, holding hands and skipping along the side of the road on their way home from school. Louise knew every turn in the road and every gas station shanty.

Passing the genocide memorial sites in all of the villages, Louise often reflected on the horror that had unfolded in her country only ten years ago. One million people murdered in a hundred days. How did it happen? It was a terrifying nightmare. To Louise, the idea of enmity between Hutu and Tutsi made no sense. She didn't care who was taller or who was supposed to have a broader nose. When she fell in love with Jean Pierre, the fact that he was a Tutsi was a minor detail. She fell in love with the man, not a tribe. Her experience as a medical doctor reminded her on a daily basis of the reality of genocide and the continued suffering of the survivors. Even though ethnic differences meant nothing to her, at times, as a Hutu, she felt shame. Louise was a healer, not a killer, but she felt guilt that her people had committed crimes against humanity. Of course, in 1994, as a young woman, she was powerless to stop the killing. Sometimes, on these long bus journeys, she thought of the many good friends she had lost, and this fortified her dedication to use all her skills to help those who had survived.

The bus juddered as it climbed the steep inclines of the higher hills, past weary women carrying jerry cans on their heads and bold cyclists balancing heavy bags of flour on their backs. The ancient vehicle was crammed with sleepy commuters on their way from Gisenyi to the capital city. Every seat on the bus was taken. The woman sitting beside her rested her head on Louise's shoulder as she slept. When she was working night shifts at the hospital, Louise made this journey three times a week. A permanent job in a Kigali hospital was her goal, but opportunities were hard to come by and it seemed that older male doctors always made the front of the queue. On the three-hour journey, Louise used the time to decompress and reflect after the pressure of patients and procedures on the night shift. She needed to leave the stress behind in Gisenyi to be fully present for her family when she got home.

Suddenly the bus jolted as it swerved to avoid an elderly motorcyclist who was wobbling from side to side with scores of sugar cane strapped across his back. The woman beside Louise wakened with a start.

'Alice!' she cried.

'It's okay, Patricia,' said Louise, 'just the usual bumpy ride to Kigali.'

Patricia sat up and looked around to get her bearings. She had been dreaming of being in a hospital, cradling her baby girl. Bernard was visiting and they decided to name their newborn Alice after his great-grandmother, the dressmaker from Rugunga. When she realised she had been dreaming, Patricia felt a familiar deep rip in the depths of her abdomen. This time, reality was the nightmare and she longed to drift back into the beauty of her dream. Here she was on a bus home to her empty house in Kigali, far from her long-abandoned home in Gisenyi, accompanied by a kind stranger who had paid the bus fare.

'Thank you for being kind to me, Doctor Louise,' she said.

'You slept for three days, sister,' Louise replied, 'but your time to go home just happened to coincide with mine.'

'Thank you for looking after me and buying my bus ticket, but you know…'

'Yes, I know. We have talked many times in these past few days. You are going to say you do not wish to live,' said Louise, 'but you are a strong woman, Patricia. You survived genocide. You survived the past ten years. You survived Lake Kivu. You are a survivor.'

23

Patricia did not have enough energy to argue, and there was something intriguing about the doctor that comforted her. This educated woman did not know Patricia and she had no good reason to help her. She had been doing her job in the hospital, and she did not have to pay the bus fare and escort her home. This genuine compassion sparked a glimmer of hope within Patricia.

'Thank you, Doctor Louise. It is good to know there is some love in the world.'

'The world is full of love, Patricia, more love than hatred.'

'Not in my world, sister,' said Patricia.

'There is enough love in the world for all of us,' said Louise, 'and I believe God has saved you for a reason.'

'God abandoned me,' said Patricia. 'Three poor fishermen and you, kind doctor, saved me.'

Louise put her arm around Patricia's shoulder.

'Listen, Patricia,' she said, 'I promise you each day will get a little better. I'll take you home to Gikondo now and buy you some food. Then we can meet tomorrow afternoon at the park at the Cercle Sportif, near where I live in Kiyovu, and we can talk about the future.'

'No, Doctor Louise, you have done enough,' said Patricia. 'My bus stop is first and I can make my own way home.'

'I need you to promise me you will not harm yourself,' said Doctor Louise. 'I do not want all my work to be in vain.'

Patricia nodded and as the bus approached her stop, she stood up quickly. Louise offered her a bunch of notes contained in a tender handshake.

'No,' said Patricia.

'Yes,' said Louise. 'A little gift. For food. See you in the park, tomorrow at three.'

Patricia got off the bus and walked towards the busy market to buy some food. The friendly greetings and the vibrant colours of the fabrics on sale did little to cheer her. She fled to Kigali in 1995 to forget the horror in Gisenyi. She settled in Gikondo because the rent was cheap and there was work at the nearby market. It was an existence but it was a shadow of her former life. She had left all her dreams and ambitions behind. On the way to the market, she passed the alcohol store and paused outside for a moment, wondering if this was a better place to spend the money. On the steps of the store, a group of drunken men were listening to Congolese *soukous* music on a dusty cassette player. She could pay to drink to forget too, she thought. Then she remembered her sister, Amina, who was also cursed to survive the genocide. Amina had witnessed her family's massacre too. Over the next five years, Amina drowned the trauma with alcohol and died a slow, anaesthetised death. In her heart, Patricia blamed the Hutu devils as if they had cut Amina's throat with their bloody machetes. She remembered the day she found her sister's cold body. Amina had choked to death on her own vomit. Patricia shuddered at the memory and reminded herself that if she wanted to leave this world, she would do it with dignity. She put away thoughts of drinking away her life and used Louise's money to buy a bag of *posho* and some mangoes in the market. When she finally arrived back in her tiny, empty two-room house in Gikondo that night, she was too exhausted to do anything but sleep.

Chapter Seven

At 3.30pm the next day, there was no sign of Patricia. Sitting on a bench near the tennis courts at the Cercle Sportif, Louise waited and hoped. Children were practising tennis shots and dreaming of sporting glory. The sun was shining on happy families enjoying the cool waters of the swimming pool. Observing the joy in the faces of the children, Louise wondered how the horror of ten years ago could have happened here. On a day like this, it seemed unimaginable. She was convinced that it was hatred and division propagated in the decades before 1994, and not just the shooting-down of the presidential plane that finally led to the genocide. Eyes closed, lost in these thoughts and also enjoying the warmth of the sun on her face, Louise did not notice Patricia arriving and quietly sitting down beside her on the bench.

'Hello, kind Doctor,' said Patricia. 'Don't worry, I'm not going to throw myself into the swimming pool!'

Louise opened her eyes and smiled.

'I knew you would come,' she said.

'I came to say thank you, Doctor,' said Patricia, 'because you are a good woman.'

'I was just doing my job, sister,' said Louise, 'and I think you deserved a little kindness. How are you feeling today?'

'Do you really want to know?' said Patricia.

'You can be honest with me,' replied Louise, as a small group of playful children scampered past.

'When I awoke today in my empty house,' said Patricia, 'I lay in my bed and thought about all that has happened.'

'Yes?' said Louise, scanning Patricia's face for an emergence of hope.

'And I realised I still have no reason to live.'

Louise took Patricia's hand.

'There is always something to live for, Patricia,' she said, nodding towards the boys playing tennis.

'On the surface, all looks well today, Doctor, but how many of those boys are "the children of bad memories"?' asked Patricia. 'Born nine years ago of mothers raped by Hutu devils and infected with HIV?'

Louise hadn't thought of it this way and as she looked around at the children playing and laughing in the park, she realised Patricia's grim assumption was a possibility.

'Children bring us hope, Patricia,' she said.

'It is good to have children,' said Patricia, 'but there is no greater pain than to lose your children.'

Patricia spoke with resignation and without tears. Her children were only memories now. Just a lovely dream from a time long gone. The two women sat in silence watching the kids playing tennis until Louise turned to Patricia and took her other hand as well.

'I lost a child too,' she said.

'Oh no!' said Patricia.

'But not like you, Patricia. For two years after the genocide, I looked after a group of orphans whose parents had been murdered. I loved those kids. They still stay in touch with me to this day. Eventually, we found homes for all of them, but then I began to long for children of my own. Jean Pierre and I were so excited when I was expecting our first baby. But, Patricia, my firstborn died at the same hospital where I worked. It was pneumonia. The treatment was not good like today. I was there with other doctors treating my own baby, day and night. I was with her until the last breath. She was beautiful. She was my blood. She was not yet one year old. She was so small and she died in my arms.'

'I am sorry, Louise,' said Patricia. 'What was her name?'

'Her name was Josephine,' said Louise, wiping tears from her eyes.

'My little girl was called Alice,' said Patricia, 'and my baby boy was…' she stopped and caught a breath, as if saying his name caused a piercing pain '… my baby boy was Innocent.'

The two women embraced and Patricia felt strangely safe. It was a long time since Patricia had felt safe.

'I spent the next two years without a child,' said Louise. 'I thought I would never be able to have children.'

'I do not understand why God allows the worst things to happen to good people,' said Patricia.

Louise turned to Patricia, taking both of her hands and looking straight into her face.

'Patricia,' she said, 'there is day after night and light after darkness. Today, I have two children, Kevin and Ngabo.'

'Kevin and Ngabo?' said Patricia. 'Two boys? That's wonderful! I would love to meet them.'

'They are a blessing,' said Louise.

'All my blessings are gone,' replied Patricia. 'Stolen from me by Hutu devils.'

She turned her face away.

'Patricia?'

'Yes, madam?'

'Those Hutu fishermen who rescued you from the lake are heroes, not devils.'

Patricia shook her head but Louise continued.

'And when I first saw your beautiful face, I was determined that you would live. Please tell me. Why do you still want to die?'

'Do you really want to know my story?' asked Patricia. 'It is a heavy burden you may not want to carry.'

'Yes,' said Louise, 'tell me what happened. I am here for you.'

Patricia shook her head and sighed, then looked into Louise's eyes.

'Are you sure?' she asked. 'I have never told anyone my story before.'

Louise nodded.

Patricia looked up at the sky and closed her eyes. Then, wiping a tear from her eye, she took a deep breath and began to share her story for the first time.

CHAPTER EIGHT

'It was the night of 6th April 1994. Bernard had been repairing the roof of our house all day. It was always leaking after a storm. By nine o'clock, Alice was in bed sleeping and I was feeding Innocent when my dear friend Felice came running into our house in a panic. She told us the president had been killed and the Interahamwe commanders in Gisenyi were blaming Tutsis and telling crowds of Hutu men to go out and kill all Tutsis. They ordered the men to spare no one. Felice said they had already started killing Tutsis in Kigali. Hutu men from all the villages in Gisenyi were joining with the militia. We could not believe it. Our worst fears had come true. Bernard said not to panic, as our Hutu friends would protect us and we could escape to Congo.

'The killing started the next day. Everyone started to hide or flee from the attacks. When we left our home, I could not believe my eyes. I saw gangs of men with machetes roaming the streets. Carrying Innocent on my back, I covered Alice's eyes with my hands as Bernard worked out the best route to safety. The army and the Interahamwe were everywhere. They set up roadblocks, checking identity cards, and no Tutsi was permitted to pass. We decided it was safer to return home until Bernard could find a way out. He left with his brother to look for a safe route, but they were separated at a checkpoint where militiamen were hacking women and children to death. Many of our friends tried to escape through the forest but the Hutu devils hunted them. When Bernard returned to the house, he said there were hundreds of dead bodies piled beneath the trees. He was in shock at the blood, the screams, the dead bodies everywhere. Oh my God!'

Patricia paused for the first time, but just for a second. She was recounting a story she had replayed in her mind for ten years. It was as if a dam of memories had burst.

'The National Gendarmerie told Bernard's other brother and sisters to go to the Red Commune near the Ruliba cemetery, at the foot of Mount Rubavu. My aunts and uncles fled there too with all of their children. The Gendarmerie assured them the Mayor had said it would be a place of safety. The Mayor was my uncle's friend so he trusted him. But it was a trick by those Hutu devils to round up as many Tutsis as possible. When they arrived at the Red Commune, all were killed and thrown into a giant pit in the ground. They even killed a Hutu nun there. After nightfall, Sister Felicita was helping Tutsis escape across the border on paths she knew into Congo. She helped my little brother, Albert, to escape. But those devils captured that courageous woman and the people she was hiding and took them to the commune. Her own brother was the commander. Good and evil in the same family. They forced her to watch the murder of the people she had been hiding. Then they killed her too and dumped her in the pit like rubbish.'

'That is terrible, my sister! Take a breath now. Are you sure you want to continue?' said Louise.

'I cannot stop,' said Patricia.

She took a deep breath and continued.

'My sister and her husband tried to hide in the marshes with many others. They lived like wild pigs, drinking swamp water and crawling in the slime. But eventually the hunters with machetes discovered them. Most of those poor souls were murdered in the mud. Amina survived by pretending to be dead as her dying husband lay on top of her.

'My father came to our house and begged me to follow him and my mother to find refuge in the church. He said we would be safe there because the church had always been a place of sanctuary and God would protect us. Bernard began to gather our most precious belongings and I packed food and clothes to take with us to the church. Isabelle and Felice went ahead with my parents, and hundreds of our friends and family crowded into the sanctuary. But once the church was full of people, before Bernard and I arrived with the children, Father Jean, yes, our parish priest, the man who married us, the one who baptized our children, that Hutu priest of the Devil opened the gates to the militia, and, oh my God, Doctor... they attacked our families with grenades and guns and machetes. They killed everyone. They raped the women in front of their children in a church! They slaughtered everyone in front of the altar, beneath the cross of Christ! And poor Felice, oh my God...'

At this point, Patricia stopped, shaking her head and then holding her head in her hands for a few minutes. But she was not finished. The floodgates had opened.

'Oh, Louise, it was terrible in those days. The shouts and screams, the blood, the hatred in the eyes of Hutu men I had known all my life, raping their friends' wives, butchering whole families like ferocious hyenas, throwing infants to the ground, the look of terror on the faces of the little children… I'm sorry, Doctor Louise, I must stop, it is too much for you,' said Patricia.

Louise was sobbing now as she embraced her trembling friend.

'I went back to the church only once. It's a memorial site now. I looked at the piles of skulls, hoping to recognise my family from their teeth, but it was impossible. There were too many skulls, so many bones and clothes and shoes and Bibles, piles of them…'

As Patricia's mind drifted to her memories of the church, she paused again. The two women held each other close. They cried together, cheek to cheek, Hutu and Tutsi tears flowing together on their faces.

'I'm so sorry,' said Louise, 'I feel shame.'

'No, Doctor, you are no devil,' said Patricia. 'They killed good Hutus like you too.'

'I remember the screams,' said Louise. 'We hid away for weeks. I cannot forget seeing all of the dead bodies decomposing under the papyrus or dried out in the sun. We were the lucky ones. So many friends gone, whole families, and I do not know what happened to most of them. It's okay, Patricia, please stop if this is too painful.'

'But I must continue,' said Patricia, composing herself once more. 'I must tell you my story. You need to know why I do not wish to live. I have to tell my truth.'

For the first time, Patricia was telling someone her story, and once she had begun, she could not stop.

'Take your time, sister,' said Louise.

CHAPTER NINE

'We decided to go back to our home. There was nowhere else to go. There was danger everywhere. Every way out was cut off. Bernard gathered timber from the farm and nailed it across the windows and doors of our house. I remember the sound of the hammer on the nails and the sound of gunfire outside. I tuned into RTLM radio. They had been spreading hatred for months. The presenter said there remained Tutsis in our area who had not yet been killed. He directed that roadblocks be reinforced so no one would escape. Then they played that hate-filled song, encouraging them to exterminate us:

"IYee Tubatsembe tsembe.

IYee Tubatsembe tsembe.

IYee Tubatsembe tsembe."

'I told Alice we were playing a hiding game and she must be very quiet. Innocent was fast asleep in spite of the banging and shooting. Bernard kept watch through a small gap in the barrier at the front door. I kept an eye on the back of the house through a gap in the timber across the window.

35

'I saw them first. A mob of devils. The Interahamwe were searching the houses nearby. They had machetes, clubs and knives. They were shouting and dancing as if they were drunk in their lust for blood. I had never seen men like this before. It was as if the Devil was alive within them. I recognised their leader, Sylvestre, wearing a sash of bullet cartridges, and his friend Claude. They were Hutu extremists from the next town. I knew they hated us. For many years, they had told Hutus that Tutsis were going to do this to them! But all along it was them wanting to do it to us!

'I could feel Alice's thin little body shaking. Bernard switched off the lights and that evil radio station and I held Alice and Innocent close to my breast.

'"Mama, why are men shouting?" asked Alice.

'"Shhh, little one, they are drunk and dancing," said Bernard, placing his forefinger on her tiny lips.

'As we peeked out through the door, we saw a familiar figure with the Interahamwe. He was talking to that wicked shit Sylvestre and pointing out all of the Tutsi houses. We could not believe our eyes. It was Bernard's friend, Damascene Hakizimana. His friend from childhood, the friend he chewed sugar cane with as a teenager, the friend he played football with as a young man, the same friend he had farmed mangos with this year. Damascene had joined the devils! He was helping them find Tutsis to kill and he was carrying a club in his hand. We looked at one another. We dared not speak. We did not want to frighten Alice or make any noise that would draw attention to our home. But as we looked into each other's eyes, we saw hope disappear. Bernard was stunned and fell back from the door. Outside, the Interahamwe shot bullets into the air. Innocent woke up and began to cry.

"'Papa, what's going on?" asked Alice.

"'Damascene will not betray us. He is my friend," said Bernard.

'I will never forget the look of panic and disbelief on my dear husband's face. He took Alice's hands and spoke to her.

"'My little one, you are safe with Mama and Papa. Everything will be all right. Okay?"

'My precious Alice nodded and Bernard kissed her, for the last time.

"'Hide in the box in the kitchen," said Bernard.

'We had planned this. I would hide in the wooden box in the corner of the kitchen and Bernard would defend us.

'The rest, Louise, is too awful.'

'That's okay, I know,' said Louise. 'You have told me enough.'

But Patricia could not stop talking.

'Even from inside the box, I could hear them talking outside our house.

"'Give me the fucking list, Damascene," I heard Sylvestre shout.

'Then I heard Damascene, my husband's so-called friend, betray us.

"'Next is Bugingo Bernard and Uwera Patricia. They are Tutsi. This is their house."

'Alice was holding me tight and Innocent would not stop crying. I prayed to God the sound of his cries were muffled by my embrace within the box.

'Then it started. Big stones smashing at the door and the windows. Then silence. Bernard remained still.

'Sylvestre banged on the front door, shouting, "Bernard and your wife, Patricia! We know you are inside and you know we are here to do our work. We have worked hard hunting other snakes like you!"

'The other men cheered.

'"We are getting tired now. So, help us out and kill your children. We don't need cockroaches in the next generation. When you're done, throw their bodies outside and then kill yourselves. You have five minutes."

'There were more cheers. They expected Bernard to execute his family and then to kill himself.

'Bernard came to the box and took me and the children in his arms. He held us so tightly we were like one person. Oh, Louise, I never felt his touch again.'

For the first time while telling her story, Patricia broke down completely. She sobbed uncontrollably. Louise stroked her face and her hair, to try to comfort her. Louise was sobbing too. She felt so much pain and sorrow from Patricia's broken heart. The two women sat on the bench sobbing and embracing as children continued to run past, playing in the park. When the tears stopped flowing, Patricia sat upright and quietly and dispassionately finished her story, as if it was happening that day.

'They start shooting at the house. They break down the door. I hear a single shot in the living room. I hear my husband fall to the floor. Claude opens the box and drags us out. His breath smells of beer. There is blood on his hands. He hits me on the back with his machete, and other men pull my children from my arms. The pain in my back is excruciating.

'"You think a cockroach can escape from a predator like me? Eh…?" says Claude.

'He stands on my hand and pours beer on my face. I am lying there, bleeding, looking for my children, hearing their screams and cries. I hear the men cheering and Damascene is standing there with a club with nails, laughing with them. He does not look me in the eye. Louise, I watch as that devil Sylvestre strikes my beautiful Alice with his cold, sharp machete. He cut my angel. She falls to the ground like a little lifeless doll. Innocent is crying and that wicked monster Claude lifts my baby and throws him against the wall. No more crying. Innocent is gone. My children are on the floor, dead beside me. I cannot move. I feel warm blood on my back. I feel I'm dying. The mob leaves, celebrating as they go. But Claude remains. He turns me over and… and… says, "Not even worth raping!" He spits on me and runs away with the other devils, leaving me bleeding, surrounded by the blood of my family.'

Finally, Patricia stopped speaking. Louise held her close and they sat in silence. In the past ten years, Louise had heard many stories of the genocide, but she had never heard a story told so intimately, with all the detail of the horror and brutality a loving family had suffered. Patricia rested against Louise on the park bench and, exhausted, she fell asleep. The sun was still shining, the children were still playing, and Patricia, in spite of everything, was still here and still breathing. Louise lost track of time and when she finally looked at her watch, she realised two hours had passed. It was quiet in the Cercle Sportif now and the sun was going down. Patricia raised her head from Louise's shoulder.

'Now you understand my nightmares,' she said.

'Your story is worse than all of my nightmares,' Louise replied. 'The wickedness that wounded you is hard to imagine.

'I'm sorry, so sorry,' she added.

Louise felt her words were weak and useless.

'After ten years, I still see one man in my memory,' said Patricia.

'Which man? Sylvestre or Claude?' asked Louise.

'No, not them. Those two men are in hell now where they belong. Sylvestre got the death sentence and was executed in public in 1998. I saw him shot in the head the same way he shot my Bernard. I felt nothing. Claude fled to Congo, but my little brother found him there and got our revenge. Albert never told me what he did to him, but he says he made him suffer for what he did to me and my children.'

Louise raised her eyebrows but no further detail was forthcoming.

'No, the man I see most clearly in my memories is Damascene, my husband's friend. He betrayed us and then he ran away to escape justice. He got away with it. My brother told me he was seen in Kigali after the genocide. He dare not show his face in Gisenyi. That man is a coward and a traitor. Damascene didn't pull the trigger or wield a machete that day, but he is responsible for the murder of my family.'

Louise was thoughtful for a few minutes. Then she stood up, took Patricia's hand and they walked towards the bus stop.

'Would finding Damascene, and bringing him to justice, for the sake of Bernard and your children, give you something to live for?' asked Louise.

Patricia nodded.

'I want him to look into my eyes and see what he has done,' she said.

'My husband is a police officer,' said Louise. 'I will talk to him. I will try my best to make sure this man is caught. He will be punished for his crimes. I promise you, Patricia, he will go to prison. You will have justice.'

'Doctor Louise,' replied Patricia, 'for me, the only justice is to kill the devil!'

CHAPTER TEN

On the same day, just a few miles away, in a small house in Kimironko, Kalisa was dancing as usual.

'Please, little brother, no more Michael Jackson!'

'I do the best moonwalk in Kigali!' replied Kalisa.

To prove the point, he moonwalked brilliantly into Damascene's bedroom, with his ghetto blaster on his shoulder, while singing along to *Bad* at the top of his voice. There was barely enough floor space to walk, never mind dance, because Damascene's bedroom was in disarray. Unfolded clothes and pairs of shoes were scattered across the floor. Damascene was busy rummaging through his wardrobe, trying to choose the right clothes to pack into a single large suitcase sitting on his bed.

'The sooner you find a girl and go off and get married, the better,' he said. 'You can dance with her in every room, all day long, when you have your own house.'

'Ah, but you would miss me, big brother, and my contribution to the rent! And you have not married either.

Admit it! You know you would be lonely without me!' said Kalisa.

He fast-forwarded the CD, got down on his knees and started mocking his brother with another Michael Jackson song: '*You are not alone…*'

Damascene shook his head and turned his back on his brother.

'Will you ever grow up?' he said, as he continued to stuff trousers and shoes into the bulging suitcase.

'*You are not alone…*'

'You're not a child anymore, Kalisa. Stop acting like one. You're twenty-five years old now,' said Damascene.

'*You are not alone…*'

Kalisa turned up the volume and continued singing along until Damascene snapped and snatched the ghetto blaster from his brother and switched it off.

'You know you're not leaving, don't you?' said Kalisa. 'You never do.'

'I can't stay here!' said Damascene.

'How many times have I heard you say that, brother? How many times have you packed this suitcase? But you never leave, Dammy. You know you must stay here with me. Just be happy, brother, just like Bobby McFerrin always says!'

Damascene stopped packing, sat down on top of a pile of clothes on the bed and put his head in his hands. Kalisa lifted the ghetto blaster back onto one shoulder, pressed a few buttons and continued singing and dancing, this time to *Don't Worry, Be Happy*.

'So fucking stupid!' shouted Damascene.

Kalisa's efforts to lighten the mood had clearly failed. Damascene hurled the suitcase onto the floor and kicked

43

it across the room. Kalisa set down the ghetto blaster and started to pick up the clothes that had spilled out across the floor.

'I need to move from here,' said Damascene, spinning around before sitting down on the bed again with his head in his hands.

Kalisa turned off the music, left the bedroom and came back a few moments later with a large glass of beer for his brother.

'We've been through all this before, Dammy,' he said. 'Where would you go?'

'Congo, Tanzania, Burundi, somewhere, anywhere?' said Damascene.

'Are you crazy, brother? Drink your Primus and all your troubles will disappear.'

Damascene took a long drink of beer, but he knew by now that alcohol didn't work. It only made him feel better for a while. Kalisa sat down on the bed beside his brother. For years, it had been just the two of them. Damascene was like a father as well as an older brother. All Kalisa wanted was for his brother to be happy and free.

'Let me tell you something, one more time,' he said. 'They are not going to find you. It's been ten years. No one knows you here in Kigali. We are a long way from the people of Gisenyi, and I bet most of your accusers are still refugees in other countries.'

Damascene continued to shake his head in despair.

'Listen, brother, the government is hunting in those countries you keep talking about fleeing to. What if you go to Burundi and they find you there?'

'I know,' said Damascene.

'So let us keep working hard and saving our money and then we can fly far away to the USA and disappear, and maybe even hang out with Bobby McFerrin.'

Damascene sighed and nodded.

'You are so stupid, my little brother,' he said, 'but sometimes you can be a little wise at the same time.'

'I'm like Michael Jackson,' he replied, 'I'm bad!'

Damascene could not stop himself laughing. He often wondered how such a joyful kid had survived growing up through terrible times. He patted his brother on the shoulder, gently. The brothers sat quietly on the bed and shared a few more glasses of beer.

'Anyway, let me ask you something I've never asked you before,' said Kalisa. 'Why did you do it?'

Damascene thought for a moment and then he held up his glass full of beer.

'You see this glass?'

'Hmm.'

'The glass was Rwanda. The good beer is the Hutu people. The foam at the top is the Tutsis. Our leaders taught us we did not need Tutsi people lording over us at the top. We should not be demeaned by them anymore and never fear them again.'

He poured some beer from the top of the glass, spilling it onto the floor.

'What we had to do was pour out the Tutsis.'

Kalisa shook his head.

'Brother, I can tell that you don't even believe that old rubbish,' he said. 'It sounds like something that idiot Sylvestre used to say in the cabaret in Gisenyi. I'm sorry, but you were the stupid one. Did you really think you

45

could kill all Tutsis? Did you ever really believe that was possible?'

'I am wondering,' said Damascene.

'The men you thought were our greatest patriots are now dead or world-famous criminals!' said Kalisa. 'Do you regret it?'

Damascene gulped down the rest of the beer.

'Yes, of course I regret it. I betrayed my closest friends. I watched them die. I see them in my dreams every night. I attacked strangers with a club of nails too. So many, I can't remember how many. So much blood.'

'But you were an educated man. How could you allow people to take a machete to butcher a human being?'

'Too much politics. Too much loyalty to my people, little brother,' said Damascene. 'Too much fearing what others would do to us and believing too much in the words of powerful men. Too much hatred and madness. Too much, too much. You were lucky to be a child, busy playing football with balls made of banana leaves and your silly dancing and dreaming of being an American superstar. I was ordered to betray my Tutsi friends first, and after that, they said, killing a stranger would be easy. It was true but it was wrong.'

The brothers sat in silence.

'But, what else could I have done? I had no choice,' said Damascene. 'I am a victim too, and what about all the people they killed afterwards? I am telling you, little brother, I did what any man would do. I am not guilty and I will never surrender.'

CHAPTER ELEVEN

'Louise, my love, it's time to get up,' whispered Jean Pierre.

Louise rolled over in bed to check the time on the clock on her bedside table. Warm sunshine touched her face through the light net curtains. She was still tired and felt so comfortable, so she turned over in the hope of a few more precious minutes of sleep. After weeks of working night shifts at the hospital, the nights at home in her own bed never seemed long enough. Jean Pierre was already up and dressed in his police uniform. The wife and husband juggled their work shifts and, along with Louise's mother, took turns to look after the children. Today, it was Louise's turn to stay at home. She looked forward to these special days with Kevin and little Ngabo, but sometimes she was so exhausted that she dreamed of another few hours in bed. The idea evaporated as soon as the children burst into the bedroom.

'Good morning, Mama!' cried the boys, jumping up onto the bed.

'I've given them breakfast,' said Jean Pierre, handing Louise a cup of coffee. 'You'd better hurry or they will have eaten everything!'

'Oh, children, have you finished your breakfast?' asked Louise.

'You love bed, Mama, and we love food. Next time, we will finish all the food before you wake,' said Kevin.

Louise and Jean Pierre laughed.

'Okay, Papa's going to work now. You can go and play in the garden for a while,' said Louise.

The children hugged their father and disappeared in a whirlwind of energy in the direction of the garden.

'They are more demanding than a night shift at the hospital and the police station put together!' joked Jean Pierre.

Louise got up and examined her face in the mirror, checking for any creeping signs of age. Jean Pierre noticed a sadness on her beautiful face.

'Is there something wrong, my love?' he asked.

'Yes, Jean, remember the woman who almost drowned in Lake Kivu?'

'Of course,' said Jean Pierre. 'She was very lucky to survive. Saved by fishermen and the best doctor in Rwanda!'

'I met her again yesterday and she told me her story,' said Louise.

'Oh, my love, what have I told you about getting too involved in the lives of your patients?' said Jean Pierre. 'You can't save everybody.'

'But she told me her story, Jean,' said Louise. 'It was awful. The genocide. Her husband. Her children. She suffered so much.'

'Like many, many thousands, my love. I remember it well. How could I forget? And I see trauma every day too, but you can't help them all,' said Jean Pierre.

'I know, but if I can help one person, that will make a world of difference to her,' said Louise. 'She is a beautiful woman, all alone. She has lost hope, Jean. I saved her life, and I don't want her to lose it again.'

'Well, you cared for her in the hospital,' said Jean Pierre. 'You paid her bus fare back to Kigali and you listened to her story. Help her to connect with IBUKA or AERG or one of the other survivor funds that help widows of the genocide, and they will look after her. What more can you do?'

'I need your help, Jean Pierre,' she replied.

'My help?'

'Yes, I need you to find a perpetrator. The man who betrayed her. The man who haunts her dreams.'

'Really?' said Jean Pierre. 'Where is he?'

'She doesn't know what happened to him. He might be in prison, he may have fled the country, but he could be living free in the community somewhere in Rwanda.'

'What is his name?'

'She said his name is Hakizimana Damascene.'

'Okay,' said Jean Pierre, kissing Louise before starting to leave. 'Hakizimana Damascene. I will check in work today. I can look through the lists of names spoken in testimonies by the survivors in the Gacaca courts[7] and see if he shows up anywhere.'

'Jean Pierre!' called Louise as he reached the door,

---

7   Community courts used to clear the backlog of genocide cases.

'please help me to help her. Maybe her soul will… will be free, if she finds out that he faced justice and is in jail.'

On the way to the police station, Jean Pierre recalled the years he preferred to forget. He knew he could tell his wife anything, but he never shared the details of what happened to him as a boy when his family fled to Burundi with thousands of other Tutsis. Louise was also unaware of the brutality her husband experienced in 1989 as a teenager when he travelled to Uganda to join the Armée Patriotic du Rwanda. The horrors Jean Pierre witnessed and the pain he inflicted when returning to Rwanda as part of the liberating Rwanda Defence Force in 1994 were memories he promised himself he would never share with his wife and children. In spite of the nightmares, he decided that these memories must remain buried and forgotten, like so many people in this broken land.

When he arrived at his office, Jean Pierre could not remember making the journey through the morning rush-hour traffic in Kigali. He picked up the phone and called Louise.

'Okay, my love,' he said, 'I will do it. I will find Hakizimana Damascene. It is my job.'

CHAPTER TWELVE

'No, thanks, madam,' said Damascene, head down, eyes averted, declining an offer of fresh beans.

He was at Kimironko market to buy bananas, *manioc* and potatoes for the week ahead. Damascene's dark mood contrasted with the brilliant colours of fruit and fabric surrounding him. He felt he must be vigilant here. He dare not allow his senses to be seduced by the smells and sounds of the market. For Damascene, there was no more relaxing, no more enjoying. Over the past decade, he had honed his skills in staying under the radar in a high-risk public location. He scanned the face of each man arriving on bicycles and motorcycles, their backs piled high with sugar cane and bags of flour. He listened for the accents of the women competing for the attention of passersby to claim their mangos and avocados as the freshest produce and the best price. He tuned out the joyous sound of laughing children, playing games at the feet of the adults, oblivious to the commerce happening above. Damascene looked around the market shiftily. He

51

constantly feared being recognised but Kalisa refused to do all the shopping and they had to eat. Damascene rarely spotted a familiar face from the past in the busy streets of Kigali, but the fear of being identified as a *génocidaire* was paralysing.

An angry woman shooed away a hungry dog from her poultry stall and it sniffed at Damascene's bag of bananas.

'Go away! Go!' he shouted, and kicked the skinny dog. It ran away yelping with its tail between its legs.

He skirted the stalls on the periphery of the market until he found a seated old man selling *manioc*. He quickly purchased a supply for the week. He had almost completed his clandestine shopping expedition when he spotted a new potato seller in a remote corner of the market. He did not want to be known here, so he was always on the lookout for new sellers. As he walked across the market towards the stall, he felt the strained plastic handles of the heavy bags force furrows into his hands.

'Welcome, sir,' said the woman selling potatoes, without looking up.

'Ahh... Thank you,' replied Damascene. 'How much for a kilo of potatoes?'

'It's 120,' she answered.

'Give me two kilos, please.'

The woman weighed out the potatoes.

'Give me your bag, please, sir,' she said.

Damascene opened one of his plastic bags and she placed the potatoes inside, looking up at his face for the first time.

'How are you, sir?' she asked.

'Am good, madam,' he replied. 'You're new here?'

'Yes, she replied, 'I moved here from Gisenyi last month with my family.'

Damascene tensed immediately. He attempted to look unperturbed, but his fists clenched around the handles of his bags.

'Gisenyi? I have never been in Gisenyi', he said. 'I believe it is near the beautiful Lake Kivu. I would like to visit one day.'

This was the response he had prepared many years ago for any encounters of this kind. However, something about the swiftness of Damascene's reply caught the woman's attention. She stopped counting out his change and looked at him more intently.

'I am from Gasiza, Bushiru,' she said, now observing Damascene's reaction closely.

'I am from Ki… Kigali,' replied Damascene. 'Us city boys don't get to travel much.'

'That's not a Kigali accent. You sound more like me than a city boy!' she said.

Damascene did not want to speak again. The woman's eyes narrowed. A memory of a terrible story flickered in her mind. A flash of recognition crossed her face. She pulled back the plastic bag and took back her potatoes.

'What's wrong?' asked Damascene.

'Get away from me!' she said quietly. 'There are many filthy dogs in this market today. But I remember you, and you are the filthiest dog in this place.'

Damascene felt his heart thumping in his chest.

'Have I not paid you correctly?' he asked, attempting to appear innocent.

His mouth dried up and beads of sweat dotted his brow.

'I know what you did,' she said. 'Stop your pretending. I say go now or I make a noise right here, right now. Take your money and get out of my sight!'

The woman threw his money back on the ground and spat at Damascene's feet.

'I know who you are and I know what you are! You are the one who betrayed his Tutsi neighbours to the machete men!'

Damascene did not pick up the cash but panicked and walked away, nonchalantly at first, but then faster and faster, with his head down. Then he began to run, past the clothing and charcoal stalls, bumping into several people on the way. In his haste, he pushed into an elderly Twa woman who was carrying a large bag of avocados. She lost grip of her shopping bag and the avocados spilled out across the ground.

'Sorry!' he cried, head down and moving on.

Passersby shook their heads in disgust at the recklessness of this man who didn't even stop to help an old woman pick up the contents of her bag. Dashing towards the street, Damascene almost collided with a pedicab, stacked with bags of beans.

'Fuck you, man!' shouted the driver.

Damascene just wanted to flee. This was the day he had feared for years. This nightmare of his future was just as powerful as his worst nightmares about the past. When he got to the street, he began to sprint, spilling fruit and vegetables out of his bag and into the red dust.

He arrived back at the house, breathless and sweating. Kalisa was outside the house, sitting on the steps washing his trainers and whistling a Lucky Dube song. Damascene slammed the main gate and locked it with every chain and padlock he could find.

'What's up, brother?' asked Kalisa, looking curiously at the empty plastic bag in Damascene's hand.

Damascene sat down beside his brother, catching his breath and glaring at the ground.

'What's going on, Dammy?' said Kalisa, putting on his shoes.

'There was a woman at the market,' said Damascene.

'At last!' said Kalisa, chuckling. 'You got yourself a woman! Does she have a sister for me?'

Damascene ignored his brother's jokes.

'It's happened,' he said, 'I told you this would happen.'

'What happened?' said Kalisa.

'A Tutsi woman from Bushiru recognised me at the market!'

Kalisa stopped joking and gave Damascene his full attention.

'Are you sure, Dammy?' he asked. 'You're not being paranoid?'

'She remembered me. She threatened to turn me in.'

He never shared his fears with his older brother, but this was the day Kalisa had been dreading.

'Then you must disappear, my brother,' he said. 'There is no other way.'

'I've decided already,' said Damascene. 'For many years, I've thought about what to do if this day should come. Tomorrow, after work, I will go. The boss still owes me my money for the week. Then I will go. He will pay me tomorrow and immediately after work I will go. I will get a bus...'

'A bus to where?' asked Kalisa.

'Congo.'

'Do you think you won't get caught in Congo?'

'Don't worry. Remember my friends Bugingo and Karangwa? They are still in Congo. They were involved in the genocide too and they fled there in 1994. I can find them and join them with the FDLR rebels and we will fight our way back into Rwanda.'

Kalisa shook his head and closed his eyes.

'Wrong, wrong, wrong, brother!' he shouted, getting to his feet.

Damascene was taken aback by the strength of his younger brother's response.

'What do you mean? It's a good plan!'

'Let me tell you,' said Kalisa, 'you are my own brother and I have kept this terrible secret for as long as I can remember. But look at you! Look at your life since 1994. It has stopped like an old broken clock! Look at your soul, brother! You are a broken man, scared, guilty, insecure and full of shame. And now you are going to run away and join with some crazy rebels for some cause you don't even believe in anymore, and you will make it even worse and probably get killed!'

Damascene did not reply. He simply stared at the ground and listened.

'I love you, brother. Think twice! If you go back to fighting and killing, how much more blood will be in your nightmares? You will never have peace.'

Kalisa grabbed his brother by the arm.

'I am begging you,' he said, 'when you reach the Democratic Republic of Congo, just go and get a normal job and find a good woman. Just work and try to forget. Leave this place and let it go. Then maybe you can forgive yourself and set yourself free.'

Damascene looked up at his brother with tears in his eyes.

So much younger but so much wiser, he thought.

'Thanks, little brother,' he said. 'Give me your hand.'

Kalisa took his older brother's hand and seemed to raise him up to his feet.

'You are right, Kalisa. You are right.'

CHAPTER THIRTEEN

'Thank you, boss,' said Damascene to the head engineer at the construction site in Kigali.

His well-worn and paint-splattered overalls were testament to the fact he had worked here as a labourer, along with his brother, for the past three years.

'We will miss you here, Damascene,' said his boss. 'You have always been a good worker, a hard worker.'

'Thank you very much, boss,' said Damascene.

'Your brother wastes far too much time singing and dancing during lunch breaks, but you, sir, toil like a man who needs a purpose or a penance!'

Damascene laughed.

You have no idea! he thought.

'Just remind me at five o'clock and after work I'll pay you for the last week,' said the head engineer.

'Thank you, sir, I really need that money today,' said Damascene.

'Don't look so worried, my friend,' said the boss. 'Back to work for one more day. I'll see you later.'

Damascene returned to the scaffolding around the brand-new building he and Kalisa had been painting for the past few weeks. Noticing the look of relief on his brother's face, Kalisa quickly jumped down from the scaffolding. He handed Damascene a paintbrush and smiled.

'Will someone be speaking Lingala soon?'

'*Mbote. Malamu*,' said Damascene.

Kalisa shook his brother's hand and the two men laughed as if they were boys again. However, as they steadily climbed up the scaffolding to resume painting the exterior of the office block, Kalisa felt unconvinced that this opportunity would give his brother the freedom he longed for.

After a few hours of work, Damascene stopped, gazed across the skyline of Kigali and called to his brother.

'When I reach Congo, I think I am finally going to be free.'

'Free?' said Kalisa.

'Yes, my brother. I'm going to get a job with one of the mining companies. I'm telling you. I will work hard. I will claim refugee status with the UNHCR in Congo. Then in no time I will be flying off to Europe or America!'

'Good luck, Dammy,' said Kalisa. 'But remember, you can run and leave a place behind, but you can't leave behind what is running inside of you.'

Damascene stopped painting and glared at his little brother.

'Are you trying to tell me that I won't have freedom?'

'Who took your freedom?' replied Kalisa. 'You lie in bed in fear every single night. You feel unsafe here every day. Is all of that really going to change in Congo?'

Just then, the brothers noticed a police car arriving at the main gate of the construction site. They watched in silence as a policeman got out of the car and started speaking to their boss. Damascene felt a deep sense of dread in the pit of his stomach.

'This can't be happening,' he said. 'Not today, not now.'

'Stop panicking, brother. It will be nothing to do with us,' said Kalisa, uncertainly.

The head engineer turned his head and pointed towards Damascene and Kalisa on the scaffolding. Damascene gasped. He felt his heart thud in his chest. The past was finally closing in on him. Three more policemen got out of the car and followed the police officer walking briskly towards the scaffolding. For a second, Damascene felt the urge to jump off the scaffolding and run for his life, but he knew it would be impossible to escape. Sensing this danger, Kalisa put his hand on his brother's shoulder and the two men slowly climbed down from the scaffolding.

'I am Chief Inspector Uwimana Jean Pierre of Kigali CID,' said the tall police officer.

Louise's husband had been true to his word.

'Who is Hakizimana Damascene?' he asked.

Damascene looked down and walked forward. 'Here I am, sir. How may I help you?'

He offered a handshake to the police officer.

Jean Pierre did not shake Damascene's hand. Instead, he nodded to his colleagues and continued. 'You are suspected of participating in the genocide against the Tutsi in 1994.'

Damascene did not look up.

'I don't know what you are talking about, sir,' he said weakly.

'You don't know what—'

'But sir....' interrupted Kalisa.

'Shut up, boy!' shouted Jean Pierre, 'I am talking to this criminal in front of me, not you!'

One of the other policemen stepped forward to stand in front of Kalisa, and another police officer shoved him back so hard that he fell to the ground, scraping his elbows along the rough cement. The head engineer shook his head and began to walk away.

'I am not a criminal!' said Damascene in the direction of his departing boss.

Jean Pierre handed Damascene a lengthy warrant paper.

'I am here to arrest you. To take you out of the community and to the place where criminals belong.'

'I am not a criminal. I am not guilty,' said Damascene, scanning the warrant paper.

'Well, Hakizimana Damascene, the prison has teeth and if you are guilty, it will chew you up and after many years, if you are lucky, it might spit you out.'

'Are you trying to scare me?' asked Damascene.

Jean Pierre stepped forward until his face was within an inch of Damascene's face.

'Are you scared?' he whispered.

Damascene was shaking.

'This is what fear feels like,' said Jean Pierre, 'and yet I do not carry a machete, like the cowards of 1994.'

'I did not carry a machete. I am an innocent man,' said Damascene.

Jean Pierre nodded towards his colleagues. They pushed Damascene to the ground, restrained him and put him in handcuffs.

'Let's go,' said Jean Pierre, thinking of how glad he would be to tell his wife later that today he had finally apprehended the man who caused so much pain to her friend Patricia.

Kalisa lay on the ground and stared as Damascene was taken away in handcuffs and bundled roughly into the police van. Noticing the feeling of warm blood on his elbows, Kalisa sat up. He wanted to raise a hand to wave to his brother, but his arm felt too heavy and he could not move at all. For the first time in his life, Kalisa was overwhelmed by a feeling of being completely alone. He could barely see the whites of Damascene's eyes looking out of the window of the police van as he was driven off to face justice. He noticed how desperately sad and resigned to his fate his brother looked. He understood that his brother's worst nightmare had just become reality. Kalisa knew their lives would never be the same again.

CHAPTER FOURTEEN

In the gloomy prison cell, Damascene sat hunched on the floor staring at his bare feet. He noticed his cuffed hands were still shaking. He felt angry and afraid but, to his surprise, his dominant emotion was relief. For ten long years, he had dreaded this scenario and although he never admitted it to Kalisa, he always felt this day of reckoning was inevitable. In his darkest nights of sweats and terror, he had begged God to bring forward this day, as an alternative to going to his grave and to the punishment of hell for his transgressions.

Jean Pierre arrived at the cell with two police officers who picked him up from the floor like a bag of garbage.

'Come with me,' said Jean Pierre, as if Damascene had a choice.

The officers bundled him down the dark corridor and into the interrogation room containing one chair, opposite where the Chief of Police was seated. The officers sat him down. Without looking up, the Chief of Police read from the papers in his hands:

'Hakizimana Damascene, born 22nd June 1969 in Gisenyi, second son of five children of the Late Hakizimana Gregoire and Nyinawayezu Francine. High School educated at Lycée de Kigali and then studied Engineering for two years at Université Nationale du Rwanda. Worked in construction on buildings in Kigali and Gisenyi. This was your life until 1994.'

Damascene did not speak or move. He sat still, head down, eyes fixed on his bare feet.

'Then,' continued the Chief of Police, 'after 1994, nothing. The strange case of a disappearing man. How odd that for the past ten years, by pure coincidence, since the days of the genocide, this man no longer exists.'

The Chief of Police stood up, bent down and, drawing close to Damascene's face, read from the various documents.

'These are the eyewitness testimonies of the survivors.'

Damascene could not look up.

'They testify that Hakizimana Damascene participated in the genocide against the Tutsi and was part of a mob that killed more than forty-five men, women and children between April and May of 1994 in Gisenyi.'

'Wrong, sir,' replied Damascene in an unconvincing whisper.

The Chief of Police stared into his eyes, but Damascene could not meet his gaze.

'Wrong? Eh…?' he said.

'Yes, sir.'

'Really?' said the Chief of Police, so close now that Damascene could smell the curry on his breath. 'Stand up!'

The Chief of Police kicked away Damascene's chair and began to steadily raise his voice.

'Listen to me, brave killer of women and children. The souls of your victims cry out from their graves because you move freely in the streets of Kigali. Their widows and orphans cannot wait for the moment they see your dirty face in jail.'

'You are wrong, sir,' said Damascene.

'Your fellow killers fled to the Democratic Republic of Congo, but you were afraid to go with them because you are a coward and you knew the RDF[8] would hunt you down and bring you to justice. Am I wrong?'

'You are wrong, sir.'

'Hakizimana Damascene. You butchered Tutsis in 1994.'

'Wrong, sir.'

'Okay. Let's see if I am mistaken,' replied the Chief of Police, nodding to Jean Pierre to open the door behind Damascene. 'Let's see who is right and who is wrong here.'

A young police officer opened the door and escorted a woman into the room. She stepped closer and stood alongside Jean Pierre, who placed an arm around her shoulder.

'Turn around!' commanded the Chief of Police.

Damascene turned around. In an instant, he saw a familiar face from both his childhood and his nightmares. It was Patricia. He remembered the sight of the blood of his old friend, her husband, Bernard, splattered on the walls of their home. He recalled the screams of her little girl

---

8   Rwandan Defence Force.

and the final cries of her baby boy. These sounds had been slashed into his soul. He closed his eyes and remembered the cheers of the mob as he left her to be beaten and raped. Damascene stepped back in shock, fear and shame. Nothing could have prepared him for this moment. This was the opposite of their last fateful encounter. On this occasion, it was Damascene who was helpless and shaking with fear.

'I do not know this woman, sir,' said Damascene, realising as he spoke how unconvincing he sounded.

Patricia did not move. She did not cry or shake. The ten-year-old machete wound on her back seemed to gnaw at her body, but she stood tall and strong. She looked into the face of the man who had betrayed her. Her husband's best friend who stood by approvingly as her family was slaughtered in front of her. Patricia had been preparing for this meeting for days now, ever since Doctor Louise had told her that Damascene had been apprehended and a witness was required. She looked into the face of the man from her nightmares, but this time she was not the powerless victim. This time, it was his turn to suffer. Today was the day to kill the devil. Suddenly, unexpectedly, and to the shock of everyone in the room, Patricia grabbed Jean Pierre's pistol from his holster and pointed it at Damascene's forehead.

'Patricia, don't! Don't do it!' called Jean Pierre.

'Please put the gun down. Put the gun down, Patricia,' said the Chief of Police, reaching out one hand to wave for calm and another hand to offer to take the gun.

This was not what Patricia had planned, but as soon as she saw Damascene's face, all of her nightmares came flooding back and ten years of hatred and a thirst for revenge consumed her. She stared at Damascene, with her finger on the trigger.

'You deny that you even know me? Hutu devil!' she cried.

For the first time, Damascene looked up and into Patricia's eyes. He saw pain and hatred.

'Patricia,' he said.

'Do not speak my name!' she cried, pointing the gun at his head.

Damascene realised this was the justice he deserved. He accepted his fate and awaited the darkness. Hot tears of vengeance fell from Patricia's eyes as she touched the trigger. This was for Bernard, for Alice, for Innocent, for all her family and friends. She was deaf to the words of Jean Pierre and the Chief of Police pleading with her to drop the gun. This was justice!

Damascene looked up and nodded at Patricia, as if to give his executioner permission to pull the trigger. Accepting his punishment and his fate, Damascene closed his eyes and bowed his head. It was then that Patricia noticed something familiar in the way he lowered his head. She recognised a fragment of the man who had been her husband's best friend. He had bowed his head in prayer this way on the day of their wedding and at Alice's christening in the same church a few years later. She felt the cold steel of the trigger on her finger. She had dreamed of this revenge as vividly as the nightmares of this devil's evil deeds, but Patricia could not pull the trigger. Her hands began to shake and she began to weep. She dropped the gun and Jean Pierre quickly retrieved the weapon and placed it back in his holster. The Chief of Police held Patricia as Damascene sank to his knees.

'Don't worry, good woman,' said the Chief of Police. 'This killer will see justice. I promise you.'

Damascene looked up at Patricia with tears of confusion on his face.

'Sign here, madam. Confirm that this is the man,' said the Chief of Police, handing Patricia her written testimony.

'I want you to tell him this,' said Patricia, in a strong and defiant voice. 'Today, I am proud to be Tutsi. I am proud that my parents were Tutsi. We were supposed to be wiped from this earth. But look, Hutu devil! I am still here! And today you are like a beaten dog on the ground. You only live because I chose not to pull the trigger.'

Patricia signed, confirming the identity of the genocide perpetrator, Hakizimana Damascene.

'Thank you, Madame Patricia,' said the Chief of Police, nodding firmly to Jean Pierre to take her away, before any further incident.

Jean Pierre began to lead Patricia out of the room. She walked slowly as if in a trance but then for a second she looked back at Damascene. He was crouching like a chained and beaten animal on the floor. Suddenly she lurched back towards him once more. Swiftly, Jean Pierre placed his hand over his gun to keep it securely in his holster and he held Patricia back. Patricia spat in Damascene's face. Damascene simply looked into her eyes for a moment but had to look away as the shame overwhelmed him. Patricia turned her back in disgust and strode out of the interrogation room. Hunched on the floor, Damascene vomited onto his bare feet.

Chapter Fifteen

Back in Jean Pierre's office, Patricia sat at the desk reviewing her witness statement. Her heart was still racing and she tapped her right foot furiously on the floor as she read and re-read the document. Finally, she took a deep breath, lifted a pen from the desk and once more added a signature slowly and firmly to the bottom of the page. This officially confirmed her full testimony against genocide perpetrator, Hakizimana Damascene. Jean Pierre examined the documents to ensure that all was in order and added the testimony to his files.

'Thank you, Madame Patricia,' he said. 'Now, please come with me.'

Patricia did not reply but followed Jean Pierre to the car park, where Louise had been waiting anxiously while the drama had unfolded inside the police station. Jean Pierre looked at Louise, raised his eyebrows and shook his head slightly as Patricia got into the car.

'How did it go?' asked Louise.

Patricia did not reply.

'Let's say it was eventful but ultimately successful,' said Jean Pierre.

'Oh, I see,' said Louise, getting the message that further elaboration would not be helpful in this moment.

'Make sure she is all right,' said Jean Pierre, tapping the roof of the car.

'I know,' said Louise, looking back at Patricia in the rear-view mirror. 'She will be okay, won't you, Patricia, my dear?'

Patricia did not respond but stared out of the car window, lost in painful memories and powerful emotions. It had been yet another traumatic day for Patricia. Louise kissed her husband, wound up the window, started the car and drove off in search of a quiet restaurant where the two women could talk about what had just happened.

When they sat down at a table in a nearby restaurant in the city centre, it was clear that Patricia did not want to talk or eat. As Louise began to take her meal, Patricia played with the fork on her empty plate.

'Please, Patricia, have a brochette, you must be hungry,' said Louise.

Just then, a smiling middle-aged woman approached Louise.

'Doctor Louise!' she said.

'Hello, Ingabire,' replied Louise, standing up to give the woman a hug.

Patricia ignored the warm exchanges between the two women and gazed out of the restaurant window at the new tall buildings on the Kigali skyline.

'It's been a long time,' said Ingabire.

'How is your husband?' asked Louise.

'My husband is okay now, thanks to you, Doctor Louise. He's back working in the brewery now.'

'Is he still on the medication?'

'Yes, but he's fine. The old fool will live forever!'

Ingabire noticed Patricia and offered her hand.

'Hello, I am Ingabire.'

'Hello,' replied Patricia, but she held back from shaking the Hutu woman's hand and continued to stare out of the window in the direction of the new buildings across the road.

'Her name is Patricia, she is my friend,' said Louise in an attempt to rescue the awkwardness.

Ingabire and Louise chatted for another few minutes until Louise was interrupted by an incoming phone call. She hugged the woman goodbye and sent good wishes to her husband.

'It's him,' said Louise to Patricia. 'Hello, Faustin? Yes, we're here in one of the restaurants... yes, I'll show you which one we are in. I'll come out to meet you in the car park. See you in two minutes.'

Louise got up quickly and left the restaurant with her phone still at her ear. Patricia remained alone at the table, staring up at the building across the road. A little boy sitting with his parents at the next table noticed and stared in fascination at the sad woman who was gazing out of the window.

A few minutes later, Louise arrived back at the table accompanied by Faustin. Her food and handbag were exactly as she had left them, but Patricia was gone. Louise looked around the restaurant. She felt immediately that something was wrong.

'What's happened?' asked Faustin.

'She was here with me a minute ago,' she replied.

Together, they started looking, asking everyone at the nearby tables if they had noticed where Patricia had gone. Finally, they spoke to the parents of the boy who had been watching Patricia. The child was looking out of the window now as his parents were finishing their meal.

'Excuse me, have you seen the woman who was sitting here with me at that table just a few minutes ago?' asked Louise.

The parents shook their heads.

'Sorry, madam,' said the father.

'I saw her,' said the little boy unexpectedly, still looking out of the window as he spoke.

'We tell him not to talk to strangers,' said the father.

'Where has she gone?' asked Louise.

The boy did not reply but pointed out of the window. Louise looked through the window and caught a glimpse of Patricia outside, running through the front doors of the entrance to the skyscraper across the road.

'Oh my God!' she cried, and ran out of the restaurant.

Faustin followed close behind. The street was busy with pedestrians and the traffic was heavy with trucks and taxi buses as Louise tried to follow Patricia. She moved as fast as she could, darting between the cars and running towards the entrance of the building. Faustin got held back as a large group of motorcycles overcrowded the road, creating a traffic jam. Standing on the far side of the road, he looked up at the building Patricia had entered. Up on the rooftop, he could see the figure of a woman walking towards the edge.

'Oh no!' he cried, and hopped between motorcycles across the road. Cars braked and horns tooted as he dashed into the building and moved swiftly towards the lift. Louise had known instinctively what Patricia was intending to do and she was already tailing her to the top of the building. By the time Faustin made it to the rooftop, Louise was already there, calmly walking towards Patricia, who was standing on the edge and looking straight ahead.

'You don't have to do this,' said Louise. 'Please come here, Patricia, okay?'

Patricia's eyes were closed and she did not respond as Louise and Faustin crept closer.

'You won't do it, beautiful woman,' said Louise. 'There is hope for a better future.'

Patricia opened her eyes and turned her head towards Louise. 'I do not fear death,' said Patricia, calmly. 'I fear machetes, but there are no sharp blades here.'

Louise inched closer to Patricia.

'Patricia, please,' she pleaded quietly, tears running down her cheeks.

'My dear friend,' said Patricia, 'I have told you many times. I do not wish to live. Today, I saw the devil and I signed a statement to bring him to justice. There is nothing more for me to do here.'

Patricia closed her eyes once more and slowly took a step towards her doom.

'Patricia!' screamed Louise.

There were gasps and squeals from the crowd which had gathered in the street down below. Just as she was about to fall to her death, Faustin made a dive across the rooftop and grabbed Patricia's hand. He fell onto his chest, holding on to Patricia's hand as she dangled from the rooftop, her legs swaying backwards and forwards. Several police cars arrived on the street below and a group of police officers ran into the building. Faustin gripped Patricia's hand tightly but she did not return his grasp. Louise threw her entire weight on top of Faustin's legs to steady him and prevent him from slipping forward. He strained every sinew in his body and slowly he managed to pull Patricia back up onto the rooftop.

When the police arrived on the scene, they found Faustin lying exhausted and sweating beside Louise, who was also prostrate on the rooftop, embracing Patricia. Both women were sobbing and shaking. After a few minutes, the police helped Faustin and the women to their feet and began to take details of what had happened. Patricia turned and looked at Faustin, the man who had just saved her life.

'Who is this man?' she asked.

Chapter Sixteen

Patricia spent the night at Louise's house. Jean Pierre disapproved of Louise bringing patients to their home, but this was an emergency and the children got excited about any overnight guest. Patricia slept on the sofa and the next morning when Louise woke to the smell of one of Jean Pierre's breakfasts she was surprised to find Patricia already awake and outside in the garden playing with Kevin and little Ngabo as if she was without a care in the world.

'She loves children,' said Jean Pierre.

'I know, it's so sad,' said Louise.

'Patricia, my dear!' she called, as if the drama of the previous day had not occurred. 'We have to leave to visit Faustin in ten minutes.'

Patricia turned around and the smile disappeared from her face, as if she had just awakened from a happy dream. After the incident on the rooftop, Louise had explained that Faustin worked for FARG, the Fund for Neediest Survivors of the Genocide. Patricia agreed to a meeting with the mysterious man who had just saved her life, but Louise was worried that she might change her mind at any minute. When they arrived at the FARG office, Patricia was silent and initially reluctant to communicate.

'Patricia, dear woman, how many more people need to save your life before you decide to save yourself?' asked Louise.

Patricia did not reply as a receptionist ushered them into Faustin's office.

'How is she?' asked Faustin, addressing the question to Louise.

'She is in the room and I am fine,' replied Patricia.

'You gave me a good workout yesterday,' said Faustin with a laugh.

'I'm sorry,' said Patricia, looking down. 'I did not know who you were.'

'I am Gashumba Faustin. I am the planning officer for the Fund for the Neediest Survivors of the Genocide.'

'Nice to meet you... properly this time,' said Patricia with a slight smile.

'Doctor Louise has told me all about you,' said Faustin. 'Patricia, it is clear to me that you are one of the neediest survivors of the genocide. You should have had support before now. You deserve a better life and we can help you.'

'She lives in a small house she rents and she does not have enough money to take care of herself,' said Louise.

Faustin looked through a series of documents on the table in front of him.

'Patricia,' he said.

'Yes, sir?'

'I am sorry for the past.'

Patricia nodded slightly as Louise took hold of her hand.

'You cannot change the past, sir,' she said.

'In accordance with our platforms,' continued Faustin, 'you are one of the survivors we are definitely able to support financially.'

'Really?' said Patricia, surprised that anyone would be interested in supporting her after all these years of poverty and hopelessness.

'I understand that before the genocide you had a house in Gisenyi with your husband. You have a choice, Patricia. We can offer you a brand-new house in one of the *umudugudu*[9] for survivors in Kigali or we can rebuild your family home and you can live there safely once again.'

The thought of her deserted family home and all that happened there brought tears to Patricia's eyes, but Faustin's words stirred a long-forgotten feeling – a tiny glimmer of hope. Louise gripped her friend's hand more tightly as if to give her strength.

'Secondly,' said Faustin, 'before the genocide, you had started a course at university, so now you can continue your studies. We will pay for you until you complete your qualifications.'

Patricia looked up and smiled. She remembered how she loved to learn.

'I wanted to study law,' she said. 'You know, before everything happened.'

It seemed so long ago now, but there was something about resuming her studies that gave Patricia more hope

---

9   An *umudugudu* is a new village settlement built to provide housing after the genocide.

than even the restoration of her little house in Gisenyi. Her father always said she was the smartest one in the family and would become a lawyer one day.

'Not only that…' continued Faustin.

'And what?' said Louise.

'We will find a job for her back home in Gisenyi.'

Louise smiled at Patricia and for the first time she saw a glimpse of happiness on her face. Faustin went through the paperwork and Patricia signed the documents to verify her identity and to accept the support.

'Thank you, sir,' she said to Faustin, 'for yesterday and today. It is almost too much to take in, but I am very grateful for your kindness.'

'You almost broke my back yesterday, madam,' said Faustin, with a wink. 'The least you can do is give me some more work to keep me busy!'

Patricia laughed. Louise sat back in shock. She had never seen Patricia laugh like this before.

'Now do you wish to live, beautiful woman?' she asked.

'Perhaps,' replied Patricia.

CHAPTER SEVENTEEN

'Here you are, boss,' said Julius, handing Albert five thousand Ugandan shillings.

'Is that everything?' asked Albert.

'Yes, boss,' replied the little boy, looking down. 'Am sorry. It was slow today because of all the rain and the mud. We will do better tomorrow, if God stops the rain, sir.'

The other street kids, in a ragtag circle, barefoot in mud-stained shorts and torn t-shirts, nodded in agreement. When it rained in Kampala the streets churned with red mud, and here in the Kisenyi slum the ditches and open sewers overflowed into the makeshift huts and houses. Albert's gang of nine-year-olds were well aware of the violent consequences of stealing from their boss.

'If I find out any of you little snakes have stolen from me, I'm telling you, I will beat you to death!' he said.

'Please, boss,' said Julius, 'we will do better tomorrow if God blesses us and the sun shines.'

'Well, it's not raining now and I need another ten thousand by tonight,' said Albert.

'Yes, sir,' said Julius.

'If no one wants to buy weed then you'll have to steal some stuff to sell instead. Go! Now! And don't come back without money, you little shits!'

'Yes, God bless you, sir,' said Julius.

The gang of boys nodded and ran off in search of easy pickings. In the supply chain of marijuana in the slum, Albert was the middleman. If he didn't have enough money for his boss by this evening then he would be in big trouble. The threats he made to his gang of street kids were mild compared to the consequences of Albert not paying the local drug lord. Every day, Albert regretted the big mistake he made when he moved to Kampala. It started with a little weed. It was easy to find, not too expensive and it helped to block out the memories of 1994. When he was offered the role of supplier to the slum where he found shelter, he thought it was an easy way to earn money. If he could survive in the slum for a few months, then he would get a proper job, move out and start to establish himself in this new country. Albert knew that if he hadn't got so hooked on using the drugs he was selling, he would have escaped from poverty by now. Every miserable day in the slum, he regretted settling in Uganda and longed to be back home in Rwanda.

'It wasn't just the whites who left us to be cut in 1994,' he would complain to anyone who would listen, after a few drinks in the bar, 'where were you, my brothers from Uganda, when we needed you?'

He lit a blunt of marijuana and sat down on a plastic chair in front of his hut. Albert felt numb most of the time, and the drugs helped to keep the past deadened. Escaping to a temporary high helped him to forget the loss of his family in Rwanda and the horror that continued in the jungles. Although he tried, he could never forget what he did to Claude, the man who murdered his sister's family. When he tracked down Claude in the jungle in Congo, he personally executed revenge. Yes, it was justice, the bastard deserved it, he thought, but the look in his eyes, the smell of his shit and the feeling of Claude's warm blood spattering his face haunted Albert's dreams. The screams of his Hutu enemy were not different to the screams of his Tutsi family and friends. It was as if all screams were simply human. Albert needed numbness to survive.

He trudged through the mud towards the bar on the outskirts of the growing slum. He chose to live here because the rent was low and the place sounded like home, but the slum was nothing like Gisenyi. He noticed Pastor Samuel, who always made a joke about this, walking towards him.

'Albert! The man from Gisenyi who came to Kisenyi!' called the pastor. 'I have something for you, my brother.'

The pastor's continuous efforts to help street kids to go to school were bad for business, and Albert was in no mood to be preached at. However, he approached the pastor in the hope that he might want to give him some money to help him out.

'Have you some more support for a poor refugee, pastor?' he said.

'I have something more important, brother,' he said. 'It's a blessing! It's a letter from your sister, Patricia, in Rwanda. It arrived at the church this morning.'

Albert was surprised. His sister had stopped writing to him years ago. He was unsure if she was still alive. So few of the people he loved from the past were still alive. When the letters stopped, he had assumed Patricia had met a similar fate to his other sister, Amina, who had drunk herself to death.

'Thank you, Pastor Samuel,' he said. 'This is good news, for once. My sister Patricia lives.'

'Yes, it's a blessing. Come to church on Sunday, Albert, my brother,' said Pastor Samuel. 'I preach Good News every week. The Lord Jesus can take away all of your sin and pain more than a million joints of weed.'

'Yes, Pastor, thank you, I will,' he replied, with no intention of ever going to church again. Church was part of the past. Church was where slaughter was carried out under the noses of priests, beneath crucifixes.

As the pastor departed, Albert opened the envelope and read the letter from his sister:

My dear little brother, Albert,

I hope you are alive and well and you receive this letter. I am sorry I have not written to you for a very long time. I want you to know that I have never forgotten you. You are my only family in this cruel world. You are my little brother who played with me on the shores of Lake Kivu. You are my brother who sang to me and Bernard on our wedding day. You were a kind uncle to my Alice and Innocent. Please understand that I have not forgotten you. I know about what you did to that devil Claude and I am glad you brought his miserable life to an end in the mud in the jungle.

Albert, I'm sorry but my life has been so hard in these years. I tried to end my life twice. I did not want to go on. I did not wish to live and I did not want you to know I had died. I thought it would be better if you never heard from me again, and you did not get to hear about the last of your family gone too.

But, little brother, I have changed my mind. I was shown great kindness by a lady doctor called Louise. She has helped me so much. She has saved my life. Her husband is a police officer and he helped to find that devil Damascene, who betrayed us. The Hutu coward was hiding in Kigali all these years, but now he is behind bars where he belongs. Maybe we will see justice at last!

Doctor Louise also got me support to start to rebuild my old house in Gisenyi, to get some money and to go back to college again. After ten years of wanting to die, I am finally starting to want to live again. I thought this would never happen, but today I am starting to think about the future again. I cannot forget the past or forgive those who betrayed us, but I am starting to hope that I might have some future.

Please, write back to me, Albert. I want to know that you are doing well in Uganda with a wife, and maybe some children and a house and good job.
Your loving sister,
Patricia

Albert stood alone in the muddy street of the slum and wept tears of joy, grief and guilt. Joy that his sister was alive and choosing life, grief at the loss of his family and guilt that he was selling weed instead of making the most of his life that had been spared when so many others had died. He did not have a wife and children in a nice house. He had a sad life with prostitutes and drugs in the slum. Was this really an escape? As he stood in the mud and cried, *boda boda* riders passed by, splashing mud from the wheels of their motorcycles onto his face. His tears blended with mud. He dropped the extinguished blunt into the sludge of the street and stepped on it. He read the letter again and again, raindrops and teardrops smudging Patricia's handwriting. Albert felt some satisfaction that Damascene was being brought to justice but a deep bitterness that his enemy's punishment was unlikely to be the death sentence. After standing in the rain for an hour, he looked up and noticed a hint of blue sky behind the clouds. Albert placed the precious message in his pocket and continued to his house to write a letter, something he hadn't done for years.

Now that his sister had found him, he would begin a regular correspondence with home, and the feeling of connection somehow began to ease his pain.

Chapter Eighteen

The drive from Kigali to Gisenyi, along winding roads and steep inclines, took almost four hours. Eventually, they turned a hilltop corner and the expanse of Lake Kivu came into view. As she admired the sun glistening on the water, Patricia knew she was home. In spite of all the terrible memories, this was where she belonged. Her roots were deep in this red soil. The last time Patricia was here with Louise was the night the fishermen saved her from drowning. In contrast to that dark night of her soul, today felt like the first few seconds of sunrise over the mountains of Congo. Louise and Faustin were helping her to rebuild her life and Damascene was about to face justice. To add to these signs of hope, she had just received a reply from her brother, Albert, in Uganda, saying he was doing well with a good job and a nice apartment in Kampala. For a moment, she thought of her parents and grandparents and all the happy times in this place, the births, the parties and the weddings. Although their graves were never found, it somehow comforted her that the bones of her family rested in this soil.

When they arrived at the site, Patricia was the first to get out of the car. Louise, Faustin and the construction engineer remained in the vehicle for a few minutes to allow Patricia some time to collect her thoughts in private.

'My little palace,' said Patricia, as if talking to a sickly child.

The small *adobe* house was a ruin surrounded by overgrown bushes and grass. The old cowshed was a tumbledown of timber. The broken windows of her home were still boarded up and the roof had collapsed. Patricia took a sharp intake of breath at the sight of bullet holes in the walls. Ten years of sun and rain had not erased the evidence of violence.

'My little house,' she said.

A few of her former neighbours passed by, carrying jerry cans and bags of maize. Patricia recognised some Hutu women she had gone to school with. They seemed to recognise her too, but the women scurried along past the house. They could not look Patricia in the eye. Louise noticed this interaction and worried that it would discourage Patricia from wanting to return here.

Faustin joined Patricia in front of her former family home.

'This is the place?' he asked.

'Yes,' said Patricia, looking intently towards the entrance with no door. Images of the past flooded back. Happy times with Bernard fixing the roof after the latest storm and hours spent tending the avocado plants in the garden at the front of the house. Little Alice chasing the chickens through the kitchen. The day she gave birth to Innocent in the back room. Then came the darker memories. Bernard hammering nails into planks of wood across the windows, the sound of that gun and the dull thud as her husband fell lifeless to the floor. The screams of Alice. The cries of Innocent. The jeers of Sylvestre and Claude and the face of the traitor Damascene. Her head spinning, Patricia felt faint and stumbled. It was too much to bear. However, Louise was there once again to catch her before she fell.

'Just take your time, Patricia,' she said. 'Faustin says if it's too painful to return here, they may be able to provide you with a new house in the neighbourhood.'

Patricia took a deep breath, inhaled all the familiar smells of this land and stood tall in front of the wreck.

'No, Doctor Louise,' she said firmly, 'this is my home. This was always my home. The spirits of my husband and children are here. This will be my home once again.'

'Patricia, we understand this is almost too much for anyone to cope with,' said Faustin. 'We can help you to get trauma counselling too.'

Patricia's first instinct was to politely refuse this offer of help. Then she took another deep breath and tried to imagine this home restored. The voice in her heart encouraging her to live was now stronger than the voice in her head telling her to give up. Patricia nodded. Now that she had chosen to live, she would accept any help offered. She sat down on the long grass in front of the house while Louise and Faustin chatted beside the car and the construction engineer inspected the property.

After an hour of taking measurements and making notes, he concluded, 'It's possible. We can rescue this house. I'm sure of it, Madame Patricia.'

'That's good news,' said Louise.

'As long as you promise not to try to jump off the roof!' said Faustin.

Patricia laughed.

'Then you will have to come and live up there on the roof to stop me!' said Patricia.

'Okay, madam. We will rebuild your home and you can work on replanting your garden,' said Faustin. 'This place will be beautiful once again.'

'I know for certain that if Patricia commits to it, she will make it happen,' said Louise.

Patricia walked forward towards the house, running her fingers along the overgrown bushes in the front garden. She leaned against a remaining part of the house and placed her cheek against the wall.

'Of course,' said Patricia, 'and in this garden I will grow the best avocados in Rwanda once more.'

Chapter Nineteen

Jean Pierre looked up at the clock on the wall in his office. He was surprised to see the hands meeting at midnight. Somehow, in the busyness of the evening, he had not noticed darkness falling. Jean Pierre loved his job so much, he often lost track of time. Every day was jam-packed with catching criminals, supporting victims, routing out corrupt police officers and far too much paperwork. He wasn't motivated by the power of his position or driven by a zeal to punish criminals; he saw himself as a problem solver and peacemaker. Every crime was a problem to be solved and an opportunity to restore peace. It was all in a day's work and this was a typical day for him, to become so absorbed in his responsibilities that he worked too late

He switched on his desk lamp and his thoughts turned to Louise and the children at home, where he found true peace. Jean Pierre was grateful for his job and his family. His experiences of war were etched in his mind, but he kept these memories in a box with the lid firmly shut. He was glad to have a meaningful job where he could make a difference, and a busy family life to help keep the bad memories locked away.

Jean Pierre took a final sip of coffee and tidied up the papers on his desk. As he prepared to leave the police station, he placed a few important files into his briefcase and checked in with the officers on the night shift. It was a quiet night in the police station, so far. Before signing off for the day, he decided to check in on the prisoner who had dominated his time in recent weeks. Damascene was scheduled for transfer the next day. His wife's relationship with Patricia made this man's case different from all the others. He usually held the stories of survivors and perpetrators at a distance, but when Louise recounted Patricia's story, it triggered within him a deep desire for justice. Looking into Damascene's cell, he saw the prisoner was still awake, sitting on the bed and staring into space. Jean Pierre noticed something on the floor of the cell and stepped forward for a closer look. Damascene looked up as he noticed his captor's presence, but the men did not acknowledge each other. In the dirt on the floor of the cell, in large capital letters, was a word Damascene had written with his finger.

'Hey,' said Jean Pierre.

Damascene did not respond but looked down at the word on the ground.

'You have ten hours,' said Jean Pierre.

'For what?' asked Damascene, head still down.

'Transfer.'

'I'm not a criminal,' said Damascene.

'And yet here you are, behind bars for these last few weeks and on your final night in this cell you are writing in the dust on the ground with your finger,' said Jean Pierre. 'Perhaps it is time for you to face up to the past and to do the right thing.'

'What do you know of my life?' said Damascene.

'I know a great deal about life in 1994,' replied Jean Pierre.

He pointed at the word inscribed in the dust on the floor of the prison cell and asked, 'How can that be what you want, man?'

'Who says it's what I want?' said Damascene.

Jean Pierre noticed the inmate had tears in his eyes.

'It's what I must receive. If I accept it then I might be free,' said Damascene.

'Whether or not you will ever be free is not your choice. It's up to the Gacaca Court,' said Jean Pierre.

He turned to leave.

'And I don't care what you want. Justice is what I want.'

Damascene shook his head and tapped his feet on the floor frenetically as if he was trying to run. Like Jean Pierre, Damascene had spent many years with his memories closed in a box, but now the lid of the box had been opened and the feelings he had fought for years could no longer be contained.

As Jean Pierre walked out of the police station towards his car, he looked up and around him at the hills surrounding Kigali. It was a still night and the moon was full. A young couple walked past him hand in hand, laughing and flirting. On a peaceful night like this, as he gazed at the skyline of the city illuminated by the glowing lights of hundreds of homes in the surrounding hills, he wondered how genocide had happened here. It was hard to believe that ten years ago these hills were echoing with the screams of the victims. Not that long ago these streets flowed with the blood of the innocents. He recalled the day he returned as a soldier to the chaos of the city. The whole of society had collapsed. Then Jean Pierre's mind returned to his prisoner in the cell and the word he had written in the dust with his finger. He shook his head and assured himself that the justice he was bringing for poor souls like Patricia would make sure the unthinkable could never happen again.

Inside his prison cell Damascene sat on the bed, rocking backwards and forwards, replaying the events of recent weeks. He was tortured by the image of Patricia with hatred in her eyes, lunging for a gun to kill him and spitting at him on the ground. Damascene would not miss this room, but he was certain the next place would be worse. He stared at the word he had written on the floor. Jean Pierre had got it wrong; he wasn't seeking this. It was all he deserved to receive from Patricia and the families of every stranger he had attacked with his club of nails. The word was REVENGE.

CHAPTER TWENTY

Damascene jerked awake as the prison van jolted over the security ramps at the front gate of the central jail. He felt nauseous at the overpowering smell of stale sweat and weed. He hadn't slept properly since he was arrested and to avoid interaction with the other detainees in the van he had closed his eyes. He did not want to associate with criminals. He did not belong here, handcuffed with thieves and drug dealers, he thought, as he dozed off. When the guards opened the van, Damascene and the other prisoners, cuffed together, were escorted out in a line, heads down, shuffling forward to their incarceration without dignity.

As Damascene entered the prison grounds through a series of heavy security gates, he noted how high the walls were that now surrounded him. He could see nothing beyond the jail, no buildings, no horizon; only clear blue sky. He looked around at the other prisoners, all dressed in the same pink uniform, labouring in the heat of the day. He noticed how the brightness of their uniforms did not match the gloomy expressions on their faces. Some inmates were chopping firewood, while others were breaking huge rocks into stones with heavy hammers, all supervised by severe-looking guards armed with sticks and guns. A few scrawny crows were picking at scraps near the kitchens. Some of the prisoners cooking porridge in huge containers outside the kitchens raised their heads for a moment to observe the newcomers. Damascene felt the stares of a group of men in foot chains with jerry cans, waiting in line for the water tap, smoking cigarettes. There was no word of welcome, just curious glances and aggressive stares.

I do not belong here, he thought, *these men are criminals!*

The new prisoners were marched to the yard outside the warden's office and ordered to wait in line. The wait seemed endless. At one point, due to the intense heat and lack of sleep, Damascene stumbled to his knees. Immediately, a guard grabbed him by the scruff of his neck and pulled him back to his feet.

'Stand! Scum!' hissed the guard in his ear.

As time passed, to stay alert, Damascene began to examine his surroundings, desperately seeking some way out, but he concluded quickly that there was no escape. The past had finally caught up with him. After what seemed like hours, the warden emerged from his office to inspect the newly arrived inmates. He walked along the line of men, looking them up and down and occasionally shaking his head but saying nothing. When he stopped at Damascene, he looked through him and simply sighed.

He spoke only once. 'Welcome to where you belong. Just remember the biggest mistake in 1930 Jail is trying to escape.'

He nodded to the guards and went back inside. Then the new prisoners were taken to be registered, given their uniforms and assigned their cells. Throughout this process, some of the men tried to start a conversation with their newfound peers, but Damascene spoke to no one. When the time came for his first meal, he joined the long queue into the heavily guarded refectory hall. He collected his *sorghum* porridge in a tin tray and looked around at the different groups of prisoners gathered at tables across the refectory. He spotted an empty table where he decided to sit, alone. He was hungry now and began to consume the watery porridge as if it was a fine feast. After a while, two prisoners came and sat down at the table in front of him.

'Well, well, well. This new guy has a big appetite,' said one of the prisoners. 'He's eating this shit like it's not just for throwing in the trash for pigs!'

The other prisoner laughed. 'Give him a few weeks and he'll be spitting it out!'

'He'll be shitting it out tonight!'

Damascene paid no attention and kept on eating.

'I am Nsengiyumva,' said the first prisoner, offering his hand to Damascene, 'and this is my friend Lucien.'

After a short moment of silence, Damascene set down his spoon, sighed and shook their hands.

'Damascene,' he said.

Lucien looked closely at Damascene as if his name was familiar.

'Okay, Monsieur Damascene,' said Nsengiyumva, 'welcome to the 1930 Central Hotel. I hope you feel at home here, man!'

Lucien laughed again, but Nsengiyumva glared at his friend.

'It's not that funny. You don't have to laugh at every fucking thing I say!'

Lucien stopped mid-laugh. He stared intently at Damascene.

'You know, my brother,' said Nsengiyumva, 'I have been here for three years already and I can promise you this – the more time you spend here, the easier it will be to survive.'

'I won't be staying here,' replied Damascene.

Nsengiyumva shook his head and continued. 'I have already made this place like my own home, even though there are no women here. Now that, my friend, is the biggest problem here for me, and I promise you are going to have that problem too.'

Lucien laughed, but not so heartily this time.

Damascene looked up and smiled. In truth, he had not been able to sustain an intimate relationship with any woman since the genocide.

'What did you do to end up in here?' he asked.

'I sold drugs, my friend,' said Nsengiyumva. 'The best cannabis from the beautiful forests of Congo. I can get you some of the good stuff in here too!'

'I killed Tutsis in the genocide,' said Lucien, with no hint of remorse. 'Why are you here?'

'I am not a criminal,' said Damascene, returning his attention to eating the porridge.

Nsengiyumva and Lucien laughed.

'Liar!' said Lucien with a smile.

'Come on, my friend,' said Nsengiyumva, 'if you were innocent, you wouldn't be here, would you?'

'Hold on,' said Lucien, finally recognising Damascene, 'are you from Gisenyi?'

Damascene looked up.

'I know you. You were friends with my brother, Claude. I remember you visited our village after the genocide and talked about escaping to Congo. That was you, wasn't it? One of Sylvestre's boys!'

Damascene shook his head in agitation.

'It's true!' continued Lucien. 'It's you, man. I remember you!'

'Leave me alone,' snapped Damascene.

'You are a killer too!' said Lucien. 'There is nothing innocent about you. Where have you been hiding while braver men like my brother went to Congo?'

'I haven't been hiding,' said Damascene. 'I'm not a criminal.'

'I know your type,' said Lucien. 'You helped to find the cockroaches but I bet you never had the guts to lift a machete. You talked a lot and showed us where to find them but you did not cut! And then instead of fighting to take our country back, you hid among old women in Kigali!'

Damascene raised his hand to strike Lucien, but Nsengiyumva intervened and held the two men apart.

'You don't want to attract the attention of those serpents on your first day,' he said, nodding toward the guards. 'You have much to learn, my brother.'

97

Damascene looked up and it seemed as if every eye in the refectory hall was focused on him.

'You're as guilty as me,' said Lucien, spitting into Damascene's porridge and standing up to walk away. 'Enjoy your punishment!'

CHAPTER TWENTY-ONE

Damascene lay on top of the tatty mattress on his cold steel prison bed, which was not constructed for comfort. It was his first night in the jail and sleep was beyond him. Eyes wide open, he gazed through the dirty iron bars across the tiny window. He could see no moon or stars to lighten the sky. He listened to the noise of other prisoners talking, snoring or banging the steel bars for attention and realised a quiet night's sleep would be impossible here. For ten years now, he had struggled to sleep. The voices and images from 1994 often returned to his mind as he lay awake in the darkness. In his nightmares, the same scenes of horror returned each night in all their guilty gore, jolting him awake to stew in his conscious mind once again. Waking or sleeping, there was no escape from the past. He often tried to put these memories away by turning over roughly in his bed, as if turning his back on the past, but it didn't work. His former deeds refused to be squeezed back into a box to be locked away. The nightmares always returned with the sound of Claude's merciless laughter;

the face of his accuser, Patricia; her husband, his old friend Bernard; those poor little children and the screams of all the unknown victims of his club of nails. Some nights, he tried to pray, but no words came, just an overwhelming sense of shame in the presence of God.

Today, he had tried to keep his distance from his new cellmates, two wiry grey-haired men called Eric and Lambert. He didn't expect to be here for long, and so it wasn't worth spending time getting to know these criminals, he thought. His cellmates were also in bed and silent until suddenly Lambert began to sing.

'"*Tuzataha tuzataha igihe nikigera tuzataha,*
Tuzataha tuzataha igihe nikigera tuzataha."'

'Oh shut up, man!' Eric shouted, sitting up with a look of exasperation on his deeply lined face.

Lambert continued singing.

'"*Ayiwe tuzataha tuzataha igihe nikigera tuzataha tuzataha tuzataha igihe nikigera tuzataha.*"'

'I promise you, Damascene, you will soon get tired of this tune,' said Eric. 'Old Lambert here sings that same damn song every night!'

'One day, I will be free and I will have a new song to sing,' said Lambert, his eyes still closed. 'I lift up my eyes to the mountains where my help comes from. My help comes from the Lord. The maker of heaven and earth. That's what the Psalm says.'

'Oh, here we go again,' said Eric, getting out of bed and standing up. 'This is what I have to put up with every fucking night. What help do you need? Eh? Which Lord do you think can help you? Eh?'

He bent over his cellmate's bed and snarled, 'You are

a murderer. Driven by pure greed. A killer. A devil. You made children orphans. The children the Lord created and now you need His help? Shut the fuck up!'

Lambert did not reply but continued singing, more quietly now. Eric sat down on the end of Damascene's bed and put his head in his hands.

'Listening to him is punishment enough for any man!' he said.

'You are a religious man?' asked Damascene, in an attempt to engage with Lambert, but he ignored the question and continued singing.

'The only thing worse than religion is politics,' said Eric. 'So if you turn out to be a politician then my punishment will be too much!'

'I'm not religious or a politician,' said Damascene.

'Then what are you?' asked Eric.

Damascene paused.

'I don't know,' he said.

At that moment, Damascene realised he hadn't known who or what he was for years.

'Well, I suppose confused is better than evil,' said Eric, 'whatever evil is.'

'How many more years do you still have to do in here?' asked Damascene.

Eric sighed.

'Fifteen more years… and I am forty-five years old,' he said.

'And him?' asked Damascene.

'This stupid preacher man? He has twenty more years and he's fifty-five years old. He believes in life but the old fool would be better to pray he dies in peace soon.'

Damascene nodded but did not reply. He had already learnt in a short space of time that you could talk about Lambert as if he wasn't there. Eric seemed volatile and dangerous and he hadn't worked him out yet.

'And what did you do to end up in here?' he asked Damascene.

As Eric stared at him and examined his face, Damascene hesitated.

'I—'

Suddenly a prison guard banged on the bars of their cell door.

'You dogs in there! Shut up!'

The conversation stopped. Damascene was relieved. Eric was soon snoring but Lambert continued his song as a whisper until eventually Damascene drifted back into his nightmares once again.

CHAPTER TWENTY-TWO

When the day of the *gacaca* court finally arrived, a crowd of more than a hundred people gathered from across the region of Gisenyi to witness justice delivered for their friends and relatives who had been murdered in the genocide. It was a rainy day and the colourful umbrellas in the crowd belied the mood of the gathering. These sombre village hearings had been a familiar scene across Rwanda for the last two years. The *gacaca* court in Rwanda had a long tradition as "people's courts". For generations, disputes and conflicts in the villages had been resolved in this way, but never before on this scale. These community courts had the onerous responsibility of seeking truth, justice and reconciliation in many thousands of cases. Sitting on a bench under the palaver tree at the front of the gathering, with a wooden table in front of them, were the six judges: people of good character (rather than legal training) who had been chosen by the community to preside over the *gacaca* court. The men and women – who had been given this responsibility by their neighbours – each wore sashes in the colours of the Rwandan flag. In front of the judges were two separate wooden benches where the witnesses and the defendants were seated. Behind these main protagonists, scores of people were sitting on the ground waiting quietly for the grim proceedings to begin. Patricia, accompanied by Doctor Louise, sat rigidly on the witness bench, staring straight ahead and holding Louise's hand.

'I am here with you, beside you all the way,' said Louise.

Jean Pierre had asked Louise to ensure that Patricia did not repeat the incident with the gun at the police station, but Louise reassured him that Patricia had moved on since that day. It was true. The more Patricia looked to the future, the less she was driven by the past, but in the days leading up to the tribunal she had decided that she did not want to even look upon Damascene or the other prisoners. The very thought of these men disgusted her. She regarded them as cowards unworthy of being mentioned in the same breath as her late husband, Bernard. However, in the moment, she felt compelled to look the devil in the eye. She glanced over at the defendants' bench and caught Damascene's gaze. He quickly turned his head away in shame. For a second, Patricia recalled their teenage years when she thought this boy Damascene had the kindest eyes. She dismissed the memory in an instant.

Damascene's younger brother was also present for the hearing. Kalisa sat with his head down, his chin on one hand, not wanting to be here but certain it was his fraternal duty to be present. Since Damascene had been arrested, Kalisa had to work extra hours to pay the rent and, in spite of his naturally optimistic spirt, on some days he felt shattered and completely alone. In the past six months, he had begun to visit certain underground bars in the city to explore if the feelings he sometimes felt were for real. He would never have taken such a risk with Damascene around. In fact, Kalisa enjoyed the freedom of having the house to himself. Today, he was glad to see his brother but ashamed to be associated with what Damascene was here to account for. To this day, he could not understand or accept what his brother had done. Damascene smiled at him but Kalisa could not return his usual smile. His focus was on his old friend Patricia, who allowed him to look after her chickens when he was just a little boy. He loved those hens and he remembered how Patricia used to invite him into her home for a delicious meal of *isombe* made from cassava leaves from her garden. Patricia looked over at him for a moment but seemed not to recognise the young man he had become in the past ten years. This was not a gathering of strangers, but a grim reunion of former friends and neighbours.

The chairman of the *gacaca* court stood up in front of the desk and opened the proceedings.

'Please let us keep quiet and continue with *gacaca*. Let us pray...'

The murmurings in the crowd ceased; both witnesses and defendants on the benches sat up and the court began its painful work of testimony and conviction. Eventually, it was Damascene's turn.

'I am asking the next man here, Hakizimana Damascene, to stand up.'

A flurry of whispers of recognition echoed in the crowd as Damascene arose, head shaved and shivering in the rain in his flimsy pink prison uniform. It was so long since he had been imprisoned that Damascene was momentarily distracted by the fresh smell of the wet grass, but the pleasure was brief.

'This man is suspected of being a participant in the genocide against the Tutsis in 1994. We would like to ask anyone who knew him during the period of genocide and before the genocide to stand and testify to all he knows about him.'

The whole *gacaca* court was quiet. No one stood up. Damascene remained standing, shivering with his head lowered, holding one arm across the other like he used to when he was scolded by his teachers at school. Patricia felt her heart thumping in her chest. Kalisa glanced towards her, hoping she would not testify but knowing that she must speak. For five minutes, no one stood up. Louise did not move and gripped Patricia's hand. The murmuring in the crowd began again and the judges looked at each other, as if preparing to move on to the next accused. Finally, slowly and deliberately, Patricia let go of Louise's hand. She stood up, straightened her back and raised her head high. She took a deep breath and began to speak steadily and clearly.

'I know him,' she said, and so began her harrowing testimony.

Patricia spoke uninterrupted for thirty minutes, telling every terrible detail of her story. She paused only once, after she shared the horror of the slaughter of her children, but she remained strong throughout. She was determined not to break down. She wanted all present to see that she was a survivor and not a victim. This was her time to tell her story to the world, and having decided that she wanted to live, she was determined to get justice for her family. The crowd remained silent and the judges took notes, occasionally wiping tears from their eyes. When he heard the details of all that had happened to Patricia that night in 1994, Kalisa could not hold back his tears. In the quiet of the crowd, Damascene could distinguish the sobs of his little brother. It was unbearable. As Patricia calmly explained the role Damascene had played in the murder of her husband and children, the accused began to sway like a reed in a breeze, longing to be blown away into oblivion. She spoke with intensity but not with anger, and she never raised her voice. Nothing she said was new information to Damascene, but the words Patricia uttered, with such courage and dignity, added to the burden of guilt he felt.

'The government betrayed me,' she said. 'My neighbours betrayed me, life betrayed me, and more than anyone else, this man betrayed me.'

Patricia's powerful account of what Damascene always knew to be the diabolical truth seemed to strip away years of denial. A decade of reasons, excuses and justifications was swept away in half an hour. As Patricia completed her testimony, she looked directly at Damascene. He felt her eyes drill into his soul and he could not return her gaze. When Patricia sat down beside Louise, she felt a sense of victory.

In the next few minutes, three more witnesses stood up and accused Damascene of attacking people during the genocide.

'He was in Sylvestre's gang,' said one witness. 'This man was the one who carried a club of nails. He played a part in many attacks in my neighbourhood. They slaughtered men, women and children.'

The public exposure of his brutal crimes seemed to crush Damascene. With every accusation, he bowed lower under a burden of disgrace. Patricia felt satisfaction at his humiliation and anguish but unexpectedly, she also noticed a feeling of pity for the dejected, shivering figure in pink swaying uncertainly on his feet like a dejected little boy. Doctor Louise put her arm around Patricia and whispered soft words of encouragement. Kalisa was so overwhelmed with shame that he got up and ran out of the court. Damascene noticed his brother's departure and looked after him as if he had just lost the last broken fragment of his life. As the proceedings continued, both Damascene and Patricia sat motionless, lost in memories and overwhelming emotions, and when the court closed they both noticed that they could not recall a single word spoken after their own case was heard.

Damascene returned to the jail in the prison van. Seven convicted prisoners from the *gacaca* court sat with him in the vehicle, in silence, all with their heads bowed as if praying or wishing their life away. Damascene began rocking backwards and forwards in his seat, clutching his knees to his chest.

'Twenty-five years, twenty-five years, twenty-five years…' he muttered.

One of the guards, hearing these whimpers, cocked his rifle and pointed it at Damascene.

'Twenty-five years, eh?' he said. 'That's not enough for a devil like you. So shut your fucking mouth right now or I will set your dismal future on fire.'

CHAPTER TWENTY-THREE

'I'm home!' said Jean Pierre.

'Papa!' squealed Kevin and Ngabo in unison.

The boys, dressed in cosy pyjamas, sprinted towards Jean Pierre and hugged one paternal leg each.

'Easy, easy,' he said, 'and how are my little ninjas today?'

'Me first!' said Kevin, pushing his little brother out of the way.

'No, Papa, me first!' cried Ngabo.

'Both together!' said Jean Pierre.

He scooped his sons up into his arms for a shared hug and kissed them both on their heads. Louise emerged from the kitchen and Jean Pierre knew immediately from the look on her face that he was unacceptably late.

'Dinner was ready an hour ago, Jean Pierre,' said Louise.

She was glad to see him but it had to be said. The unpredictable hours and an unspoken undercurrent of danger in his job were a constant stress to Louise. The couple were in love and the family were happy, but under the peaceful exterior, Jean Pierre and Louise fought their own internal battles. She tried to control her worries, the same way Jean Pierre controlled his memories of the past. As she watched the children embrace their father, Louise had a deep sense of gratitude and noticed afresh how handsome her husband looked in his navy blue police uniform. As he removed his police beret, Louise kissed him on the cheek, and the family moved as one to the sofa where the children had been watching the DVD of *The Lion King* for the one hundredth time.

'What's in the bag tonight, Papa?' asked Ngabo.

'Guess what.'

'Hmm... chocolates?'

'Nope.'

'I know,' said Kevin. 'Today is Thursday. Papa gets us biscuits on Thursdays!'

'Correct! Big round of applause for Kevin,' said Jean Pierre.

'I'm the smartest!' said Kevin.

The whole family clapped hands and chuckled as Jean Pierre began to dispense the bag of biscuits to the children.

'Hold on, dinner first, then the biscuits!' said Louise.

She got up to return to the kitchen to rescue the overcooked meal. Jean Pierre followed and put his arm around her.

'I'm sorry, my love,' he said, 'I will try harder to get away on time.'

'How many times have I heard that promise?' said Louise.

'Well, I promise again, I will get better,' said Jean Pierre. 'I love my ever-patient wife!'

Louise laughed and kissed him.

'Help me serve this food,' she said, 'and you are cleaning up after.'

The family gathered around the dinner table, chatting and enjoying the food, and eventually the biscuits. When the meal was finished, the boys helped their father to tidy up.

'It's bedtime, boys,' said Jean Pierre, 'but before you go to bed, tell me, what did you learn in school today?'

'We learnt how to draw a cow!' said Ngabo.

He darted from the table to find his school bag and returned with his work of art.

'That's a beautiful cow!' said Jean Pierre.

'It looks more like a goat!' said Kevin.

'It's perfect,' said Louise, noticing the sibling rivalry. 'What about you, Kevin? What did you learn today?'

Kevin thought for a moment and looked very serious.

'The teacher taught us the history of genocide against the Tutsis in Rwanda,' he said.

Louise and Jean Pierre looked up at each other. This was a new part of the curriculum, an unthinkable lesson in their schooldays. They had discussed how to explain the genocide to the children when they were old enough; Mum is Hutu, Dad is Tutsi and we are all Rwandans. However, the school curriculum had beaten them to it.

'What did they tell you about the genocide?' asked Jean Pierre.

'Well,' began Kevin, taking a deep breath, 'Teacher said the Belgiums came here and took over Rwanda and they divided us by Hutu, Tutsi and Twa…'

'Yes,' said Jean Pierre. 'That's right, boys. They made it up. It wasn't a real ethnic difference…'

But Kevin was in full flow and continued. 'The Tutsis were hated and escaped from Rwanda in 19 erm... something...'

'1959,' said Louise, nodding for Kevin to continue.

'But when they tried to come home... erm... the Hutus didn't want them and hurt the Tutsis who were still in Rwanda and umm...'

'That's not nice,' said Ngabo, putting his hands over his ears.

Kevin tried hard to remember what happened next. He stared up at the ceiling with his little brow furrowed.

'Then, what?' asked Jean Pierre.

Ngabo got up from his seat and sat on his mother's knee, sucking his thumb, like he always did when he was anxious or tired.

Suddenly Kevin remembered the next part.

'Then in 1994, the airplane of the President was shot down by a missile and it crashed and he died and the next day the killing started and over... erm... one million Tutsis were killed by guns and machetes.'

Ngabo put his tiny hand across his mouth in horror.

Jean Pierre nodded at his sons and looked at Louise with sadness. Louise and Jean Pierre wanted to protect their children from all the darkness in the world, but they also knew how important it was to remember and to learn from the past.

'That's what happened, boys. It was a terrible time in our country and very sad for many people,' said Louise.

'Well,' explained Kevin, 'the teacher said we must learn from history and bring a change because we are still young and... erm... it must never happen again to anyone ever, ever.'

Little Ngabo looked upset.

'Is it going to happen again? Will it happen to us, Papa?' he asked.

Jean Pierre took his son's small hand.

'No, my son, you are safe. It will never happen again. Do not believe people who tell you to hate someone who is different from you.'

The boys looked up with wide, bright eyes and nodded at their father.

'Just work hard to achieve your dreams and do not waste time on divisions,' said Louise.

She kissed the boys on the head.

'What about us, Papa?' asked Kevin. 'Are we Hutu or Tutsi or Twa?'

'We are Rwandans,' he replied. 'We are all Rwandans and you should be proud of being a Rwandan.'

Later that night, Louise and Jean Pierre lay in bed looking up at the ceiling, reflecting on the conversation with their sons.

'I hope we said the right things,' said Louise. 'They know you were a soldier. There will be more questions soon.'

'I know, but I think we told them enough for now,' said Jean Pierre.

'Jean Pierre, my love,' said Louise, 'there are many things about those days you have never told me.'

'It's better that way,' said Jean Pierre. 'The past needs to stay in the past.'

'Sometimes I worry about you,' said Louise.

'You don't need to worry about me,' said Jean Pierre, kissing Louise on the cheek.

113

After a few moments of silence, Louise spoke again.

'I was thinking about Patricia when Kevin was speaking. It's not just a history lesson for her.'

'It's a whole new world for Patricia now,' said Jean Pierre. 'Twenty-five years in jail for that guy Damascene and now FARG taking care of her home and her studies.'

'She finally wants to live and at last she has some hope for the future,' said Louise.

'Thanks to you, my dear,' said Jean Pierre.

'I just stood with her and held her hand until she chose to live again,' said Louise.

'But there are so many others like her that still need counselling and help,' said Jean Pierre. 'I hear sad stories every day. The need is overwhelming. There are so many survivors and so many men who have been in prison.'

'What is the government doing for them now?' asked Louise.

'Well, the latest idea is for local leaders to organise clubs to unite survivors and perpetrators,' explained Jean Pierre.

'Really? That's amazing,' said Louise. 'I never thought such a thing was possible. There is so much hurt and anger. How can those survivors talk to the people who killed their families? I have spoken to patients in the hospital who told me they still shake with fear when they have to pass a Hutu on the path. One poor old woman told me she stopped going to Mass in case a Hutu killer sat beside her.'

'I've heard some incredible stories already,' said Jean Pierre, 'survivors and perpetrators from the same village, sharing their stories, perpetrators apologising and asking for forgiveness, and survivors letting go of their anger and forgiving their neighbours.'

'That sounds like a miracle,' said Louise. 'Some people are so strong! After all the terrible things that happened, this gives me hope for our land.'

'It gives me hope for the whole world,' said Jean Pierre. 'I hope our boys will learn about the reconciliation as well as the genocide.'

'In some ways, it's more important,' said Louise.

'Do you think Patricia would go to such a meeting, or is it too soon?' asked Jean Pierre.

'I don't know,' said Louise. 'I just pray Patricia gets better and finds a good husband and maybe gets some peace in her heart.'

Jean Pierre smiled at his wife.

'Are you saying a husband can bring a woman some peace?' he asked.

Louise smiled and exaggerated a roll of her eyes.

'Yes, most of the time,' she said. 'As long as he does what he is told!'

She smiled and stroked Jean Pierre's hair.

'Just like you do for me.'

CHAPTER TWENTY-FOUR

The brand-new curtains swayed in the gentle breeze that wafted through the recently restored window. Patricia lay on the bed gazing up at the photograph of Bernard in his finest suit, taken on the day of poor Felice's wedding. This was the first picture to be hung on any wall in the newly restored house. The renovations had taken a year to complete. As the construction work continued, Patricia noticed that with every repaired row of bricks she felt a little more healing. In the living room was an assortment of fading photographs of the whole family on one of their happy picnic days on Lake Kivu. These small square snaps seemed to come from a different life, another time, another world. Once the house restoration was completed, Patricia had moved in with what little she owned. She had just enough furniture to feel comfortable and after the years of depression in the cramped apartment in Kigali, she was glad to be home. This was where she belonged. The place of her ancestors. It felt like a new beginning, but the past lived here with her too, both the many happy times and that one terrible night. She felt closer to Bernard, Alice and Innocent than at any time in the past ten years, but the more she felt the presence of her family in their home, the more she felt alone.

She admired Bernard's photograph, framed in musave wood, strong and reliable, just like him. She remembered how striking he looked on that day. As was her habit, she began to speak to her husband.

'I miss you, my love. I still love you with all my heart, and I miss you and the little ones every day. I'm glad to be back home here with you once more, but I feel so alone in this dark world.'

Hanging beside the photograph was the beautiful red, white and black *imigongo*[10] her sister, Amina, had created and given to Patricia for her birthday the year before the genocide. Every surviving object from before 1994 represented a part of an old fairy tale that was supposed to lead to a happy every after. In reality, her life was transformed into a horror story that never truly ended.

'You will not believe it, my love, but I have enrolled as a student at university now. You always said I was too smart for just growing avocados! I have a girl that helps me with the garden now and I've even made some new young student friends too. Just you watch, husband, I will earn my degree. One day, I will be a lawyer. I'm doing it for you… But I will miss you at my graduation.'

---

10   *Imigongo* is an art form popular in Rwanda, traditionally made by women using cow dung. Often in the colours black, white and red, popular themes include spiral and geometric designs that are painted on walls, pottery and canvas.

The sense of loss flicked her smile to a frown.

'He is now in jail,' she continued.

Her face darkened.

'That Hutu devil, your so-called friend.'

She shuddered, as if wanting to shake off some filth. Then she continued to confide in Bernard.

'I thought justice would bring me peace, but not yet. I am starting to heal but I am still not satisfied. While you rest in peace, my love, that devil must pay.'

Patricia looked into her dead husband's eyes. They were the kindest eyes in the world, but as she gazed into his soul she was surprised to sense a tender rebuke of her hatred for Damascene.

'I love you,' she said, and drifted off to a half-sleep mixed with treasured memories and terror.

The next day, just as Patricia was finishing her final lecture of the afternoon, there was a fierce rainstorm. Patricia and the other students without umbrellas sheltered under the eaves outside the main entrance to the university. Grace arrived, splashing through the muddy puddles and grabbing hold of Patricia's arm as she joined her under the eaves.

'Hey, sister, I was looking for you earlier,' said Patricia. 'I have my first big exam next week and I need some advice from a mature student.'

'Mature? Even though you are ten years older than me, Grandma!' laughed Grace, shivering in the damp air close to Patricia.

'Be careful or I'll throw you back into the ocean!' laughed Patricia.

She held her new friend close for warmth.

'Where were you?'

'I had to see the professor about my project. He says I need to be more ambitious, and being a girl is no excuse!'

The friends rolled their eyes and laughed.

'How are we going to get home?' said Patricia. 'This rain is here for the whole day.'

'Hold on, sister,' said Grace.

She jumped back into the deluge and dashed towards the front doors of the university. 'I will find us an umbrella!'

Patricia smiled at the energy and good humour of her young friend. Grace's zest for life reminded her of the young woman she used to be. She trusted her earnest fellow student, but Patricia had little confidence that Grace would find them an umbrella. She took a deep breath and stepped out into the rain. Patricia tramped through the mud with determination. She had braved worse than a little rain, she thought. These days, she noticed how minor discomforts such as rain, a late bus or being sold bad *posho* seemed more tolerable after all she had endured. Suddenly, to her surprise, Grace grabbed her arm again and gathered Patricia under a freshly sourced umbrella.

'Where did you find an umbrella, Grace?' said Patricia.

'Oh, I can be very resourceful!' she replied. 'There's a boy in first year who adores me and would do anything to make me happy!'

'Does he not know you have a boyfriend at the church?' said Patricia.

Grace chuckled as Patricia caught sight of Grace's admirer, Nkurunziza, emerging from the main entrance holding his books over his head to keep the rain off.

'It must be love,' she said. 'Poor boy! You'll break his heart.'

'Why did you leave without me and an umbrella?' Grace asked. 'Look at you! You are soaking wet!'

'I've got no time for climate change,' said Patricia.

'Aren't you scared of the rain?'

'Why would I be scared of the rain?'

'Sometimes, I don't understand you, Patricia. You are a mystery to me.'

Patricia laughed and put her arm around her friend as they walked in the rain beneath the shared umbrella towards the bus station.

'Honestly, Grace, I'm not scared of anything anymore. I'm not a little girl, I'm not a wife and I'm not a mother. No one needs me anymore, so I have nothing to worry about.'

'I need you,' said Grace, stopping and smiling, 'you're my wise old mama!'

Once again, Grace made Patricia laugh. She couldn't help herself. Even on the days when Patricia was determined to be sad, Grace had the ability to make her smile. When the women reached the bus stop, Patricia stopped and looked up at the clouds, as if she was detaching from the world.

'You were just a little girl, sweet Grace, but you know it rained when over one million people were dying. It rained and rained and rained. But all the rain in the world could not wash away the blood. If God wants to take people away, then let it rain.'

'Oh, Patricia, my sister, sometimes you are too sad,' said Grace. 'You must come to the concert at my church next week. It will cheer you up, I promise you.'

Grace searched in her bag and on finding an invitation handed it to Patricia, who examined it closely.

'A Christian concert at church?' said Patricia. 'That's not my idea of fun!'

'Well, I met Rwibutso at church, and his father is the pastor,' said Grace. 'Papa says he is organising the praise and worship concert to bless God, but he wants to bless all of us too. Come along, Patricia, it will be a happy day and we can give thanks to God.'

It was a long time since Patricia had thanked God for anything. She was angry at God for what had befallen her family. Bernard was a good man who went to church, sang in the choir and taught in Sunday school. Where was God when he prayed to Him to protect his family? Churches were supposed to be a refuge, but her family and friends had been slaughtered in the very churches they had fled to for safety, betrayed by wicked priests and fellow believers. Every time Patricia walked past a new church being built beside the site of a church destroyed in a genocidal massacre, she felt sick. She believed the churches where people were betrayed by fellow Christians deserved to remain as rubble forever. She felt angry at the thought of Hutu Christians standing in church thanking God for the forgiveness of their terrible sins. In fact, Patricia no longer believed in God. She still believed in the Devil because she had experienced evil, but she saw no evidence of God in her life.

'How many of us cried out to God to send us help?' she once told Doctor Louise. 'And God sent us more machetes!'

In spite of these feelings, she respected Grace and felt enlivened by her innocent faith. She did not want to offend her newfound friend, so she kept these thoughts to herself.

'Thank you, Grace,' she said. 'Sounds good. I'll come to your concert. Just don't expect me to sing or dance!'

'I promise you, my church is a good place, sister. It's where I met Rwibutso. Who knows? You might meet a boyfriend there too!'

Both women laughed as Patricia's bus arrived and she left Grace standing, smiling in the rain under the umbrella.

CHAPTER TWENTY-FIVE

Patricia stood outside the church listening to the sound of singing inside. Now that she was here, she was unsure if she was prepared to go inside. She sat on the grass and closed her eyes. A passerby may have assumed she was praying before entering the sanctuary, but Patricia was not communing with God. She was remembering. As the sound of joyful voices wafted through the little windows of the church, Patricia thought of her parents and her dear friends Isabelle and Felice, entrapped and murdered in their own church, betrayed by their priest, abandoned by God. Quietly, she turned away from the church and spoke to her parents, not to God.

'My dear momma, I miss you every day. I'm doing okay now. I have chosen to live. My little house is fixed and, Papa, you will not believe it, but your daughter is at university now. Today, I'm meeting my friend at church. I know how much you loved the church, but, Momma, I don't think I can go inside. I haven't been in a church for ten years. Our church in Gisenyi is a museum now, a memorial, with the clothes and bones of all those we loved still resting there since the day… from that day…'

Just then, Patricia noticed a familiar tune coming from within the church. It was *Amazing Grace*, her mother's favourite hymn. Tears ran down her face as she continued to pray to her mother.

'Are you sending me a message, dear Momma? *I once was lost, but now I'm found*? Do you want me to go inside?'

Patricia opened her eyes, stood up and walked slowly towards the front door of the church, tears streaming down her face. On opening the door, she was enveloped by the warmth of the gathering and the volume of the singing. Just inside, Grace was waiting to meet her.

'I knew you would come,' she said, hugging her friend.

Grace led Patricia to her seat at the front of the church. As they walked hand in hand up the aisle, she felt her mother's favourite song wrapping her in a safe embrace.

'"*Through many dangers, toils and snares,*
We have already come
T'was Grace that brought us safe thus far
And Grace will lead us home."'

'Are you keeping me safe and leading me home?' she whispered to Grace.

The two women chuckled as they sat down beside Rwibutso, who shook Patricia's hand politely and welcomed her to his father's church.

'You are very welcome here, Madame Patricia. I hope you enjoy the praise and worship,' he said.

As the singing continued, Patricia kept glancing at Grace beside her. She noticed the sincere smile on her friend's face as, eyes closed, she sang and raised her hands in worship. Silently, Patricia said her own prayer, not to God but to her mother.

'Thank you, Momma. Thank you for sending me Grace. I feel safe with Grace.'

As the praise band played the next song, Patricia remained seated, praying to her mother and father, to Isabelle and Felice. Grace and Rwibutso and the whole congregation rose to their feet and lifted their hands in praise.

"*We give you all the glory,*
We worship you, our Lord,
You are worthy to be praised."

When the band leader announced the final song of the concert, Patricia opened her eyes. It was as if she had awakened from a dream where she was back at church with her mother and father beside her, her friends sitting behind her and Bernard singing in the choir. She felt the old familiar pain returning as Rwibutso's father, Pastor Robert, made his way to the pulpit. He stopped to shake hands with an elderly man in the front row.

'That's my grandfather,' said Grace, 'and my father is the man sitting beside him. I want you to meet them after the service.'

Everyone sat down to listen to the preacher deliver an epilogue.

'Praise be to almighty God and blessings in the Name of Jesus!'

A wave of "Hallelujahs" flowed from the front of the church to the back row, echoing back to the pulpit as Pastor Robert began to speak.

'Let the church of God say Amen!'

'Amen!' was the response of a hundred voices.

'The Word of God says in Deuteronomy 33, verses 29 to 30,

"Blessed are you, Israel,

Who is like you?

He is your shield and helper and your glorious sword,

Your enemies will cower before you and you will tread on their heights."'

People around Patricia stood up and began clapping their hands and shouting, 'Praise the Lord!'

Why did God not protect my family from their enemies? she thought.

Pastor Robert continued to share his closing remarks.

'Brothers and sisters, this morning, as I prayed about the message to share with you today, the Lord spoke to me. He told me to tell you this. The Lord will save you from your enemies, yes! But listen, my friends! The Lord wants you to forgive your enemies too.'

Patricia felt a sudden urge to cover her ears.

'In the prayer that Jesus taught us to pray, he said,

"Forgive us our trespasses as we forgive those who have trespassed against us."'

I knew I shouldn't have come here! thought Patricia.

'I am asking myself,' continued Pastor Robert, 'do we love our enemies as Jesus said we must?'

The mood in the church was sombre now. Many people here had lost loved ones in the genocide. This was not a comforting message. Rwibutso shifted uncomfortably in his seat and looked at Grace.

'There's a time and a place,' he whispered to Grace. 'He always does this at just the wrong moment.'

Grace felt the change in atmosphere too and was aware of Patricia bristling beside her.

'But what if this is the word God wants us to hear today?' she whispered to Rwibutso.

Abruptly, Patricia picked up her bag from the bench and ran out of the church.

'Stay here,' said Grace to Rwibutso.

She followed Patricia outside and eventually caught up with her.

'Hey, sister, what's wrong?' she asked.

'What's wrong with me!' Patricia replied, still walking away. 'Really? What's wrong with me! What's wrong with your pastor?'

Patricia strode on in anger. She needed to get far away from those words as quickly as possible.

'It's just a little preaching,' said Grace, catching up again. 'Please tell me, Patricia. What is the problem?'

Patricia stopped and turned to Grace.

'What does your pastor know about forgiving your enemy? He survived! You know what happened to me! I'm sorry, Grace. I know he is your boyfriend's father but you should go back in there right now and tell him that he and his god are wrong!'

Grace appeared pensive and took a deep breath.

'Stop, Patricia,' she said, 'I've something important to tell you.'

'Please don't tell me that God will help me to forgive. I cannot forgive those devils,' said Patricia.

'Listen, sister,' continued Grace, 'I never talk about it, but I want to tell you something.'

Grace began to cry.

Patricia had never seen her happy-go-lucky friend upset like this before and she was shocked.

'What is it, sister?' she asked.

Grace paused for a moment and then took another deep breath.

'They killed my mother too,' she said, so quietly that Patricia thought she had misheard.

'What!'

'They killed my mother in the genocide, and my aunt and my uncle. My father and my grandpa in the church are the only ones who survived.'

'Grace!' said Patricia. 'You lost your mother!'

The two friends sat down on a little wall at the side of the road.

'Yes, I don't remember much about it. I was just a little girl. When the genocide began, my family was visiting Kigali for an Easter conference with the churches. I remember everyone being happy, singing at church, and then one day everyone was scared and running away. The next day, my mother wasn't there anymore and we hid in a swamp. It was horrible but my father said we were playing a game. I asked him if Momma was going to catch up with us and play hide and seek in the swamp with us. He whispered, "Of course she is." Eventually, we escaped that dirty swamp and came home. My father said we were the lucky few, but I never saw my mother again.'

'Oh my God, Grace,' said Patricia, 'I am so sorry.'

'It's why I will never trust white people,' said Grace.

'What?' said Patricia.

'My father told me we were staying near Kicukiro. The UN were evacuating whites from the school nearby.

My mother left us and ran up to their trucks and begged them to take us too. She believed the foreigners would help us. They refused and drove off, abandoning us to the Interahamwe in the streets. In all the chaos, my mother got separated from us. If she hadn't put her faith in the *muzungu*, she might have survived. But black lives are not important to white people.'

'Oh my God, Grace, I had no idea,' said Patricia.

'I only tell my closest friends,' said Grace. 'This story is a part of me, but it's not all of me.'

Patricia embraced her young friend and they wept together.

After a while, Patricia spoke. 'Now you understand why I cannot forgive. You have suffered from those devils too.'

'Yes, I do understand,' said Grace. 'I understand the pain and the loss, and the deep rage and the desire for revenge. I had all of those feelings too. I understand.'

'So when you hear a pastor tell you to forgive, you know it's just fine religious words. You know it's not possible. You know you could never forgive the genocide perpetrator who killed your own mother.'

After a short pause, Grace took both of Patricia's hands and looked into her eyes.

'Yes, I forgave him,' she said.

Patricia let go and stood back, demonstrating just how much the idea repelled her.

'I forgave him,' said Grace.

Patricia got up and walked away. She stomped her feet in angry disbelief.

'You forgave the devil that killed your own mother?'

Her beautiful face was contorted to ugliness, and tears of anger ran down her cheeks.

Grace called after her. 'I forgave him, sister. And God can help you to forgive too.'

Patricia finally did what she had felt the urge to do all day long. She put her hands over her ears and ran away. As she fled, the sound of the Hutu Interahamwe singing vile songs of hatred replayed in her head. As she ran, her mind was filled with images of Damascene holding a club of nails; sweating, pointing and mocking. Machetes. Gunfire. Bernard. Alice. Innocent. Felice. Dead Tutsi bodies in the street, in the fields, in the swamps. Bodies floating on Lake Kivu, a dead baby floating in the Nyabarongo River. Blood in the hills. Blood in the church. Blood in her home. She screamed and ran on and on, but she could not escape the terror in her mind. Arriving home, she slammed the front door behind her and threw herself on the bed.

All night long, she was tortured by terror. Every time she awoke, the same words reverberated in her mind: *I will never forgive. I hate those Hutu devils. As long as I live, I will never, never forgive.*

Chapter Twenty-Six

It had always been there. The guilt, that is. Even though Damascene had buried it away for years, like the bodies of so many missing victims of the genocide. He had crowded it out of his mind by busyness and diminished its power by political justification. For eleven years, he had also tried to dampen the truth crying out in his heart by the deadening effect of alcohol, but in his pure soul Damascene knew he had committed great wrong. Ever since childhood, he had known the difference between right and wrong.

'Damascene is a good boy. He will never let me down,' his mother would say.

He was glad his parents had not lived to witness his shame. Night after night, and week after week, as he lay awake on the straw mattress of his prison bed, more and more vivid memories of the genocide returned to haunt him. At first, there was just a hint of guilt, then a trickle of conscience, but as months blurred into years in prison, he could no longer hold back the dam of memories and he was overcome with a flood of regret and remorse. It reminded him of how the hatred had overtaken him as a young man. At first, it was just a resentful thought about Tutsis, then a joke over a beer and an unchallenged slur among Hutu friends. The mistrust was fed by political leaders, amplified by RTLM radio screaming 'Cockroaches!' and 'Snakes!' and blessed by hate-filled clergy, until a deep fear that if we do not destroy them first they will annihilate us finally possessed him. In the darkness of the prison cell, as Eric snored and Lambert sang, Damascene was tormented by flashes of horror with him wielding his club of nails. Nevertheless, the memory that haunted him most was the betrayal and slaying of his friend Bernard and his dear children.

Patricia is right, he often thought, *I am a devil*.

Life in prison was a mixture of hard labour in the sun by day and pure boredom by moonlight in the evenings. He rarely engaged in conversation with other prisoners during work and outdoor exercise. He avoided Nsengiyumva and Lucien in the dining hall and, even after three years of sharing a cell, Damascene maintained a distance from his cellmates. Eric wanted to talk about history and politics. Damascene listened to many nighttime lectures about the destruction and division of Rwanda by the colonialists and the latest political controversies Eric gleaned from the daily newspaper.

'Of course, when the colonialists tell the story of the genocide,' Eric explained, 'they don't mention how the Belgians divided us by ethnic group in the first place. There is no talk about the Belgian priests who helped in the genocide, or the secret role of the French soldiers. No, it is all about tribal African savages because *bazungu* are superior in their minds! White history for white minds!'

Eric regarded the government's Unity and Reconciliation Programme as a way to maintain political control of the masses rather than a genuine attempt to build the identity of one community of people.

'Oh yeah, it's all about "One Rwanda" these days,' he would say. 'That's one Rwanda under a military dictatorship that will not tolerate any political opposition! Just watch what happens to any poor soul who dares to speak out against our reconciling president!'

Sometimes Damascene agreed and sometimes he disagreed, but he refused to take the bait of any argument and rarely engaged with Eric. On the other hand, Lambert prayed on his knees every night. He read aloud from a battered old Bible and continued to sing hymns in his bed until the guards told him to shut up. Eventually, Damascene got used to the quiet singing and regarded it as a lullaby that might just help him to sleep, rather than a nightly irritant that kept him awake as much as the belligerent mosquitoes. For two years, Lambert invited Damascene to join him at the prison chapel on a Sunday morning, and every week Damascene declined.

'Even if there was a merciful God, I'm beyond saving,' he would say. 'The only thing that will save me now is as much *ikigage*[11] as I can drink!'

However, one Sunday morning as he lay in bed looking out of the window of his cell, a small red-billed firefinch alighted on the window sill. He hadn't seen one of these beautiful little birds since he was imprisoned. They were everywhere in Kigali but Damascene had almost forgotten

---

11   *Ikigage* is a Rwandese traditional beer made from *sorghum* malt and local plants.

what they looked like. The bird seemed to peek into the prison cell through the bars as it pecked for insects around the base of the bars on the window. The sun was shining, and in the distance, Damascene could hear the sound of children playing. For a moment, he felt an unfamiliar lightness in his spirit.

'Well, my brother,' said Lambert, 'you know what I'm going to ask you?'

'He stopped asking me years ago,' said Eric. 'He knows what I think of churches and their fat pastors who are paid by a corrupt government to advance their politics of forced reconciliation.'

'Okay, just this once, for you,' said Damascene, winking at the little bird.

Eric sat up in surprise, shaking his head, and Lambert smiled.

'I knew you would open your heart one day, my brother,' he said.

'It can't make me any more unhappy,' said Damascene.

'Bring me back some wine from the communion cup,' mocked Eric.

In the small prison chapel, the inmates, clothed in clean, identical uniforms, sat in orderly rows. Damascene lingered alone in the back row as Lambert took a seat at the front. To his surprise, Damascene appreciated the quiet atmosphere in the chapel, but he wanted to remain unseen under his dark cloak of shame. Just as the service was about to begin, a familiar figure crept into the back row beside him. It was Nsengiyumva, the same prisoner who put on a public show of cynicism to all the other prisoners every day. Noticing Damascene, he looked embarrassed, as if his wife had spotted him entering a brothel.

'Today,' said the priest, 'our guest preacher is brother Gasongo from Prison Fellowship Rwanda.'

Damascene looked up at the tall pastor, who was dressed in jeans and a t-shirt. Although Gasongo had a benevolent smile, Damascene expected to be unmoved by his words.

'Brothers, I want you to know this,' he began. 'No matter what you have done and how you may feel, God has not let go of you. God's mercy is everywhere and, as it says in 1st John 1 and verse 9, "If we confess our sins He is faithful and just to forgive us our sins and to cleanse us from all unrighteousness". Listen, dear brothers, I know you have done great wrong, but God's forgiveness is always there for you.'

Damascene heard the words but they did not connect to his heart.

But I am a devil, he thought. *Who forgives a devil?*

Then, as if speaking directly to Damascene's thoughts, the pastor said, 'No, you are not a devil!'

Damascene looked up.

'I know your heart is broken. You always remember and you regret every wicked thing you did. You see yourself as a devil who deserves to be locked up in this place forever.'

Damascene stood up. It felt as if the pastor was speaking only to him.

'You treat yourself like an unrighteous demon. But what I am here to tell you is that God is full of mercy for each and every one who confesses his transgressions.'

Damascene felt a sudden wave of emotion overwhelm him. He tried to hold it back, as he did not want to appear weak to his fellow prisoners, but he lost control and began to cry, quietly at first, until he was overwhelmed by sobs of pain and remorse. Other prisoners turned around to see what was happening, while Nsengiyumva found the situation too uncomfortable and quietly left the chapel. At the end of the service, Pastor Gasongo approached Damascene and asked him his name.

'Why are you crying, my brother?' he asked.

Head down, still weeping, Damascene replied, 'I have done great wrong. I betrayed my friends. I let them die. I joined the mob. I attacked men, women and children with a club of nails. I knew it was wrong but I was too weak to resist. I am responsible for the shedding of innocent blood.'

Gasongo put a hand on Damascene's head and prayed silently.

'I do not deserve to live. I am a filthy beast. A devil.'

Gasongo sat down beside him and put an arm around his shoulder. Damascene flinched at the touch of kindness.

'You are still a human being,' said the pastor. 'You can be forgiven, my brother. You can have mercy from God and perhaps from the widows and orphans who suffered because of you. If you confess to your sins.'

Damascene shook his head. The pastor was kind, he thought, but he was speaking of the impossible.

'Look, Damascene,' he continued, 'you can change. I believe it is possible. I have seen many men like you transformed. You can be a part of bringing a change for our people. This is still your country, brother. You destroyed it once, but you can contribute to rebuilding our land.'

Damascene looked up. He wanted to believe these words.

'Go, Damascene. Go! Starting from today. Do it. Do it now.'

After Gasongo had prayed with him, Damascene returned to his cell with Lambert. Eric could see that Damascene had been crying.

'Oh God, no! I warned you not to go there. It looks like you have lost your mind,' said Eric. 'Don't be fooled by Lambert here. Forget about God. You don't need that nonsense. The church just wants to control you, just like the politicians they bribe. All you need to do is to erase what is in your memory. Rub it away. Just don't go there. Works fine for me.'

Ignoring Eric, Damascene sat on his bed, took out a notebook from under his pillow and began to write. At first, he didn't know where to start. He began and stopped and then tore up the paper and threw it in the bin. He lay back on the bed, crying tears of frustration. He was ready to give up. Neither Lambert nor Eric tried to intervene. Then Damascene remembered the pastor's final words to him before he left the chapel:

Do it right now! Let your country know what is in your heart at this moment and you can stop the pain. Do it now!

He looked up and noticed the red-billed firefinch was back on the window sill, as if expecting a progress report. Damascene sat up, turned over a new page and began to write. Once he began writing, he could not stop, until finally, that night, exhaustion cradled him into a deeper sleep than he had known for many years.

CHAPTER TWENTY-SEVEN

'Quick, hide in here, Pastor Samuel is coming!' said Albert to the two young women who had just presented their takings from the previous night.

Rachel and Matusi stepped into the dusty shack where Albert stored the weed for the street kids to sell. In the slums of Kampala, prostitution and drug dealing were complementary business ventures for Albert. Selling their bodies was not the first choice for Rachel and Matusi, but their father had disappeared long ago and there was no money for food, never mind school, for the two sisters.

'*Oli otya*?' said Pastor Samuel.

'*Gyendi*,' replied Albert.

'I have another letter from your sister in Rwanda,' said the pastor, handing the latest correspondence to Albert.

'Thank you. You are the postman as well as the pastor,' said Albert, standing in front of the firmly closed door.

'I think you prefer me as postman,' said Pastor Samuel. 'You still won't come to church or change your ways.'

'I'm beyond change, Pastor,' said Albert.

'How is your sister?' asked Pastor Samuel.

'She is doing well, sir,' said Albert. 'She is studying at university now.'

'You see! An example to you, Albert,' said Pastor Samuel, raising his eyebrows. 'If a woman can do this, think of what a man like you could do!'

Albert shook his head.

'Do you plan to return to Rwanda?'

'No, sir, I have made my life here in Uganda.'

'But, Albert, this is no life. I know of your business interests here. I saw you hide those poor girls in this hut you sell weed from, using little kids. You can do better.'

'I don't know what you're talking about, Pastor,' said Albert. 'I'm just a humble businessman and I help out the poor kids on the streets.'

'You can hide who you are from me, brother Albert, but you cannot hide from God,' said the pastor.

Albert laughed and shook his head lightly as Pastor Samuel held his gaze.

'I could never return. My life is here now,' he said.

'But look at how your sister has recovered.'

'My other sister died. My parents died. Most of my friends died or disappeared in Congo.'

'Listen,' said Pastor Samuel, 'maybe your sister needs you.'

The conversation was interrupted by a noisy gang of street kids, arriving, out of breath, at the door of the hut, almost knocking over Pastor Samuel.

'Please, boss,' said Julius, 'the witch doctor chased us. He says he will curse us for selling weed.'

'Don't listen to him,' said Albert, and then looking at

Pastor Samuel, as if to include him in his next comment, 'No one believes in all of that superstitious religion anymore.'

'But, boss...' said Julius.

'Get back to your work, or I will beat you like a snake!' growled Albert.

Julius and the other boys ran off again down a nearby alleyway, scattering a pile of rubbish at their feet as they escaped the wrath of both their boss and the witch doctor.

'They're just kids,' said Pastor Samuel, shaking his head and wandering off.

'You have a sister in Rwanda?' said Matusi, popping her head around the door.

Albert nodded and sat down on the step to read the latest letter from Patricia.

'Does she need you?' said Rachel, as the two women sat down beside him.

'I'm the last thing she needs,' said Albert.

'I would not like to be all alone,' said Matusi, putting her arm around her sister.

Albert was happy to know his sister was doing well, but he still needed to forget Rwanda. Life in Kisenyi was tough, but at least here he could bury the memories, contain his fury and control the overwhelming desire for revenge. He opened the letter and smiled as he read of the new life his sister was creating. In this letter, Patricia told him about her efforts, tilling and sowing, to bring her garden back to life again.

I will grow the best avocados in Rwanda once more, she wrote.

When Patricia wasn't studying, she had been working hard for months to restore the garden at her home. It wasn't an easy job to do alone. The house had been fully repaired two years ago, renovated by builders through the government grant. However, restoring the small piece of land surrounding the house was down to Patricia. The garden was too small to be considered a farm, but it was large enough to grow a healthy crop of avocados to both eat and sell. In her old life, the burden of tilling, planting and harvesting was shared with Bernard, and then with a little assistance from Alice, who considered being allowed to help out as a sign that she was very grown up. The garden had been neglected for so long that none of the original plants remained. All had shrivelled and died, like Patricia's former life here. Bernard's old shed had collapsed in a heap of rotting wood. The soil was hard and lifeless now and so Patricia had to start all over again. For the first few years back home, Patricia did not have sufficient energy to start to work on the garden. It was enough to have a home again, but slowly, as Patricia began to feel herself come alive again, she developed a desire to see life growing around her once more. While working in the garden, she started to notice the sound of the hummingbirds and the smell of eucalyptus.

'I will grow the best avocados in Rwanda once more,' she repeated, with every dig of her spade.

The shed at the back of the house remained as a ruin. Bernard had constructed this large wooden outhouse as a secure place for his garden tools, a small storehouse for the annual crops as well as a small section that served as a chicken house. Patricia missed the company of her hens and planned one day to earn enough money to rebuild the outhouse and purchase a few chickens. As

141

well as producing eggs, she was certain that the sound of the rooster and the cluck of the hens would bring the whole house alive again. As she laboured in the sunshine, she thought about the most recent letter from Albert in Uganda with all the wonderful news he had shared about his family and business. Of course, she longed for him to return to Rwanda, but she was happy to hear that Albert was settled in Kampala with a good job in one of the new telecom companies. She smiled when she thought about his beautiful wife, Matusi, and their son, Julius, and the new home he was building for them near Lake Victoria. *Maybe one day*, she thought, *if he doesn't visit me, I will go and visit him.*

Chapter Twenty-Eight

'How are you, Dammy?' said Kalisa.

He took off his baseball cap and set it on the table.

'I feel good today, little brother,' replied Damascene. 'Today is a good day.'

Kalisa smiled broadly. This was so different from the Damascene of recent years.

'Really? I never thought I'd ever hear you say that again!'

Every month, for the past three years, Kalisa had visited his brother in prison. He didn't enjoy the visits. He retained a sense of shame for the crimes of his brother. Some of the other prisoners mocked him for his bright clothes.

'Here comes the Fresh Prince of Bel-Air!' they shouted.

As time went by, Kalisa noticed how most of the other prisoners had different family members visiting, while he alone came to see Damascene. The visits were short, but in the limited time together, Kalisa noticed a gradual change in Damascene. In the first year, there was nothing but anger and despair, and often the two brothers simply sat together across the table, heads down, in silence. Even Kalisa's attempts at humour, including a Michael Jackson moonwalk dance in front of the disapproving prison wardens, did not raise a smile.

'Uh oh! It's the crazy little brother again,' they said, each time Kalisa arrived for a visit.

Then last year, Damascene told his younger brother all about his experience in the prison chapel. He told Kalisa that since that day, he had started to write down all that was in his heart. He never shared the writing, but Kalisa began to notice a change in his brother. It was almost imperceptible at first, but gradually he detected a lessening of anger and despair, then a growth of remorse and shame and now even a hint of hopefulness. As the years passed, Damascene started to ask Kalisa more about what was going on in his life. The conversations now included lighter moments when Kalisa shared his excitement about some success at work, his favourite new song or his latest romance. For the last twelve months, Damascene had updated Kalisa on the regular meetings in the prison chapel and his insights from counselling with the Prison Fellowship pastor. Damascene stopped making excuses for his actions. He finally told his brother there was no justification for what he had done. Kalisa was amazed at the transformation in his brother. He was taking responsibility for his crimes. Then he began to talk about seeking forgiveness from his victims. The old rhetoric, justifying his actions and blaming others for all the pain he inflicted, began to fade.

'It's good to see you again, little brother. Tell me about the latest music, no need to dance, though, and tell me about your latest girlfriend!' said Damascene.

Kalisa smiled.

'It's all good, Dammy. And you know that Uwase has been my only girlfriend for more than a year now! Apart from Beyonce, of course! Everything is beautiful, my brother! Now do you really want all the details?'

Damascene laughed and paused, before asking, 'Have you been following the news about all the prisoners who have confessed in public and asked for forgiveness?'

Kalisa nodded. He was glad to move on from questions about his imaginary girlfriend.

'Yes, everyone's talking about it,' he said. 'It's all over the newspapers and on the television. It's very controversial. Some people say it is the new Rwanda, and the government says this is the way forward, but others are saying it's not real and not even possible.'

'I've been discussing this inside here with many of the other genocide perpetrators,' said Damascene.

'And what are they saying?' asked Kalisa, 'I have seen on television where some prisoners have confessed. They have been released and gone back to their villages to build houses for destitute survivors.'

'Well, some perpetrators, like that guy Lucien from Gisenyi, say they will never confess,' said Damascene, sighing. 'I was once one of them, brother, but now my heart has changed.'

'But, Dammy, I hear also of some prisoners who confess but who do not tell the whole truth. They ask for forgiveness but they are only thinking of themselves. They

145

are not sincere. They just want to say the right things to be released from prison.'

'Little brother, they may be released from these prison walls but they will never be free until they truly confess… and unless they are forgiven.'

'But how can they live again in the villages with the families they hurt? How can they work in the same fields, sit in the same church pews, stand together cheering at the same football match? The shame and the hatred are too much. There will be revenge killings, I'm sure of it,' said Kalisa.

Damascene looked into his brother's eyes intensely.

'I see some prisoners who want to confess, just to heal the shame and hurt in their own hearts, but that is not me, my brother.'

'I know,' said Kalisa.

'I want to tell the whole truth, for Patricia and her surviving family – I think her brother, Albert, also survived. I do not even know the names of the other families I hurt but Patricia was my friend. For three years, I have spent sleepless nights in this dark place, thinking about every detail, crying and sweating until my sheets are damp and cold. I want to confess it all and ask for forgiveness. I know I do not deserve her forgiveness, but I have decided I must confess and… I leave the rest to God.'

Kalisa was not surprised. His brother had changed so much in the last few years. He seemed to be returning to the man he once looked up to as a little boy, before their lives were torn apart by genocide. Kalisa stretched across the table and hugged Damascene. It was the same way Damascene had always embraced Kalisa whenever he fell and cut his knees as a little boy.

'This is a good step, my brother,' he said, 'but I must tell you this.'

'What's wrong?' asked Damascene.

'After you went to prison, I began to feel guilty too for keeping your secret, while survivors like Patricia were in so much pain and sorrow.'

Damascene shook his head. 'No. You were just a kid.'

'But, Dammy, I did wrong too. I could have accused you myself or asked you to hand yourself in, or—'

'No!' Damascene interrupted. 'You were an innocent child. I am responsible. But you know, little brother, I think I can finally be free now. If I expose the whole truth and someone seeks revenge and I die, at least I know I will rest in peace.'

'Time's up!' shouted the prison guard.

'I don't want you to die, brother,' said Kalisa, now crying. 'There has been too much death in this land. I pray you will confess and Patricia will forgive you. She was always a good woman. She was kind to me when I was a kid.'

'I pray that one day she will forgive me,' said Damascene.

'If you do confess, soon you will be out on parole,' said Kalisa. 'You can work in the community and together we will be a part of rebuilding our nation.'

Damascene's eyes widened at the thought of a brighter future.

'I can see it, Dammy. Soon, we can begin our lives again.'

'I pray she will forgive me,' said Damascene.

'Okay, Michael Jackson. Get out of here. Go!' shouted the prison guard.

CHAPTER TWENTY-NINE

'This is very good,' said the warden, raising his eyebrows in genuine delight.

He continued to read the document. 'This is what is needed in the Rwandan community. This is what I pray for.'

Damascene was standing in the warden's office for the first time in four years, as the warden read his handwritten confession. He remembered the warden from his first day in the prison and noticed how his hair had greyed at the side since the day he inspected the new arrivals outside. The warden was seated behind a fine wooden desk, the most impressive piece of furniture Damascene had seen in all of his years in this prison. Behind him, on the wall, a large framed photograph of HE Paul Kagame, President of Rwanda, looked down upon the scene.

'I have one question I must ask,' said the warden.

'Yes, sir?' said Damascene.

'Is this the whole truth?'

'Yes, sir. I promise you, it is written from the bottom of my heart. For the past two years, I have written and rewritten this confession. Every night in my cell, I have considered these things. I have tried to find the right words that tell you how I feel about everything I did in the genocide.'

The warden nodded.

'It is not easy for a genocide perpetrator to accept all his crimes against the Tutsi people and to make a full confession of this kind.'

'I promise you, sir, I do this not for me, but to make things right for those who have suffered because of me.'

'They suffered a great deal because of you,' said the warden.

Damascene bowed his head. The written confession did not remove his burden of shame.

'Tell me this, Hakizimana Damascene. Will you be able to confess before the people of Rwanda and in front of the ones whose relatives you helped to kill?'

Damascene took a deep breath and swayed slightly as he responded. He had imagined this encounter for many months and now he was standing here before the chief warden, turning his desire to confess into reality. He felt the enormity of both the crimes he had committed and the words of confession he had so carefully written.

'Yes, sir. I will do it with all my heart,' he said.

'In this office, I have heard half-truth confessions and half-assed apologies. I have listened to some who will say anything just to get out of here. I have been disgusted at others whose only concern is to rid themselves of the mental torture of their guilt.'

149

'I mean every word, sir,' said Damascene.

The warden scanned other documents on the desk, including the annual reports on Damascene's behaviour.

'Well-disciplined and hardworking… Co-operative… Keeps himself to himself… Accepted counselling.

'Okay,' he said, having made the judgement that this man's confession was full and genuine.

'The latest report I have received is that in the past six months, more than one hundred and twenty genocide perpetrators, prisoners like you from different regions of Rwanda, have written letters of confession asking for forgiveness.'

Damascene looked up, surprised to hear the number of others who had confessed. His cellmate Eric had mocked his desire to confess so many times that Damascene began to doubt if forgiveness and reconciliation were really possible.

'It's those bloody Belgians that need to apologise for the genocide,' Eric told him. 'The colonisers brought the problems to this country, so I'm waiting for their confession, not yours. But I know I will have a long wait!'

The warden stood up.

'Early next year, we are going to have a meeting with the National Unity and Reconciliation Commission, FARG, Prison Fellowship Rwanda, AERG and the Rwanda Governance Board to take this whole process forward. The President wants us to build a new Rwanda as one people. You will be part of this process.'

Damascene looked up at the photograph of the President and nodded again. He was amazed to hear of the number of organisations apparently committed to finding a way to recover from the genocide through public confession and forgiveness. A few years ago this had seemed impossible, but now it was actually happening.

'You guys who have accepted all your charges, if you are willing to go back to the community and rebuild your country, you may be released. Go back and build reconciliation. Do not provoke survivors. Take the hoe to your overgrown fields. Forgive your unfaithful wives and bake bricks for grieving widows.'

'Yes, sir,' said Damascene. 'I was a builder. I will use my hands to rebuild.'

'However,' said the warden, 'you must also give more information about where the bodies of Tutsis are buried. And you must give us the names of the other perpetrators. The ones who have not yet been brought to justice. You know they need to be punished too.'

'I know, sir,' said Damascene. 'I am ready to confess everything I can remember. I will tell what I know about where people were buried and I will also tell my Rwandan brothers and sisters who the other killers were. I will go back home and work hard. I am not married. There is no one waiting for me.'

'Perhaps, if you are lucky, you will find a wife,' said the warden.

He shook Damascene's hand. It felt like a mark of respect. It was a long time since Damascene had felt respected by anyone. He knew there was more he must remember and the remembering would be painful. He realised there was much more he must tell. His experience of the past year had taught him that with each confession of every detail, he would feel a further cleansing of the filth that had clogged his heart for so many years. Damascene was fixed in his belief that he did not deserve to be forgiven, but today he believed, at least in his own heart, the truth could one day set him free.

Back in his cell, Eric was unimpressed.

'I'm telling you, brother,' he said, 'all this talk of forgiveness is meaningless. It's a foreign import from the international NGOs that did nothing to stop the genocide in the first place. Those prisoners are all just pretending to forgive, because of the money from white hypocrites and all their fancy, corrupt NGOs and, of course, because our president, the dictator, says so!'

'I believe forgiveness can happen,' interrupted Lambert. 'Look how God has forgiven me for all my sins.'

'And yet you are still here for killing an old woman in a robbery! You didn't need a genocide to behave like an evil bastard. Loser!' said Eric.

'I will pray for you, Damascene,' said Lambert. 'God can forgive you and if you confess to your victims, they might forgive you too. I believe it is possible, brother.'

'Thank you, brother,' said Damascene. 'Perhaps the world is not as dark and cynical as you believe, Eric.'

'I'm telling you,' said Eric, 'forgiveness is impossible, so don't waste your time and lose what dignity you have left begging for it!'

CHAPTER THIRTY

It was a hot, sunny day in the land of a thousand hills, as hundreds of people gathered in Gisenyi for the neighbourhood General Assembly for Unity and Reconciliation. As men, women and children arrived, families sought out the best seats in the cool shade under the vivid green leaves of the trees. Fourteen years had passed since the horrors of the genocide and nowadays words and actions of forgiveness and reconciliation had become as commonplace as cassava leaves and papaya in Rwanda. The people sat together on rows of low benches, side by side, not as Hutus and Tutsis but as Rwandans. This was the work of the National Unity & Reconciliation Commission (NURC), established by the Rwandan government to avoid history ever repeating itself. For years now, the government focus had been on replacing Hutu and Tutsi ethnic labels, imposed by the colonisers, with a national Rwandan identity.

Patricia did not want to be here, but Grace had persuaded her to come along. She agreed to attend the meeting on the clear understanding that she was not there to participate but simply to observe and learn. She made her feelings about reconciliation very clear.

'If all the Hutus and Tutsis were to tell the whole truth,' she said, 'about how they really feel inside, not what they are supposed to say for unity and reconciliation, there would be another genocide!'

Doctor Louise had come along too for moral support, always looking out for Patricia and supporting each step on her journey of healing. Now that Patricia had graduated, Louise had helped her to get a job as a legal secretary in a legal practice in Gisenyi, where Jean Pierre's sister was a solicitor.

'I cannot forget, so how can I ever forgive?' Patricia whispered to Grace as the proceedings began.

'Just try to have an open heart, sister,' said Grace.

Patricia was aware that Damascene would be here today to make a public confession of his crimes.

When the NURC had contacted her to explain that Damascene would be a part of the process taking place today, she gave a curt reply.

'He just wants parole,' she said.

The first *génocidaire* was invited forward to make his speech. He was a small, thin man in his forties with haunted eyes and a haggard face. His appearance represented no threat to anyone. The man spoke slowly and quietly, but just loudly enough so all those present could hear his words. The thin paper trembled in his hands as he began to read his confession.

'My name is Ndagije. On the morning of the genocide, I went with Mudenge and joined the mob. We attacked the house of Jean Baptiste, where he was hiding with his wife and children. We pulled Jean Baptiste from the house, Mudenge knocked him to the ground and I killed him with a machete. He was buried with the others in the fields beside the swamp.'

There were quiet gasps and sobs in the crowd. Ndagije looked up to the heavens and stopped until there was silence again, not in a demand for attention but to take a breath to empower him to complete this ordeal. Patricia observed the man closely, scanning for indications of insincerity. She also noted the reactions of the people listening to his words.

So many Hutu-lovers here! she thought. *A disgrace to the memory of their Tutsi families.*

'We slaughtered their cows and stole from their houses. We screamed insults and mocked those who pleaded for mercy. We became devils. For many years, with every beat of my heart, I have regretted what I did. I have no peace when I remember what I have done.'

'He deserves no peace. I have no pity for that weak little man,' whispered Patricia.

'I believe he is sincere, my sister. Can't you see his pain?' said Louise.

Patricia examined the man closely to try to see what she was missing.

'Devil!' she said, under her breath.

'I have decided to confess what I did. I apologise to the wife of Jean Baptiste, Ilibagiza Francine. I apologise to all of you, my fellow Rwandans. I do not deserve mercy for the evil I have done. I cannot take back the suffering I have inflicted upon Ilibagiza Francine and her children.

But today I beg her from the bottom of my heart. Please forgive me.'

Ndagije seemed even smaller and thinner now as he folded his letter and bowed his head. It seemed as if a slight wind would blow the man away. As soon as he finished, a woman stood up in the middle of the crowd. She wrapped her *kitenge* around her waist and began to walk forward. Watching the woman approach the front of the crowd, Patricia spotted Damascene sitting on one of the benches with some of the other prisoners. He was looking straight at her. Patricia felt his gaze as a kick in her stomach, but she returned a stare. Francine now stood at the front of the gathering, only a few feet apart from Ndagije, and addressed her community.

'Last year, when this man was released on parole from prison to work in the community, I was frightened when I saw him in my neighbourhood again. Me and my children were still afraid of him. When we met in the street, he would see us and go the other way. Or if we saw him first, we would do everything to avoid him. But one day, he took the first step. He asked if he could speak with me. Eventually, one day, I agreed and he came to my home to confess and ask for my forgiveness. My dear friends, I want you to know that I could not speak to him that day, but in my heart I forgave him.'

There was complete silence as every ear, including Patricia's, attended to these remarkable words.

'When I forgave Ndagije, for the first time since that day of genocide in 1994, I felt at peace. I suffer every day at the loss of my dear husband, but the hatred has left me. The turmoil in my head is over and I have peace in my heart.

Today, this man is begging for forgiveness once more. He is apologising to me and all Rwandans gathered here. But I want you all to know I have already forgiven him.'

Ndagije knelt before Francine, bowed his head to his chest and clasped his hands behind his back. Francine gestured to him to stand up and when he arose she embraced him.

So quick to swallow false apologies! thought Patricia, feeling more and more alone in this crowd, and becoming more and more angry.

The crowd began to applaud gently as Ndagije returned to his bench, taking a handkerchief from his pocket to wipe away his tears. Damascene and the other prisoners shifted uncomfortably on their benches. Francine remained standing at the front of the meeting, the most humble and yet the most powerful figure in the gathering. Her children rushed forward to embrace her. As Grace and Doctor Louise stood up to join in the applause, Patricia could take no more. She pushed past the others in her row who were standing and applauding and began to flee. Her departure route took her straight past Damascene. He looked up towards her with a pleading in his eyes. He wanted her to stay. He needed her to hear his words. He had spent a year preparing for this moment. She stopped, scowled and spat at Damascene.

'Devil!' she growled, and ran from the meeting in a flurry of anger. Grace followed Patricia but Louise remained to hear Damascene's confession.

'Bugingo Bernard was my friend,' he read. 'We played football and climbed trees together. I was at his wedding to Uwera Patricia. I grew mangos with him.'

It was just after noon now and Damascene felt the strong sun's relentless heat on his head as he spoke.

'For years, I listened to and believed words of hatred towards Tutsis. I no longer trusted them and I feared they were planning to remove us from our homes and our land. I felt a fear and hatred towards them. I told my Hutu friends that all Tutsis were bad, even the ones we knew who appeared to be good. I talked to the other men in my village about what we would do if the Tutsis threatened or attacked us. Then the genocide began and on that night Sylvestre and Claude came from the next town asking which Hutu men were prepared to fight for our lives. They said the Tutsis had killed our president and planned to destroy us. I was afraid for my family. The Interahamwe arrived in our community and gathered us together. They told us if we were not with them we were against them and must die too, like Tutsi cockroaches. I could have said no. I might have died. Perhaps it would have been better for me to die than to betray my friend. But I was weak and I agreed to help them to find the Tutsis in my neighbourhood. I forged a club of nails and joined the mob. Sylvestre gave me the job of identifying all the Tutsi homes. I made a list and went along with the Interahamwe, pointing out the homes where my Tutsi neighbours lived. All of the families were gone. Those poor souls were hiding in the church, thinking they were safe. The mob was angry and some of the men with guns, like Sylvestre, were firing bullets in the air. We had found no one to kill, and every empty house we found made us more angry. Then we came to Bernard's house.'

Louise sat rigid on the bench. Four years ago, she had heard this same story from Patricia's point of view and she could never forget it. A woman with a large yellow fan, sitting beside her, sensed Louise's response and fanned some cooler air in her direction and offered her a drink of water.

'I pointed to the house and the mob attacked. They started shooting at the house. They broke down the door. When I entered, Claude was holding Bernard down and Sylvestre shot him in the head. The mob began to cheer and laugh and I joined in. Then Claude...'

Damascene faltered for the first time. He fell to his knees, perspiring heavily and trying to control the tears streaming down his cheeks.

'Continue, brother,' called Ndagije from his bench.

There was a moment's silence in the meeting. It lasted for ten seconds but it felt more like an hour. The oppression of the heat seemed to match the heaviness of heart that surrounded Damascene. He remained on his knees and continued.

'Then Claude killed... the baby, Innocent, and Sylvestre killed the girl, Alice... with a machete. Claude attacked Patricia. I thought she was dead. I betrayed them. I am as guilty as the men who did the killing. I carried my club of nails and joined in the killing of many others. I have spent five years in prison for my crimes and if I spend the rest of my life behind bars, it will not be enough. Bernard and Patricia were my friends and I betrayed them. I have come here today to confess my sins before my Rwandan brothers and sisters. But most of all, I have come here to beg for forgiveness from Uwera Patricia. I can never do anything that will repair the damage I have caused you. I have inflicted on you, a good person, more suffering than

159

I could ever know. But I want you to know that for every day I live in shame on this earth, I will be sorry for hurting you and your family.'

Damascene's knees ached as he knelt on the ground with his head bowed and choking back tears. But this time there was no response in the crowd. Patricia was gone. No one stood up to accept his apology. No one offered him forgiveness.

'Thank you, brother,' said Pastor Gasongo, who had been sitting on the front bench listening to every word. The Prison Fellowship pastor had watched Damascene's transformation over the past few years and today was the culmination of all his support, prayers and counselling. The pastor wanted to offer Damascene forgiveness, but he knew that only Patricia had the right and the power to forgive.

Finally, when the long meeting ended and the community began to disperse, hot, exhausted but somehow lightened in spirit, Louise approached Damascene, just as the prison guards were leading him away.

'I am a friend of Patricia's,' she said. 'Give me your letter, please, and I will pass it on to Patricia.'

Damascene hesitated to let go of the letter. He had wrestled over writing these words for years and this was his one and only copy.

'I will help her to read it,' said Louise. 'She needs to hear your words.'

'Thank you,' said Damascene.

Damascene assented and let go of the letter. He had let go of so much today, and the burden of shame had lessened.

'Thank you,' said Louise, noticing in the brief exchange that Damascene was not a monster or a devil but just a man.

As Damascene lay in his bed in prison that night, he felt relief that he had finally confessed his sins and sought forgiveness.

'God bless you, my brother,' said Lambert. 'I will pray for you and for that poor woman.'

'Sounds like a great big performance by all of you guys just to make politicians look good,' said Eric. 'Politicians who don't give a fuck about you or any of us!'

When silence fell in his cell, Damascene looked up and out of the small window towards a full moon in the sky, and he noticed that although his burden had lightened, his deep sadness persisted. Yes, he had asked for forgiveness, but in his soul he believed that he should not and would not be forgiven.

CHAPTER THIRTY-ONE

Patricia arrived in the car park outside her office in her new red Volkswagen Golf. After three years of successful study she had completed her degree, secured a good job in the best legal firm in Gisenyi, and after a year of earning a good salary she had bought her first car. She ached for the chance to share every new accomplishment with her parents and with Bernard. Every day, she hoped somehow they were looking down upon her and celebrating how she was rebuilding her life. Patricia was very grateful for the new life she was creating, but today, as she arrived at work, she was not happy.

'Hello, madam!' said the security guard.

Patricia did not respond and, lost in thoughts of yesterday's events at the General Assembly for Unity and Reconciliation, stomped into the office. Her colleagues looked up and, realising immediately that it was one of Patricia's "bad days", did not attempt to initiate a conversation. Jean Pierre's sister, Jacqueline, looked over the top of her computer screen to observe her latest recruit. Patricia had turned out to be an excellent legal secretary and Jacqueline was investing in her further training, but some days the unpredictable mood swings were hard to handle. Jacqueline liked a quiet, businesslike office but not a dark, silent atmosphere. The firm had just secured a new contract with a big construction company in Kigali and she was considering Patricia for the project team. Oblivious to her impact on the people around her, Patricia sat down and took a deep breath, hoping that the detail of today's "to-do" list would distract her from the anger she felt towards Damascene and all those men she had witnessed making public confessions the day before. She followed her daily routine, poured a glass of water, opened her diary and logged on to her computer, hoping to become so absorbed in the business activities of the office that the pain and hatred could be quashed for another day. Patricia's phone rang.

'Hello.'

'Hi Patricia, it's Grace.'

'Hi.'

'I ran after you yesterday but I couldn't find you,' said Grace.

'I do not wish to talk about this. I am at my work,' said Patricia.

Suddenly she became aware of the other people around her in the office. She noticed Jacqueline looking in her direction and felt her cheeks warm with embarrassment.

'Can we meet for dinner tonight? I just want to talk,' said Grace.

'I am sorry, I have another appointment,' said Patricia.

'Oh, maybe at the weekend then? I've got a new job,' said Grace.

'Congratulations,' said Patricia.

'Thanks, I just thought we should talk about...' said Grace, but Patricia hung up.

She tutted heavily, slammed down the phone and escaped to the restroom to try to take control of her feelings. She now regarded this little toilet in the office as a haven, somewhere to flee on a day like this when the churn of her emotions became overwhelming. She was still angry at Grace and envious that her father and grandfather had survived the genocide while she had lost everyone. It was easier for Grace to forgive because one day she would have children who would have a grandfather and a great-grandfather, she thought. She hid there for twenty minutes until she composed herself and returned to her desk. In spite of her efforts to be inconspicuous, everyone in the office had noticed, especially Jacqueline.

By the time Patricia got home that evening, her mood had lifted a little. She loved her new job because the work was so absorbing that it numbed the pain. That afternoon, Jacqueline informed her she would be part of the new project with Fame Construction Company in Kigali. Jacqueline had decided that Patricia's talent and potential outweighed the risk of emotional breakdown. Patricia appreciated the support of her boss and did not want to let her down. As she prepared her delicious *umutsima*[12] for dinner, *Museke Weya*[13] came on the radio in the kitchen. The programme broadcast the same message of unity and

---

12 *Umutsima* is a traditional Rwandan dish of corn and cassava.

13 *Museke Weya* is a popular radio drama whose main objective is to promote reconciliation, peaceful co-existence and trauma healing in post-genocide Rwanda.

reconciliation she had heard the day before at the open-air NURC meeting.

After she had eaten and cleaned up, she settled down to another evening alone in front of the television watching *Kanyombya*[14] and occasionally laughing out loud. She began to doze off before the end of the latest episode but before she could descend into one of her dark dreams, she was awakened by the familiar voice of President Kagame giving a speech on the television news.

'As we remember, we must do whatever is in our power to build a solid future.'

Patricia had little time for politicians, but she admired the President for establishing the work of FARG, which had helped her and other genocide survivors so much. Here she was in her restored home, with an education, a career and a nice little car. So she resisted the urge to change the channel and tuned into the words of the President.

'We must build strong building blocks today so as to build a strong tomorrow.'

This message was similar to the one Patricia had heard the day before at the neighbourhood assembly and also on the radio earlier this evening. The encouragement to build a better tomorrow seemed to be everywhere. She felt as if she could not escape from it. The President's words seemed to be directly addressed to her.

'We must try to have a clear and contented heart. We should work hard and work in happiness, and we should even allow ourselves smiling faces.'

Patricia switched off the television and lay back on the

---

14 A popular television comedian in Rwanda.

sofa, reflecting on the words she had just heard. These were the same sentiments she had heard from so many Tutsi neighbours and Hutu genocide survivors at the public meeting the day before. She wanted to repel these ideas but resistance was becoming more and more exhausting. Patricia was starting to feel weary of holding on to hatred, and she noticed how this seemed to push away the people who cared about her. She winced at the thought of hanging up on lovely Grace. Alone and in private, without pressure from anyone, Patricia could not deny a feeling of hopefulness that sprung from words of unity and reconciliation. What if she accepted this idea? How could she begin to think of her Hutu tormentors as human beings, never mind fellow Rwandans? What was the future for Rwanda in being divided? What was the future for her own life, holding on to hatred? When she retired to bed that night, she did not endure one of her terrible sleepless nights of anguish. Her mind was active and she could not sleep but it felt different. It seemed as if she was untangling a bunch of knotted cords, subconsciously reordering her life. She noticed that a new outlook was seeping into her being.

On Friday afternoon, Patricia had arranged to meet Doctor Louise in the same park in Kigali where they began their chats four years earlier. Once a month, they met at the same bench near the tennis courts at the Cercle Sportif for a catch-up. Patricia enjoyed hearing how Louise's boys were growing up and Louise wanted to know all about Patricia's new job and new car. It was a perfect place to meet. The sound of laughing children was always in the air. Waiting for Louise to arrive, Patricia watched a father playing ball with his young son. She naturally thought of Bernard and Innocent playing like this, if only God had given them the chance. On the grass, a group of boys were playing at traditional African dances, using their bags as improvised drums and falling over in fits of laughter. Patricia laughed along with them. Sitting on the grass nearby, two boys were absorbed in a game of *igisoro*[15] and two little girls were chuckling and playing with their dolls. One of the girl's toys reminded her of Alice's favourite doll; the one with the sky-blue dress Alice carried everywhere and took to bed with her every night. Patricia was admiring how the little girls were sharing their toys, when their parents arrived with some ice cream.

'This is the future for us,' said one father to the other. 'Look at our children, Hutu and Tutsi playing together, and laughing together.'

'Little Rwandans,' said the other girl's mother.

As Patricia observed this interaction, she realised she could not tell which family was Hutu and which was Tutsi. She reflected again on the words of the President, the message on the radio and the testimonies at the open-air NURC meeting. She wondered if she was destined to be left behind. Just then, Doctor Louise arrived and the two women greeted with a warm embrace.

'I'm sorry for rushing off like that and leaving you at the meeting, Louise, when you had come to support me,' said Patricia.

'Patricia, I love you, my sister, and I do not blame you for being upset after all that you have suffered,' said Louise.

---

15 *Igisoro* is a board game played with pits and seeds.

'I do not wish to forgive,' said Patricia.

'I know, Patricia, I know,' said Louise, 'but I also remember sitting here with you on this very spot, when you said that you did not wish to live. Then one day, in your own time, you made a choice that you did want to live.'

Patricia nodded slightly at the gentle wisdom of her friend.

'Maybe one day, in your own time, you may also choose to forgive.'

'I do not wish to forgive,' said Patricia.

'I have something for you,' said Louise, and she handed her Damascene's letter of confession.

CHAPTER THIRTY-TWO

It was the last Saturday of the month, Umuganda, a tradition revived by the Rwandan government, and now mandatory for all Rwandans, to bring the community together to rebuild the country and encourage reconciliation. On this Umuganda Day in Gisenyi, everyone was busy tidying the streets, building and repairing community facilities, digging wells and planting trees. In the same places where, sixteen years ago, machetes had been used by Hutus to kill Tutsis, today Hutu and Tutsi neighbours toiled together with machetes to cut back overgrown bushes. Patricia was helping a team of men who were digging a ditch and cleaning up a natural well, to install a tank and tap that would increase the clean water supply for the community. Patricia was keen to help because last year the outcome of a similar project was an improved water supply for her garden and prized avocados. She also wanted to give something back to the community as acknowledgment of the help she had received. Today, her job was to carry jerry cans of water on her head, backwards and forwards, to help quench the thirst of the labourers who were sweating in the heat of the sun. She was bringing workers water so they could bring water to the whole village. As the team worked together, everyone playing their part, they sang together.

"*We will build Rwanda,*
We will build it,
Children of Rwanda,
And we will make a paradise for the whole world,
We will build,
We will build Rwanda.'"

After three hours of intense activity, the volunteers gathered together for a public meeting addressed by the village leader. Patricia sat at the back. Today, she was wearing sunglasses, not just to protect her eyes from the glare of the sun, but to hide her eyes, swollen with a night of tears, after she had read and re-read Damascene's letter of confession.

'I want to make sure all of you can hear me at the back,' said the village leader.

'What? Yes, we can hear you! What did you say? What?' shouted the elderly man sitting beside Patricia.

'Thank you, brothers and sisters, for your contribution to rebuilding our country of Rwanda,' said the village leader. 'I would like you to welcome a special guest to our village on this Umuganda Day. Doctor Rulinda is a delegate of the National Unity and Reconciliation Commission. I would like to invite him to come forward now to address our community.'

The villagers applauded as the NURC delegate stepped forward. He raised his fist in the air and called to the crowd.

'*Intore!*'

'*Ijabo riduhe ijambo!*' the crowd responded.

'*Intore!*' he repeated, louder this time.

'*Ijabo riduhe ijambo!*' replied the crowd, standing up, matching the increase in volume and raising their fists in the air. Patricia stood up and applauded but did not join in the cheers.

'Thank you,' said Doctor Rulinda, gesticulating to the crowd to be seated. 'I thank you very much for your zeal and determination here in Gisenyi. I can see that you are very enthusiastic to serve our country through Umuganda and other public activities.'

Patricia removed her sunglasses and listened intently. Since reading Damascene's letter, her resistance to talk of reconciliation had somehow softened and she leaned forward, hoping to hear a message to help her decide how to respond.

'I want to talk about unity and reconciliation between Rwandans today,' began Doctor Rulinda. 'I say Rwandans because I see no Hutu, no Tutsi, no Twa. All I see is Rwandans. I want reconciliation and peace to flow in the hearts of Rwandans.'

Today, Patricia was more open to hearing these words, to let them in, but she could not imagine peace flowing in her heart.

'I always thank God when I see the survivors and perpetrators of the genocide against the Tutsi becoming reconciled,' said Doctor Rulinda. 'I know there are some among us here today who have followed this courageous path.'

Patricia looked around the crowd. In the past two years, she had heard more and more stories of reconciliation in

171

her community. Some of her neighbours here, Hutu and Tutsi, perpetrators and survivors, had found peace together years ago. They did not just speak to each other again. Some of them worked together and entered each other's homes. Some neighbours were rearing a cow together in the Cow for Peace initiative. Patricia often observed their interactions from a distance, curiously looking for signs of pretence or insincerity, but she found no evidence to deny that these former enemies were truly reconciled. She could see in their eyes the pain was still there, but the hatred was gone and they appeared to have found peace. Some of her friends who had suffered even more loss than Patricia herself, including poor Felice's only surviving sister, were here today, sitting beside the perpetrators they had forgiven. The NURC delegate continued his speech.

'I am a survivor myself,' he said. 'I personally lost both of my older brothers, my eldest son and many friends. Like many of you here today, it breaks my heart that we will never hear the testimony of the dead. But I am here today, Rwandans, to tell you that I have chosen to forgive the perpetrators. Of course, it was not easy. I will never forget, but I can forgive.'

'*Amina! Amina!*' cried a woman in the front row, and the crowd applauded once again.

'One of the perpetrators against my family is here with me today,' continued Doctor Rulinda.

A tall, modest-looking man, wearing a large brimmed hat, sitting beside the NURC delegate, stood up and bowed meekly to the crowd. The crowd applauded again. Patricia was astounded. She noticed a similarity between this man and the perpetrator who had begged for forgiveness at the previous public meeting. There was a humility, a quietness and a brokenness about both men.

'Today, we are friends and we share uncooked and cooked food. And today I want to tell you the truth, my whole truth...'

As the speech continued, Patricia got up and slipped away from the meeting. However, this time, she did not storm out in anger; she left to be alone in her thoughts and reflections. She walked the whole way to the shores of Lake Kivu, repeating in her mind the words she had just heard and weaving them with the words from Damascene's letter, begging for her forgiveness. She accepted that the Damascene she grew up with, Bernard's friend, the man who attended her wedding, would write such a letter and mean every word. She removed her shoes, this time to cool her feet rather than to walk to her death in the lake, and paced along the shoreline. In the distance was the familiar sight of three-haul fishing boats. She wondered if the fishermen casting their long eucalyptus rods were the same ones who had saved her. Then she pondered again on the integrity of Damascene and thought, *But how could a devil capable of such betrayal and brutality ever say anything from a pure heart again?*

Chapter Thirty-Three

She didn't consult Doctor Louise. She didn't talk it over with Grace. In fact, since hanging up the telephone in mid-conversation, she hadn't spoken to Grace for weeks. She certainly didn't have the patience for an exchange of letters with Albert in Uganda. When Patricia decided she wanted to do something, she usually pressed ahead with single-minded determination. This wasn't a result of her trauma; Patricia had always been like this. Long before Bernard had asked her for a date, Patricia had decided he would one day be her husband.

It was the Monday after Umuganda Day and on this occasion, having decided a course of action, the only advice she needed was practical. During her lunch break at the office, she called Faustin at FARG. She hadn't spoken to him for years but always remembered him for his help with the fund for survivors of the genocide.

'Hello, Faustin. It's Uwera Patricia from Gisenyi. Do you remember me?'

'How could I forget you, madam?' replied Faustin.

'The woman who taught me how to do an emergency rescue on a rooftop in Kigali!'

Patricia laughed.

'It's good to hear from you. How are you, Patricia?' he asked.

'I am quite well,' said Patricia. 'I love my restored home, I finished my degree and now I'm working as a legal secretary.'

'Wow!' said Faustin, 'I'm delighted to hear this. You are a remarkable woman.'

'I'm just me,' said Patricia, embarrassed by the compliment.

'How can I help you, madam? You're not up on the roof again, I hope!'

Patricia laughed. It was an outward indication of inner healing that now she was able to laugh at herself.

'Please, Faustin. If you keep making fun of me, I might push you off the roof next time!'

'Yes,' said Faustin, laughing. 'You are an exceptional woman.'

'I want a meeting with Doctor Rulinda from the National Unity and Reconciliation Commission.'

'Really?' said Faustin.

'Yes. He gave a speech at the Umuganda Day meeting in Gisenyi on Saturday and I need to speak to him.'

Faustin remembered Patricia's stubborn determination.

'Let me see,' he said, and after a few minutes he came back with a telephone number for the NURC offices.

'If you call this number, someone there should be able to arrange it. It might take a while, though, as he's a very busy man.'

'I can wait,' said Patricia.

She didn't have too long to wait. Three weeks later, she arranged a day off work and took the early bus to Kigali for a meeting with Doctor Rulinda at the headquarters of the National Unity and Reconciliation Commission. Patricia thanked him for his time and got straight to the point.

'How was it possible for you to sit down with that man who killed members of your own family?' she asked.

Doctor Rulinda paused for a moment, realising the importance of the question. A woman he'd never met before would not travel from Gisenyi to Kigali to ask him this question if she had not given the possible answers considerable thought.

'Everything under the sun is possible,' he began. 'For many years, my heart was not free. When he was released from prison, I used to see him in the street. I would freeze and feel sick in the pit of my stomach.'

Patricia nodded. This was how she felt the day she saw Damascene at the public meeting.

'I hated the sight of his face and I feared him at the same time. But one day he sent a message asking to meet me. I hesitated at first, because I assumed he wanted to ask forgiveness. I knew others who had forgiven perpetrators. They seemed happier, more at peace. But I wasn't sure if I could ever forgive him. I worried about how other survivors in my family would feel if I forgave him. And I certainly wasn't going to make it easy for him. But the turmoil in my mind just got worse and finally I agreed to see him. He came to my house. When I opened the door, I didn't see a monster. I saw a broken man. It was not easy for him. He could not look me in the eye until he finished speaking. He told me what he did. He said that he regretted what he did. He didn't make excuses or blame anyone else. He took responsibility for the suffering he had caused me.'

'Did you believe him?' asked Patricia.

'Yes,' said Doctor Rulinda. 'Honestly, madam, I will never forget the pain and shame on his face and the sadness in his eyes. He apologised and asked for forgiveness. I wondered if I could do this if I had killed his family. I think it took some courage. You know, many perpetrators ran away from their crimes and to this day they hide and refuse to confess their evil deeds. He made a different choice and so I believed his words. And guess what, madam.'

'Yes?' said Patricia.

'The moment I forgave him, he no longer had any power over me. I saw him for who he is. A sad, broken man who wants to do the right thing and who wants to live out his days with some peace in his heart. And I realised in that regard, he and I, perpetrator and survivor, we are just the same.'

'But how can you forget what he did, sir? Is it not a betrayal of your family?' asked Patricia.

'I will never forget,' said Doctor Rulinda. 'We must never forget the more than a million Rwandans we lost. Forgiving does not mean forgetting. We will always, always, always remember. But I believe that to live the rest of our lives in hatred and revenge, to allow what happened to happen again, well, that would be the biggest betrayal of those who we have lost.'

Patricia's throat tightened and, overcome with emotion, she coughed.

'Here, have some water, madam,' said Doctor Rulinda.

'I am sorry, sir,' said Patricia.

'It's okay,' said Doctor Rulinda, 'I know those feelings well. What do you want to ask me?'

'But you must have wanted revenge,' said Patricia.

'Madam, please believe me,' said Doctor Rulinda, 'if I had found this man in 1995, I'm sure I would have done the same to him as he did to my brothers. But we did not meet. Maybe God was protecting us both.'

'Hmm…' said Patricia, 'but, for me, it's not just what I would have done in 1995. Four years ago, when he was arrested, I tried to take revenge on the devil who betrayed my family. I took a gun and pointed it at him. I wanted to see him dead. Lucky for him, I did not pull the trigger.'

Doctor Rulinda raised his eyebrows.

'Perhaps it was lucky for you too, madam,' he said.

Doctor Rulinda got up and looked out of the window at the many people traversing the streets down below.

'If you had killed him, today out there someone would be looking for you, to avenge his death too. His brother. His son. His best friend. That's how vengeance works. An eye for an eye and a tooth for a tooth and we all end up blind and toothless.'

Patricia began to cry. The words of Damascene's letter had reverberated in her mind for weeks now:

I want you to know that for every day I live in shame on this earth, I will be sorry for hurting you and your family.

She could not deny the sincerity of his confession.

'Do you still want him dead?' asked Doctor Rulinda.

Patricia stopped crying and for a few minutes repeated

this question in her mind. Finally, she spoke, with a quiet assurance.

'No,' she said, surprising herself.

For the first time, she felt glad not to have pulled the trigger that day in the police station.

'Do you want to forgive this man?' asked Doctor Rulinda.

'I don't know,' said Patricia. 'I feel no mercy towards him. I… I really don't know what to do. What should I do, sir?'

'I cannot tell you what to do, madam, but I know this. If a cruel person hurts you and all you do is hurt them back, you have become a cruel person too.'

Patricia nodded. She no longer resisted these ideas. She knew it was the truth.

'But you can choose your response and break the chain of hatred,' said Doctor Rulinda.

On the long journey home on the bus, Patricia relived the conversation, and certain words resonated in her soul. *For many years, my heart was not free.*

She took out Damascene's letter and read it once again, in the light of Dr Rulinda's words. *You can choose your response and break the chain of hatred.*

When she arrived in Gisenyi, Patricia walked home slowly under a bright full moon. She looked up at the stars, thinking of Bernard and Alice and Innocent, wondering if somehow their souls lived on. She prayed to her mother and father to give her answers to the questions swirling in her mind. Then suddenly it struck her.

For many years, I have wanted to kill the devil. I thought the devil was Damascene, she thought.

But what if the devil is my hatred, controlling me, eating me up and poisoning me? What if the devil is within? What if this is the devil I must kill?

Chapter Thirty-Four

'I kept asking myself, what did I do wrong? Why did she hang up on me?' said Grace.

She rotated Patricia's rear-view mirror towards her face to apply fresh lipstick.

'I'm sorry,' said Patricia, keeping her eyes on the road ahead, 'you know how stressed I was. Everything I heard that day upset me, and when I saw HIM, I just had to get away.'

'I do not blame you, sister,' said Grace. 'I understand those feelings too.'

'Well, a lot has happened over the past few months,' said Patricia.

'I know,' said Grace, 'I can hardly believe it, but I know you are doing the right thing, sister. And you look more beautiful than ever!'

'Even without lipstick!' said Patricia, swivelling the rear-view mirror back into place.

It was true. These days, Patricia looked different. Everyone was complimenting her. Every time someone said, 'Oh, Patricia, you are looking so well,' she smiled because she had changed nothing about her appearance. Her clothes and hair were the same. The transformation had been happening within Patricia. As she tried to let go of the hatred, she began to notice a lightness in her heart she had almost forgotten.

'I can't believe we're doing this,' said Grace.

'I know, sister, but I just want to know how I will feel,' said Patricia.

She decelerated and pulled the car over to the side of the road. They parked at a discreet distance, opposite the construction site for the new school. Patricia put on her sunglasses and the two women looked across the road to see what was happening on the building site. Among the construction workers was a small group of men with shaved heads who looked like they had just been released from prison.

'That's him at the front,' Patricia whispered, as Damascene walked towards the front of the workers pushing a wheelbarrow. 'I've seen him here every day this week on my way to work. He must be released and on parole, since his public confession.'

'He looks sad,' said Grace.

The two women kept their heads and voices low even though it was impossible for Damascene to see or hear them inside the car across the road.

'All of those guys on parole,' said Grace, 'they put them to work like this, building schools to help them to reintegrate and do some positive work for the community.'

The two women watched as Damascene carried blocks

of concrete across the building site. He moved quickly and did not stop for a chat or a rest like the other men.

'Is he a mason?' asked Grace.

'He worked as a construction engineer before 1994 and when he hid in Kigali he worked on building sites with his brother.'

'He works hard,' said Grace. 'He doesn't even look up or talk to the others. He just keeps on working. Non-stop!'

'What am I going to do, sister?' said Patricia. 'One day soon, I will see him in the village. He must be living in Gisenyi again. I know I will bump into him. I do not know what I will do.'

'You do know he apologised at the public meeting after you left?' said Grace. 'He begged for your forgiveness.'

'I know,' said Patricia. 'Doctor Louise passed his letter to me. I know every word. I have read it a million times.'

'I can see you are still sad, my sister,' said Grace. 'Even these days when you smile more often, I can still see the sadness in your eyes.'

Patricia looked at the familiar outline of Damascene. He was older now, but the way he moved reminded her of the times he had helped Bernard on his latest building project. The way Damascene kept his head down reminded her of when they were at school together as children. One day, Damascene broke a window with the football and the principal punished him by making him build a flowerbed in front of her office. He worked hard all day long in the heat of the sun, with his head down until his work was complete. Every time Patricia saw Damascene, she glimpsed the remains of the little boy buried beneath the man who had committed genocide.

'He's just a man,' said Patricia. 'Look at him. He's a broken man, like so many other perpetrators. He's not a devil, after all.'

'That's true, sister,' said Grace. 'So many Hutu men did terrible things, acts of evil, but not all of them are terrible, evil men.'

'He looks weak not wicked,' said Patricia. 'Why have I given so much power to someone who looks so fragile?'

'Are you going to forgive him?' asked Grace.

Patricia shook her head and thought for a moment.

'I might be willing to forgive, but I cannot ever forget,' said Patricia. 'How did you forgive the man who killed your mother?'

'I decided to forgive him on the day of his public confession,' said Grace, 'but I haven't seen his face since that day. I'm not sure if I would even recognise him. I don't remember the terrible things he did because I was too young, but I cannot forget that he took my mother away from me. Anyway, at church, I was taught to forgive, and the government wants reconciliation, and so I had to forgive him. He lives far away in Kigali and I don't have to think about seeing him at the well or in the market every day.'

'I don't know how I can avoid Damascene... and we were once friends. He was at my wedding, Grace,' said Patricia.

'Do you want to meet with him one day?' asked Grace.

'I don't think I have a choice,' said Patricia.

She turned the ignition key in the car and prepared to drive off.

'What can I do, Grace? I will surely meet him in the street one day.'

'You have more courage than me, sister,' said Grace. 'I'm sure you will know what to do.'

'I do not wish to kill him now,' said Patricia.

'I know, my sister,' said Grace. 'I can see bitterness within you is dying. You are coming back to life again. You must come with me to the Survivors' Club next week. You will meet others who have had the same experience. It might help you.'

'Maybe,' said Patricia.

She pressed the accelerator pedal.

'If I can kill the devil within me,' she said, 'I might be able to live the rest of my life in peace.'

'The difference between you and me, sister,' said Grace, 'is that I forgave a stranger because I believed it was the right thing to do. But you will only forgive your friend when you decide in your heart that you truly want to.'

CHAPTER THIRTY-FIVE

'Everyone here is a Tutsi survivor of the genocide,' said Grace.

'Everyone?' asked Patricia.

'Yes, even the children,' said Grace. 'They have been badly affected by what happened to our parents and grandparents.'

Patricia nodded.

Grace and Patricia were sitting together in a circle of men, women and young people, in one of the brand-new classrooms of the school they had watched Damascene working on the previous week. For several years now, survivors' clubs had been springing up all over Rwanda. As time went by, more and more people wanted to join these meetings and share their stories.

'Madame Charlotte is the leader,' whispered Grace, nodding towards an older white-haired woman in the circle. 'You remember she was a teacher in Gisenyi?'

'Yes, I remember her,' said Patricia. 'She taught my

brother, Albert. She needed a lot of patience with him! The poor woman lost her whole family in the genocide. All of them. She is the only survivor.'

Charlotte stood up and opened the meeting with a warm welcome and a prayer. Patricia noticed immediately that although this was a meeting of survivors of terrible violence, there was an atmosphere of peace and good humour. One by one, different people stood up and shared their story, and when each person finished speaking, the whole group applauded.

'Let us all join hands together,' said Charlotte. 'Thank you all for sharing your testimonies with us today. It is amazing how far we have come. Thank you for the courage and love you have shown today. And thank you all for playing your part in the Unity and Reconciliation process in our country.'

'She's a wonderful woman,' whispered Patricia into Grace's ear.

'Each one of us can testify that our hearts have healed through reconciliation,' said Charlotte. 'I know, brothers and sisters, there are many in our land who do not agree with this path of forgiveness. We understand their pain and all we can do is pray and encourage them to follow in our footsteps one day.'

Grace squeezed Patricia's hand and she returned the squeeze.

'What we need to continue to do,' said Charlotte, 'is to build our country. We can use education and technology for development while at the same time preserving our cultures and values as Rwandans. And let us remember that unity and forgiveness have always been Rwandan values.'

The circle of survivors applauded Charlotte's remarks and Patricia clapped along with the others. She was starting to accept the idea that reconciliation was not just good for her soul but it was a duty to her country.

'Now,' continued Charlotte, 'let's welcome Mr Mugabo Jean-Paul from Prison Fellowship, to tell us more about uniting perpetrators with survivors of the genocide.'

The visiting speaker came forward and Patricia listened intently to his words.

'Thank you, madam. I would like to thank everyone who took his or her first step to come here to learn more about our values. The values of Rwanda have always been love, peace and patriotism. But today we also have reconciliation. I am happy for the remarkable reconciliation my country has achieved.'

Patricia looked around the circle as people of all ages nodded in agreement at these opening remarks.

'I want to thank the RPF, which took the first step to liberate us in 1994,' said Jean-Paul. 'They saved us when all the nations and international peace organisations were just watching and doing nothing. It was as if they were watching a horror movie.'

Patricia had not expected the speech to be quite so patriotic or political, but she liked what she heard. She remembered the shock felt among Tutsi people in 1994 when it became clear that the international community were not coming to their aid. She recalled the fear and panic that spread when the UN soldiers abandoned them as the killing got worse.

'Listen, Rwandan brothers and sisters,' Jean-Paul continued, 'our country was liberated by Rwandans. And now the work of reconciliation must be done by Rwandans too, through teaching given by Rwandans.'

Patricia kept her eyes fixed on Jean-Paul for the rest of the speech. She found the combination of the simplicity of the survivors' stories and the strength of Jean-Paul's patriotism to be truly inspiring. For the first time, she felt a fire of motivation rising within her. She loved her work and her new friends, but it was a long time since she had felt this way about anything.

'Well, what did you think of the meeting?' asked Grace, being careful not to push Patricia too far.

'I will be coming here the next time,' said Patricia.

'It's every first and third Tuesday of the month,' said Grace.

'Good,' said Patricia.

As they walked back to Patricia's car, in the distance, they noticed a well-dressed woman leaning against the vehicle.

'Who's that?' asked Grace.

Patricia quickened her pace.

'Doctor Louise!' she cried.

Louise turned round with a smile and hugged her friend.

'I was on my way back from the hospital when I spotted this beautiful little red car. I was certain it was yours,' said Louise.

'This is my good friend Grace from university.'

'Yes, we met briefly at the public meeting, remember? Before you stormed out and she ran after you?' said Louise.

'Oh yeah,' said Patricia, putting her hand over her mouth.

Grace and Louise laughed and hugged.

'It's nice to see you again. Patricia's friends need to stick together!' said Grace.

Patricia joined in the laughter and once the warm greetings were shared, she added, 'Doctor Louise saved me, you know.'

'I have good news!' said Louise. 'I just heard today, and when I spotted your car, I thought I would wait here to share it with my best friend in Gisenyi.'

'What is it?' asked Patricia. 'A little sibling for the boys?'

'Oh, no!' said Louise. 'Two boys and a husband are quite enough to look after. I have been offered a job in the main hospital in Kigali. No more night shifts in Gisenyi and no more long bus journeys through the mountains.'

'Oh, Louise, I'm thrilled!' said Patricia.

'Congratulations!' said Grace.

'Of course, you will be missed in Gisenyi,' said Patricia.

'We will still see each other,' said Louise.

'Yes, we will! Our firm has just landed a new contract with a big construction firm in the city,' said Patricia, 'and Jaqueline has put me on the project team. So I will be in Kigali more often too!'

'That's wonderful news!' said Louise. 'I tell you what. Why don't we meet up at a nice restaurant in Kigali to celebrate together? You must come too, Grace.'

'I'm there already!' said Grace.

'There are so many new restaurants popping up all over the city. But I will choose the best one for my sisters from Gisenyi!' said Louise.

'Okay, it's a plan. Let's do it, sisters!' said Patricia.

It didn't take long for Louise to organise the get-together. The restaurant table was booked and two weeks later Jean Pierre was confined to the house to help the boys with their homework while the three women met up in the city centre for a celebratory meal. Grace and Louise got on well together and the evening was full of laughter. Patricia enjoyed every minute of the evening. She had almost forgotten the enjoyment of a normal social gathering with a few close friends. After the meal, as they walked to the car park, Louise stopped suddenly and looked around.

'Hold on!' she said, looking up. 'Do you remember this building, Patricia?'

Patricia looked up at the building that she almost jumped from five years ago.

'Is that the one?' asked Patricia.

Grace looked confused.

'It's a long story!' said Louise.

'It is a very tall building,' said Grace.

'It sure is!' said Louise.

'Let's go up there!' said Patricia.

Louise was shocked.

'Not again!' she said.

Patricia laughed and shook her head.

'Just to see beautiful Kigali,' she said. 'I missed the view the last time.'

Grace looked confused.

'Okay, let's go,' said Louise.

The three women took the lift to the top floor, which was now a popular rooftop bar, teeming with young people.

'Oh good!' said Louise. 'There are enough strong young men here today that we won't need to call upon Faustin this time!'

Patricia bent over laughing, much to Grace's confusion.

The three women looked out across the growing city of Kigali. A light wind caressed their faces as they scanned the beauty of the city, neigbourhood to neighbourhood separated by hill after hill and surrounded by deep green, sunlit mountains. New concrete roads had replaced the old dust tracks and bumpy dirt roads. New modern buildings were under construction all around them. They could feel the renewal of the city. It was hard to believe that anything terrible had ever happened in this place.

'Sixteen years ago, this country was like a hell,' said Louise, 'but look at how it is now becoming a paradise.'

'We should thank God,' said Grace.

'We should also thank Rwandans,' said Patricia.

'I think you know now what you almost lost here,' said Louise.

Patricia looked down at the street far below.

'You came here to jump?' asked Grace. 'How could you?'

'Yes,' said Patricia, 'it seems like a long time ago now. Another life. I seem to have had several lives.'

Louise nodded and put her arm around Patricia's shoulder.

'I knew you would be all right in the end, beautiful woman,' she said.

'The devil within me was talking that day and I was listening to every word,' said Patricia.

She turned to her friends and, kissing them both on one cheek, said, 'Thank you.'

CHAPTER THIRTY-SIX

Patricia had often imagined this day. She had been planning what to do for weeks. She discussed it over and over again with Grace and Louise, but she declined both their advice and their presence. She did not care if her best friends thought this was not the best way. Patricia decided she must act alone. As she dressed for work in her bedroom, she looked up and smiled at her favourite photos of Bernard, Alice and Innocent. Patricia sensed the approval of Bernard's kind eyes. The time for churning words, memories and feelings was over. Today was a day for action. One simple act to change her life forever. At last, she was at peace about what she must do. Today was the day to kill the devil.

Leaving her house in the early morning, with a heavy bag over her shoulder, she stopped and listened to the soft queet-queet of the red-billed firefinches in her garden. Early morning was a good time to go to the school because the construction workers arrived early, before the streets were busy. Driving towards her destination, she chose to not turn on the car radio. She drove to her destiny in silence. Patricia parked her car beside the school construction site. Damascene had started work early as usual. She sat there and watched him hammering nails into the frame of a door, working alone, not pausing to joke with his co-workers.

For Damascene, it was just one more day of trying to labour away the pain. He prayed that perhaps a million nails hammered to build a new Rwanda would one day counterweigh the club of nails he forged in 1994. Damascene's supervisor noticed the woman in the car outside and tapped him on the shoulder.

'She's here again,' he said, 'the woman in the red car, who stops here and stares over at you nearly every day.'

Damascene looked up briefly, always uncertain how to respond. For weeks, he had wondered if Patricia's friend had delivered the letter, and if Patricia had torn it up or burned it, or if perhaps she had read his words. Since his release from prison, apart from coming here to work, he had stayed at home with Kalisa, not going out, safely cocooned from the community. On several occasions when he ventured out, survivors who knew of his crimes mocked and insulted him in the street. However, his biggest fear was running into Patricia in the shop or on the path home. He did not want to add to her pain and so when she began to park her car beside the construction site, and to look in his direction, he did not know what to do. He was confused. Did she want to speak to him or did she want to kill him? He certainly believed he deserved the latter. All Damascene could do was to try to stay focused, to keep going, to work hard, to help build a school, and nail by nail, to create a better future for the children of Gisenyi.

'It looks like someone needs you,' said the supervisor. 'Look!'

Patricia had wound down the window of the car and with one hand was beckoning Damascene to come forward. Damascene looked around to check if he was the person that she was calling. All of the other construction workers were working inside the school and so she could not be gesticulating to anyone else. Damascene set down his hammer, noticing his hand was shaking. He wiped his brow with a handkerchief and slowly began walking towards the car. Damascene had dreaded this moment for years, but he always knew this day must come. As he walked towards the friend he had betrayed, the sweat returned, but not as a result of labour. He felt his heart beating faster and faster, thumping in his chest. This was the encounter he had feared and longed for, in equal measure, for more than fourteen years. He had no idea what Patricia planned to say or do, but he was certain it was to be a moment of endings. He felt dizzy as he walked towards her. Patricia's eyes did not divert as he drew closer and closer. As he arrived alongside the car, Damascene stopped and bowed.

Head down, he finally spoke. 'Hello, madam.'

'Hello,' replied Patricia, holding her stare.

'How is madam?' he said.

'I am fine,' she replied.

'Hmm… I… I just wanted…' he began, faltering, his voice shaking.

'Get in,' said Patricia.

195

At this point, Damascene looked up with surprise, and there was Patricia his old friend, from another life. Her face was still beautiful and to his surprise he did not see the anger in her eyes. He recognised only the same still sadness he saw in his own eyes on the rare occasions he looked in the mirror. Damascene moved towards the rear passenger door of the car.

'No. Come sit here beside me,' she said, without any apparent emotion.

'Yes, madam,' he replied.

As Patricia looked straight ahead, Damascene skirted the front of the car and opened the passenger door. He looked at Patricia as if to check this was what she really wanted.

'Sit,' she said.

Damascene got into the passenger seat beside Patricia. The first thing he noticed was the bulky handbag on her lap. He wondered if it contained a knife or a gun. He could hear Patricia breathing. He was so close, he could smell her perfume. The living person he hurt so badly was almost touching him. This proximity overwhelmed him. Unable to control his emotions, Damascene began to cry. With eyes and cheeks burning, he gasped deep breaths so that he could finally speak.

'Thank you, for allowing me to be here with you, madam,' he said.

Patricia remained staring ahead and as she did not reply immediately, Damascene filled the silence with an outpouring of words.

'Madam, I know I and other Hutus did unthinkable acts, killing innocent Tutsis. I really... I truly... I regret what I have done... I know I don't deserve to be in any community. I was weak, a coward. I should have protected you. I just deserve death. All I deserve is death. Since 1994, I have never slept. The days were dark and the nights were only nightmares...'

His words poured out like water gushing from a breached dam.

'... That day, when I saw you at the Unity and Reconciliation meeting, I was fighting within my mind, struggling with what to say to you. I had thought about it so many times. Written it all down, ripped up the paper and started again, for years. I didn't know where to start. I wanted to get it right. I wrote it all down. I gave my letter to your friend Louise. I hope she gave you the letter. I hope you read my confession. All I want to say from the bottom of my heart is—'

'I forgive you,' said Patricia.

Damascene stopped, in shock. Then, thinking he had misheard Patricia's words, he began to speak again.

'For many years now, all I have wanted to say to you—'

'I forgive you,' said Patricia, now turning and looking into his disbelieving eyes.

'You forgive me?' he said.

'Yes. I forgive you,' she said.

For a few moments of silence, Damascene and Patricia looked into the pain in each other's eyes.

'No, please!' said Damascene.

'I forgive you,' said Patricia.

Damascene curled up in the seat, shaking, holding his knees to his chest, and cried. A great weight seemed to have been torn from within him.

'Thank you, madam. Thank you. God bless you. You have saved me. Thank you...' he continued, rocking backwards and forwards in the seat and pressing his forehead on the dashboard.

Patricia did not speak. She noticed how like a distraught child this man behaved, and yet he looked much older than his true age. She saw in him no threat, no danger, just brokenness. In her heart, she was aware that today she felt no anger or bitterness. It had taken so many years to arrive in this place. After a few minutes, Damascene became self-conscious of his emotional breakdown and tried to regain composure.

'I'm sorry, madam,' he said. 'I will go now.'

Patricia nodded and Damascene got out of the car, steadying himself on the pavement.

'Thank you, madam,' he said, wiping his face with his forearm.

As she drove off, Patricia lingered on the image of Damascene in her rear-view mirror, standing at the side of the road, crying and waving, becoming smaller and smaller. Once he disappeared from view, it was Patricia's turn to break down in tears. She pulled over into the car park near Lake Kivu, switched off the car engine and began to sob. She was struck by Damascene's weakness and helplessness. She noticed drops of his tears and smears of his sweat on the dashboard of the car. Reminders of his humanity. Then, as she looked across the waters of the lake, Patricia noticed a deep peace, a pure peace, envelope her heart. In the past few months, she had become aware of a newfound lightness in her soul, but today it was clear that the old heaviness was gone and it was not coming back.

She thought of Bernard, imagining her dear husband now seated beside her in the car, holding her hand and kissing her on the cheek. How she longed for his touch. Patricia looked through the windscreen towards the fishing boats on the lake.

'Bernard, my love, I have killed the devil,' she said.

CHAPTER THIRTY-SEVEN

Damascene strode into the house. Kalisa hardly noticed his brother's arrival. He was too busy watching his favourite music show on the television at full volume. Kalisa was sitting on the sofa, drinking a beer and moving in time with the latest Afrobeats hit by Kitoko. On a normal day after work, the brothers relaxed on the sofa and chatted over a few beers before cooking some brochettes together. Tonight was different. Without speaking, Damascene walked straight in front of Kalisa, switched off the television, abruptly, and sat down on the sofa beside Kalisa.

'Aw, man! Those beats are so good!' said Kalisa.

'Sorry, little brother, you know it's too much for me,' said Damascene.

'How are you, my brother?' asked Kalisa, noticing something different about Damascene, and handing him a bottle of beer.

'I am fine, brother,' said Damascene, declining the beer.

Kalisa scanned his brother's face.

'You look different,' he said. 'What happened?'

'Different? How?' asked Damascene.

Kalisa set down his beer and put an arm around Damascene's shoulder.

'I know you, brother,' said Kalisa. 'I can see when you are in pain. I know when you are eaten up with shame and I see it in your eyes when you are depressed. Today, something has happened. I can see it in your face. You look relieved, almost happy! I don't know this happy stranger!'

Damascene shook his head and smiled.

'She forgave me,' said Damascene.

'Are you okay, brother? Were you dreaming? Have you been drinking?'

'Today, she forgave me,' said Damascene.

Kalisa looked at him in wide-eyed amazement.

'Uwera Patricia forgave you? But she hates you! She thinks you are the Devil!' said Kalisa.

'She came to the construction site first thing this morning and she asked me to get into her car…'

'No way! How did you know she wasn't going to kill you?' said Kalisa.

'I didn't know. I thought she might want to kill me. I thought she had a knife in her handbag. But she forgave me.'

'Wow!' said Kalisa. 'I don't believe it!'

He hugged his brother.

'I honestly did not think this was possible. What did she say?'

'All she said was "I forgive you",' said Damascene.

Kalisa sat back in disbelief.

'Wow, man! Patricia forgives you! I've heard about this with other survivors, but I never thought this would happen to you. Are you sure she's not tricking you for revenge?'

'I can't believe I'm telling you this, but it's true. Why would she trick me like this? She must have read my letter. I'm sure of it. It's true. Patricia has forgiven me.'

'And what did you say to her?' asked Kalisa.

'I don't remember,' said Damascene. 'I think I thanked her again and again and I cried… It was a short conversation, but every word was important. I think for her as well as for me. She was different. More like the woman I remember, before…'

'This is awesome!' said Kalisa. 'Come on, brother, have a Primus. This is a time to celebrate.'

'I don't think so,' replied Damascene, declining the beer once again.

'What happens now?' asked Kalisa.

Damascene thought for a moment.

'I don't know,' he said. 'Do you think she really meant it? I'm sure she did. You don't think it's a trick? I don't know how I feel. Should I be happy or sad?'

'You look ten years younger in one day,' said Kalisa. 'This is what my eyes can see! I'll have you dancing to Afrobeats soon!'

'I have gone over it in my mind, again and again, all day long. Trying to take it all in. My brother, many years ago, I made a club of nails to kill. With every nail I inserted in that weapon, I lost another part of my soul. Today, at the school building site, I must have hammered a thousand nails. And with every one that I hammered, I think I nailed a part of my old self back together again.'

'So, tell me, brother,' said Kalisa, 'how do you feel now?'

'How do I feel?' said Damascene.

He paused and then a flicker of joy crossed his face, as if he had discovered some precious treasure for the first time.

'I feel that perhaps one day my heart will be free.'

Chapter Thirty-Eight

The heavy rain spat in Albert's face. As the thunder roared in the skies over Kampala, the streets of the slum became rivers of red mud.

'Watch where you're going, you fool!' he shouted at a *boda boda* rider, who was skirting the street and splashing mud in his direction.

'And you two won't get any business, standing there in the mud, like ugly pigs!' he shouted.

Rachel and Matusi cursed Albert under their breath and retreated from the road into the hut. Noticing the dark mood of his boss, Julius, a gangly teenager now, shooed his gang of street kids down an alleyway to safety.

'Hide, boys! The boss is mad as hell again today!' he cried.

Albert was in a fit of fury. He was angry at the sky because bad weather was bad for business. He was angry at himself for getting stuck in a life of addiction and petty crime with no family, apart from a gang of juvenile thieves and a house of prostitutes. He was angry at the police for constantly disrupting his business in spite of regular bribes. Yet, today, his overwhelming anger was directed at his sister back home in Rwanda.

The pastor had just delivered Patricia's latest letter from Gisenyi. Every letter from his sister created a certain degree of discomfort, as Patricia always asked for updates on Albert's imaginary wife and son and his fictional office job in Kampala city centre. Once Albert had established these lies, it was hard to sustain the fantasy. Apart from this challenge, the letters from home were usually a moment of joy in the midst of Albert's struggle for survival and descent into addiction. Patricia's correspondence was Albert's only connection with family and home. The letters evoked distant memories of a sense of belonging he had almost forgotten in a haze of time and marijuana. He was delighted to read of Patricia's steady progress from despair to hope and from university to work. He was proud of his only surviving family member and he looked forward to hearing the latest stories of her new friends, her new car and her attempts to replant the garden with avocados and beans.

I will once again grow the finest avocados in Rwanda!

Albert shared Patricia's initial disdain for the Unity and Reconciliation initiatives she reported in Gisenyi. He maintained that the only good Hutu was a dead Hutu. However, as the years went by, as Patricia's tone softened towards the idea of forgiveness and reconciliation, Albert felt a barrier building between him and his sister. He was certain that if only he could get her into the same room as him, he could talk her out of all this nonsense about reconciliation. When Patricia shared her experience of listening to perpetrators confessing their crimes and seeking forgiveness, Albert wrote back telling her they were snakes, trying to manipulate their way out of prison. When she included stories about meeting other survivors who had forgiven their perpetrators, he replied by accusing those survivors of being weak and trampling on the graves of their loved ones. When Patricia shared news that a son of a survivor and a daughter of a perpetrator were getting married in Kigali, Albert wrote back to say that if he was present on their wedding day he would burn their church to the ground. Patricia tried not to turn their exchange of correspondence into a long-distance argument, and while she gently disagreed, she tried to keep the content positive and happy.

I do not wish to argue, she replied to one long letter in which Albert said that any Tutsi who forgave a Hutu was a traitor.

However, Albert had not expected the contents of this letter. Today, he read Patricia's story of the day she forgave Damascene:

I forgave him. I know you will disagree, but do not question me, brother. It was the right thing to do for me, and for Damascene. Now we can exist in peace in the same community. That's it. He is forgiven. I want you to know and I do not wish to argue with you about this matter.

Throwing down the letter, he flew into such a rage that Julius, Rachel and Matusi knew they must scatter to avoid the inevitable violence of his wrath. As the years had gone by, Albert's mood swings had worsened and most of his workers had experienced a beating on more than one occasion. Two hours after first reading Patricia's letter, as he paced backwards and forwards through the mud, he was still enraged. The words of the letter repeated in his head and seemed to torture him.

'Forgive him? Forgive him?' he repeated as he circled aimlessly on the flooded road, like one of his most destitute addicts.

'Well, he'll never be fucking forgiven by me!' he shouted towards the clouds, stomping through the mud, his face burning with anger.

Passersby ignored him. He was just another voice crying out in the slum. A line of *boda boda* drivers sped by, splashing sludge all over him until Albert was covered from head to toe in red mud.

'What will we do?' said Rachel, peeking through the window of the hut.

'Don't go near him or he'll take it out on you!' said Matusi.

Albert fell to his knees and cried out to the heavens.

'Forgiveness? That's not what he will get from me! The only thing that cowardly bastard will ever get from me is a machete across his fucking throat!'

Chapter Thirty-Nine

'What if she sees us?' said Kalisa.

'She won't,' replied Damascene. 'She is still at work.'

'I think this is a bad idea,' said Kalisa. 'She only just forgave you a few months ago and now you are sneaking around outside her house. What will people think if they see you?'

'I am not sneaking. We are neighbours again. I see her nearly every day and she says hello,' replied Damascene.

He gathered pace as he walked towards Patricia's house.

'There is something here I need to show you, my brother,' he said.

Then Damascene stopped abruptly. Memories of standing here with the mob in 1994 flooded back into his mind. The same images tortured him every time he came here. Confession, forgiveness and reconciliation had not deleted the flashbacks.

'Are you okay?' asked Kalisa. 'Brother, this is crazy!'

Damascene shook his head, as if to cast out the memories.

'I'm just remembering the last time I stood here,' he said.

Damascene was learning that forgiving did not mean forgetting.

'God bless them,' said Kalisa.

'God bless them all,' said Damascene.

Kalisa noticed the resignation in his brother's voice and the deep lines on his forehead. The burden of guilt had aged him terribly, he thought.

'Why are we here, brother?' said Kalisa.

'Maybe we should leave, little brother. You're right. This is crazy.'

Damascene began to walk away.

'No. Hold on! Show me what? You said you wanted to show me something,' said Kalisa.

Damascene turned back and looked up to the sky, as if God above might give him strength.

'I remember this house well,' said Kalisa. 'I used to help Patricia look after the chickens here when I was a little boy.'

'That's why we're here,' said Damascene.

The brothers drew close to Patricia's house.

'Chickens?' said Kalisa, bemused.

'Look!' said Damascene, pointing, 'remember the storehouse and the chicken shed at the back of the house?'

'Oh yeah,' replied Kalisa, squinting his eyes towards the rear of Patricia's home.

'Look at her garden, she has replanted it,' said Damascene.

He stopped and breathed in the beautiful scents from the garden.

'Yes, it's flourishing once more,' said Kalisa, admiring the rows of sturdy avocado plants.

'But look here! The building at the back has fallen down,' said Damascene, walking past the house. 'Look! It's still a wreck after nearly fifteen years. They repaired the house for her but they never fixed up the shed. She has nowhere to store her produce and she can't keep chickens here anymore.'

'Oh yeah, I remember this,' said Kalisa.

He examined the tumbledown remains of the shed at the rear of the house.

'That's where the chickens laid their eggs. I used to love collecting them and bringing the eggs to Patricia in a basket. We used to count them in the kitchen, and she always gave me a few to bring home to our house.'

'I am going to rebuild it!' said Damascene.

'What?' said Kalisa.

'I am going to restore it. Her home is not complete without it. I will buy the materials and one day, when I know Patricia is not here, I will come over here and I will rebuild it.'

'But why don't you ask her first?' said Kalisa. 'You can't go on her property without asking her permission after… after… you know, what happened here before.'

'I do not want her to know it's me,' said Damascene. 'I want to do it for Patricia in secret. No one will know but you and me. It is a gift. I expect nothing in return. It must be a secret,' said Damascene.

'My brother, you are crazy,' said Kalisa.

'Can you keep a secret?' said Damascene.

More than you will ever know! thought Kalisa.

'Well?' said Damascene.

'I will help you and keep it all secret, of course,' said Kalisa.

He patted his brother on the back.

'But you know this is a risky thing to do.'

'You will help me transport the materials here,' said Damascene, 'but no one must know about this and I will work alone.'

'Okay,' said Kalisa, 'I'll help you get the materials. You are a good man, Damascene. Patricia will thank you and people will hear of your kindness.'

'I do not want attention or thanks from anyone,' said Damascene. 'Patricia must never know.'

'Why is this so important to you, brother?' asked Kalisa.

Damascene looked around the site of Patricia's home and remembered happier times he had spent here with his friend Bernard.

'This is my penance,' he said.

CHAPTER FORTY

'Welcome to Fame Construction!' said Ferdinand.

'Thank you!' said Damascene, shaking hands with his new colleague.

'Damascene is my older brother and this is his first day,' said Kalisa, 'and Nsabimana Ferdinand is the best engineer in the whole company! We call him Fer-Fer-Fer-di-nand! Ha ha!'

'Oh no! Kalisa, my friend, not another crazy Manchester United fan from Gisenyi!'

'He is the hardest worker in Rwanda!' said Kalisa. 'My brother never stops!'

'That's good news!' said Ferdinand. 'He will be a good addition to the team, even if he's not an Arsenal fan!'

'It's good to meet you, Engineer!' said Damascene.

'You are very welcome here, Damascene. New year, new job!' said Ferdinand. 'Let's hope 2009 is a good year for the construction industry in Kigali. Then we will be able to celebrate every football victory in style!'

The men stood at the entrance gates to the company,

joking and talking about football for a few minutes before starting work for the day. Damascene had been nervous about the first day of the new job. This was his first time back in Kigali since being released from the penitentiary. It was good to be able to travel to and from work with his brother, but he had painful memories of the city. All those years of hiding his identity and the fear of being exposed had left a scar. It was many years since the day of his arrest. He knew he was free, but the flashbacks continued to stab him. Ever since Kalisa had put him forward for this job, he had felt a mixture of excitement and dread at the thought of this first day. However, now that he was here, the good humour of his brother and Ferdinand helped him to settle in.

The morning went well, meeting colleagues in the office and learning the ropes, but Damascene was keen to get out onto a construction site in the afternoon. He enjoyed hard physical work. Intense labour absorbed him when he was on parole, building the school in Gisenyi. The harder he worked, the more he felt a return to normality. The sweat of labour seemed to soothe the wounds in his heart and he was impatient to get started today. At lunchtime, Ferdinand invited Damascene to share a table in the canteen.

'The work is good,' said Ferdinand, 'the pay is okay, but the canteen food is awful!'

'So the work is like Man United, but the food is like Arsenal!' said Damascene.

Just then, Kalisa came running into the canteen, sat down beside Damascene and began whispering in his ear.

'Oh, brother, I don't believe this!' he said.

'What's wrong?' said Damascene.

'You will never guess who is working here,' said Kalisa, looking towards the doors to the canteen.

When Damascene looked up, he froze, with a forkful of food halfway to his mouth. Patricia, accompanied by two of her colleagues, entered the canteen.

'But she works in Gisenyi. Why is she here? Has she come here to get me sacked?' said Damascene.

He dropped the fork, sprang up and fled to the restroom before Patricia spotted him.

'What's up?' said Ferdinand.

'Long story,' replied Kalisa, getting up.

He looked after Damascene and then over towards Patricia and decided to speak to Patricia first. Ferdinand shrugged his shoulders and continued eating his lunch.

'Manchester United fans!' he said.

Damascene stood alone in the men's restroom, holding on to a wash hand basin and looking into the mirror. In all his imaginings of this first day in his new job, this possibility had never crossed his mind.

I knew this was a mistake. I should have got a job in Gisenyi! he thought.

He looked at the deep wrinkles on his face and the new grey hairs on his head. For the first time in his life, Damascene noticed how old he had become. He took deep breaths but felt a deep weariness overwhelming him.

Staring into his dark eyes in the mirror, he thought, *I can't do this anymore.*

Kalisa burst through the door.

'I spoke to her,' he said.

'I can't work here,' said Damascene. 'We live in the same place and now we work in the same place. How the hell did that happen? Why did you not tell me? How could you not know?'

'I didn't know!' said Kalisa. 'It's her first day here too! If I had known, I would have told you. Do you think I'm cruel or just stupid!'

'I don't believe this,' said Damascene. 'It's bad enough she sees my face in the village these past few years, but now she has to look at me here at work in Kigali too!'

'Listen, brother,' said Kalisa, 'I spoke to her.'

'You spoke to her?' said Damascene.

'Yes, she was kind, brother. She didn't know you had got a job here. She doesn't work here and she didn't come to Kigali to get you sacked!'

'I don't believe this!' said Damascene. 'Then what is she doing here, today of all days?'

'Listen, brother,' said Kalisa, 'she told me her legal company got a contract with Fame Construction and she will be here Monday to Wednesday for the next six months. It's her first day too. Don't worry, be happy, Dammy!'

'I don't believe this!' said Damascene. 'I've only had that one conversation with her months ago in the car. What will I do?'

'Calm down, brother,' said Kalisa. 'She says it's okay!'

'Okay? How could it be okay? I am the last person she needs to see.'

'Seriously, brother, she really has forgiven you,' said Kalisa, taking his brother's face in his hands. 'She was very kind.'

'What else did she say? If she doesn't want me here,

215

I can leave and get a job in Gisenyi. That's what I should have done in the first place!'

'She told me you should not worry,' said Kalisa.

'I don't believe it!' said Damascene.

'Well, you won't believe this, Dammy!' said Kalisa.

'What?' said Damascene, just as Ferdinand entered the restroom.

'Patricia has invited us to her home. She says she wants to talk. She wants us to come over for some food.'

'Oh, I see!' said Ferdinand, winking and laughing.

CHAPTER FORTY-ONE

It was early on a Monday morning. The only sounds in the air were goats bleating and the twittering of swallows and weaverbirds. Damascene chose a Monday because he knew Patricia would be away from home all day working on the project in Kigali. The plan was to take leave from work for the day and to toil alone from early morning until early evening. He saved most of the earnings from his new job to purchase the building materials. Damascene drew up a plan for the construction of the outhouse in the same old notebook where he wrote and re-wrote his letter of confession. He designed a shelter for storing produce from the garden and a chicken coop to house some good egg-bearing hens. Kalisa remained sceptical about the wisdom of the venture.

'I know you think I'm crazy, little bro, but I must fix it!' said Damascene.

'What if some of her neighbours see you?' said Kalisa. 'They know both of you very well and they will wonder what you, of all people, are doing at her house when she is away. They might even call the police.'

'My counsellor advised me to speak to her next-door neighbours first,' Damascene explained, 'and they agreed to keep the secret. They love Patricia and they are happy to see her shed rebuilt. I think they trust me. They accept that I am trying to make amends.'

Kalisa realised that to argue would not change his brother's mind. For the first time, it occurred to him that Damascene and Patricia were equally stubborn. In spite of his misgivings, he agreed to help Damascene transport everything here to Patricia's house. Kalisa's next task was to travel to work in Kigali and text Damascene when Patricia's car arrived and departed from the Fame Construction car park. This way, when Patricia arrived home, the building would be complete and the builder would be long gone. Damascene's secret penance would be complete, and Patricia's home would finally be fully restored to all the comfort her family had enjoyed before 1994.

In spite of all his careful preparations, Damascene could not control the weather. By the time he began working, heavy rain had transformed much of the ground at the rear of Patricia's house into mud. Refusing to be diverted, slowly, step by step, as the rain poured down, soaking him completely, Damascene carried the materials up the small hill to the rear of the property, kneeling, pushing, pulling and climbing in the rain and the mud. He lost track of the hours as he lifted, sawed and hammered.

As he laboured without ceasing, he repeated one phrase in his mind: *I must fix it. I will fix it.*

The relentless downpour seemed to match his inexorable resolve to complete the task. A confluence of raindrops and sweat flowed from his furrowed brow. At midday, he did not even stop to eat, as if fasting was another sacrifice of his penance. By afternoon, he was exhausted. All that remained was to complete the sheet metal roof to make the building secure. For the first time, Damascene stopped. He stood with his hands on his hips, satisfied with the structure and certain it would be complete long before Patricia returned. Patricia's next-door neighbour arrived and, under the shelter of an umbrella, handed Damascene some water and bananas.

'You must take a break, sir,' she said. 'I will come back later with more water.'

'Thank you,' said Damascene. 'I must fix it. I can do it. Do you think she will be happy with it?'

'I know she will,' said the neighbour, waving farewell and retreating from the rain.

'Remember, she must never know it was me!' he cried.

As thunder cracked and the sky darkened, Damascene loaded three panels of sheet metal onto his back. The pounding of huge raindrops on the metal panels was deafening. He began to trudge up the hill towards the outhouse, stretching his muscles and straining against the wind. Perhaps it was a flash of lightning, or a thunderous bang in the sky that startled him, but suddenly Damascene lost his footing in the mud and fell backwards down the hill. He landed heavily on the razor-sharp edge of one of the steel panels. It sliced through his trousers and cut into his thigh like a machete. As he attempted to soften the fall with his hand, his wrist twisted back inwards and he heard the bone snap.

After the initial shock of the fall, Damascene lay on the ground in the mud. He punched the earth with his uninjured hand and began to cry tears of pain and frustration.

'I must fix it!' he cried out to the dark skies.

Blood, sweat and tears soaked his clothes. With his unscathed hand, he tore off his shirt and used it to tie a tourniquet around his bleeding leg, pulling it tight with his teeth.

'I must fix it!' he shouted, above the clamour of the storm.

He pulled himself up and then, limping and bleeding, he started to drag the sheet metal back up the hill. Using one hand, he pulled one panel at a time into place, continuously slipping back and lunging forward in a battle against pain, gravity and the elements. His naked torso was covered in mud and he looked like a deranged creature emerging from a swamp. Refusing to give up, he grunted through the pain and finally managed to drag all of the steel roof panels to the outhouse. With his injured leg still bleeding, he scrambled to the top of the structure and winched each panel up with a rope. Using a row of nails held in his teeth, he started to hammer the panels into place. As he pounded each nail, a terrible memory returned to add to his torture. He visualised the day he hammered nails into the head of a club to carry out his nighttime killing expeditions with the Interahamwe. With every blow of hammer on steel, he let out a cry of pain. It was as if every nail he struck, every cry of agony, represented one of the nails he had once driven into the head of a wooden club to create a weapon to attack people in 1994. All alone in the midst of the storm, no one heard his cries.

Finally, with the last roof panel in place, he lowered himself to the ground and fell on his back in the mud like a corpse waiting for its grave. He looked up at the sky as the rain pummelled his body and drummed on the newly attached roof. His broken wrist was now badly swollen and the pain in his thigh was searing. His whole body ached and he groaned as he tried to get up to gather his tools and tidy up the site. When at last he felt the task was complete, Damascene simply turned away and limped into the distance like a wounded animal seeking shelter in a storm. He left behind a pristine shed and chicken house. As the rain began to ease, the sound of drumming on the sheet metal roof diminished to a patter.

When Patricia arrived home, she was tired and it was dark and she did not notice the new construction. As she fell asleep, she thought she heard a strange sound outside, like a gentle beat on a steel drum. The next morning, while making breakfast, she glanced out of her kitchen window and her eyes grew wide in wonder. The new building she had longed for stood proudly before her. At first, she thought she might still be asleep and dreaming, but when she went outside to inspect her restored outhouse, she touched the fresh, damp wood and began to cry tears of joy. Initially, she wondered if the ghost of Bernard had returned in the night to make the restoration of her home complete. Then she concluded that Grace and Louise had plotted this generous surprise as a typically selfless gift.

Wait until I see those two! she thought.

The possibility of a secret penance from Damascene did not even cross her mind.

I have all I need now, thought Patricia, standing in the garden in the early-morning sunshine, breathing in the fresh air after the storm, *my home, my garden and good friends.*

Then an afterthought popped up. *And now I must get myself some chickens!*

CHAPTER FORTY-TWO

'Any sign of them?' said Grace.

Patricia pulled a curtain aside to peek out of the window to scan for the visitors.

'No sign yet,' said Patricia. 'I wonder if he has changed his mind. It will be very difficult for him.'

'Him? It's more difficult for you, my sister,' said Grace. 'Are you sure you want to go ahead with this? You can forgive someone without welcoming him back into your home, especially as it all happened in this very place.'

'My family died here,' said Patricia, 'and one day I will die in this house too. Until then, I want it to be a place of peace. Forgiving Damascene and welcoming him back here will help the cleansing of hatred from my home.'

'You are a complicated woman,' said Grace. 'You don't make life easy for your heart, but I respect your wishes, my sister.'

Patricia stared out of the same window that Bernard had looked out of almost fifteen years ago, when Damascene arrived outside with the Interahamwe.

Patricia's determination to live out her forgiveness was so intense that this memory spurred her on rather than prevented her from receiving Damascene back into her home. This was not a spur-of-the-moment decision. Patricia had considered this possibility for many months. A year ago, this day was unthinkable, for both Patricia and Damascene.

'Grace, you are the one who first encouraged me to forgive and I do not want to half-forgive him,' said Patricia. 'If Damascene and I are to live in peace once more, we must both retrace our steps from the past, no matter how painful.'

'But it's already clear you have forgiven him. You don't have to put yourself through this. Most people who forgive do not go this far,' said Grace. 'Do you remember the first time perpetrators were released from prison? They arrived back in the villages together and no one knew what would happen. We all kept our distance and somehow it worked. Most people cope this way.'

'Most people are not me. I know what I want and what I do not want. We must both face what happened here. I will not run away. This is how we will be healed,' answered Patricia.

She spotted Damascene and Kalisa walking down the street, carrying a gift and not a club of nails. She felt goosebumps rise on her neck.

'I don't know about this, brother,' said Damascene, his voice breaking with emotion as Patricia's house came into view.

'Brother, when she asked us to visit her home that first day at the office, she seemed sincere. Some women trick men into their homes and poison them for revenge, but I don't think Patricia is planning to kill you,' said Kalisa. 'If this woman wanted you dead, she would tell you to your face!'

'That's not what I'm worried about,' said Damascene. 'Here we are, standing outside the same house, asking to come in… like… like before…'

'I think she wants you to remember. She wants to remember too,' said Kalisa. 'Uwera Patricia is a strong woman. She doesn't do anything half-heartedly. It's as if she thinks the pain of remembering will help you to let go of the past.'

'If she is strong, I must be strong too,' said Damascene. As they approached the house, he took deep breaths to try to control the waves of guilt rising up within him. As he got closer, he focused on his recent handiwork on the outhouse at the rear of the house.

'It looks good, brother,' said Kalisa, looking at Damascene's bandaged wrist. 'She has no idea you did it, and nearly killed yourself in the process!'

Damascene knocked on the front door gently. In his mind, each knock echoed with the thuds on this door from 1994. Patricia opened the door. It felt unreal to be standing here. Damascene wondered if he was dreaming.

'Good afternoon,' said Patricia.

'Hello, madam!' said Kalisa, cheerfully. 'Here's a gift to enjoy. We hope you like it!'

Damascene opened the box he was carrying to reveal a bucket of six Primus beers in ice. Patricia smiled.

'Your garden is perfect as usual!' said Kalisa. 'The best avocados in Rwanda!'

'Thank you!' she said.

'Good afternoon,' said Damascene, finding it difficult to engage in eye contact with Patricia.

'What happened to your hand?' asked Patricia.

'Oh, just a little accident at work,' said Damascene. 'I broke my wrist but it's on the mend now.'

'You should have seen him that day!' said Kalisa, prompting a furtive dig in the ribs from Damascene.

'Come in, gentlemen, my friend Grace is here too,' said Patricia. 'She's a good church girl. She won't touch the beer, so there will be more for the three of us!'

Damascene struggled with the lightness of the conversation. His voice wavered as he spoke the words he had been practising for weeks.

'Madam, I want to thank you for your invitation to your home. I do not deserve to be welcomed into your home. I am not worthy of your kindness or your forgiveness and I beg you—'

'Okay. Are you coming in then?' she said, deliberately interrupting Damascene's formal speech.

'Hello, gentlemen,' said Grace.

She eyed the bucket of beers disapprovingly as the brothers followed Patricia into the living room.

Immediately, Damascene's eyes were drawn to the family photographs on the wall. He had not seen his old friend's face since 1994. He felt Bernard look into his eyes and dropped to his knees beneath the picture, wincing in pain from the wound in his thigh. Damascene began to cry.

Grace and Kalisa were taken aback and embarrassed by this dramatic move, but Patricia placed her hand on Damascene's shoulder.

'Forgive me, brother!' he said, as if praying to Bernard.

'Oh God, I knew this was a mistake,' said Kalisa. 'I am sorry, madam. We will go now.'

'Yes,' said Grace.

'No. Give him a moment,' said Patricia.

Grace and Kalisa looked on awkwardly.

'I really don't know how I can thank you for welcoming me back here,' said Damascene.

He remained on his knees, wiping tears from his face and starting to feel faint.

'I can't believe what you have done, madam. It is a miracle. I am unworthy of your forgiveness. We can leave now if you wish. Thank you, madam.'

'There is no need to continue thanking me. I forgave you and I meant it,' said Patricia. 'Now get up and have a Primus, brother.'

Grace and Kalisa were shocked at Patricia's matter-of-factness. Damascene was dumbfounded at Patricia's calm demeanour and generous words. He slowly got to his feet. Kalisa already had a beer in his right hand. He gave Patricia a high five and handed her a bottle of beer.

'Thanks, Kalisa. You always were a little rascal!' she said.

'I was a good boy, madam,' said Kalisa.

'I remember you as a little boy, chasing my chickens just for fun!' said Patricia. 'When you weren't dancing instead of working!'

'He still prefers dancing to working!' said Damascene, starting to relax.

'Do you have chickens now?' asked Kalisa.

'I am buying some chicks soon, for my new outhouse,' she said.

227

Patricia pointed out of the kitchen window at the brand-new structure at the rear of the house.

'Wow! That's impressive!' Kalisa replied.

He winked at Damascene, who returned the gesture with a wary stare.

'It was built by an angel from your church, wasn't it, Grace?' said Patricia.

Grace shrugged her shoulders and declined a beer. The others sat down together to partake. Patricia's radio was playing at low volume in the background.

'Hey, hey, wait...' said Kalisa, listening in to the DJ introducing the latest song. 'Can I raise the volume, please?'

'Sure,' said Patricia.

'It's the one and only – Michael Jackson,' said Kalisa, jumping up and turning up the volume.

'I'm not sure about Michael Jackson,' said Grace, but it was too late.

Not only had Kalisa pumped up the volume, but he stayed on his feet, singing and dancing along, looking and sounding like Michael Jackson himself. This was the only way he knew how to change the atmosphere in a room, and Kalisa felt his services were most definitely required on this occasion.

'I'm sorry, madam. You remember how crazy my little brother is?' said Damascene, shifting in his chair.

'I do remember,' said Patricia. 'He always used to wear a little baseball cap the wrong way round like a kid in America. Always singing and dancing like a Hollywood superstar!'

By this stage, Kalisa was in full flow.

"'All I want to say is that,
They don't really care about us.'"

In all of Damascene's tortured imaginings of this encounter, it had never crossed his mind that it would involve his brother performing the moonwalk! However, Kalisa's lack of self-consciousness was infectious and, with a little help from the effects of the alcohol, Damascene and Patricia relaxed into a polite conversation. They occasionally broke off the chat to laugh at Kalisa's attempts to breakdance in the middle of Patricia's living-room floor. After a few more songs, Kalisa was successful in tempting Grace to join him on the dancefloor. After a few more drinks, eventually all four were up dancing and laughing together. This was not at all what Damascene had expected and he remained somewhat stilted, but Patricia enjoyed the sense of release she felt from practising her choice to forgive with some joy.

'I have an idea,' said Patricia, taking a breath. 'Can anyone do a traditional dance?'

'Not since we danced at school,' said Damascene.

'Oh, I remember,' said Patricia, 'you were in the dance group when the archbishop visited our school.'

'Oh yes!' said Damascene, recalling a part of his life he had forgotten in recent years, 'and Bernie and I were chosen to present an *inyambo*[16] to the bishop.'

'Oh yes!' said Patricia, remembering the affectionate way Damascene always referred to Bernard.

'And Bernie let go of the rope, and the *inyambo* ran away...'

---

16 An *inyambo* is a prized breed of cow in Rwanda.

'And the teachers had to run after the cow, all the way through the muddy fields in their best clothes!'

Damascene laughed along with Patricia. It felt unreal. For so long, laughter had been just a memory for the pair. A survivor and perpetrator laughing together seemed surreal, and Grace was not sure if she approved.

'I can do any dance!' said Kalisa, not allowing a moment for a more sombre mood to emerge.

'I can believe it!' said Patricia. 'Grace, I will definitely have to teach you!'

Patricia darted to the music player, put on her favourite Cecile Kayirebwa CD and began to teach the others a traditional Kinyarwanda dance. Damascene and Grace struggled at first but Kalisa picked up the steps quickly. The atmosphere was lighter than any of them could have imagined.

In a break from the dance lesson, Patricia paused for thought in the bathroom. Looking at herself in the mirror, she wondered if this meeting was too happy and if she might be disrespecting the memory of Bernard. She walked into her bedroom and looked up at her favourite photograph of her late husband. Once again, she felt Bernard's kind eyes urging her on towards normality. She remembered happy gatherings like this with Damascene and Bernard in the distant past. She knew it could never be the same, but now that she had found peace, she also wanted a little joy.

'Are you okay?' asked Grace, standing at the open door of the bedroom.

'Yes, sister,' replied Patricia, 'I am fine. I just need to allow myself to feel joy again. It's what Bernard would have wanted.'

Grace was amazed at Patricia's resilience.

'You are stronger and more merciful than I could ever be,' she said.

Grace hugged her friend and the two women returned to the living room for more music and chat. Damascene looked worried but Kalisa was still absorbed in the music.

'Okay, one more dance!' said Patricia.

The dancing, singing and laughter continued for over an hour and then Patricia served some food. Damascene looked for any sign of anger from Patricia but the old bitterness was completely gone. It seemed like a miracle. An outside observer would not have guessed the painful history shared by this group of people. Damascene decided in advance that they would not stay late and nodded to Kalisa when it was time to leave.

'I cannot thank you enough,' said Damascene.

Patricia and Grace walked Damascene and Kalisa to the gate.

'You're welcome. You must come again,' said Patricia.

'Good lady, you did not have to speak to me or forgive me,' he said, 'but you have even welcomed me back into your home and helped me to feel human again.'

'I know,' said Patricia.

'I can never repay you,' said Damascene, about to begin another sincere speech about his gratitude to Patricia, when his brother interrupted.

'I love you, Uwera Patricia!' said Kalisa, after one too many beers. 'You are a very, very special lady! Call me when you buy your chickens and I will look after them once more!'

He began to dance like a chicken and Grace bent over, laughing.

'I think I will survive without a little dancing chicken helper now!' said Patricia.

'I will bring twice as much beer the next time!' said Kalisa.

He attempted some of the dance steps Patricia had taught him but tripped over into the garden, much to everyone's amusement.

'Don't squash my avocados!' cried Patricia.

As the brothers departed, Patricia and Grace waved them goodbye.

'She is kind and she really has forgiven you,' said Kalisa, 'unless she secretly added poison to the beer when you weren't looking! You might still drop dead any minute!'

'Ha ha, brother,' said Damascene. 'You have had too much Primus as usual, but thank you for coming with me. I could not have done this on my own.'

'You needed the king of dancing to be around to make sure you are all chilled-out, man!' said Kalisa.

He attempted a drunken moonwalk on the street.

'Listen, little brother,' said Damascene, stopping and looking at Kalisa, 'when we were young and you were just a kid, I would go out to work every day with Papa while you stayed home. I thought I was the best son because I was older and making money to buy food, while you stayed home with our mother.'

'Come on, Dammy! I couldn't go to work when I was five years old, even though I could sing and dance like the King of Pop!' said Kalisa.

'But listen, brother,' continued Damascene, 'one day, I was sitting chatting to our papa while you had gone to fetch water. We watched you coming back from the well.

The jerry can was bigger than you, but you were skipping and singing! Papa said you might be the youngest but you are the brightest one in the whole family.'

'Yes!' said Kalisa, jumping up and punching the air. 'Papa always knew I was a genius!'

Damascene laughed.

'Listen, Kalisa,' he said, 'I didn't know what he meant at the time and I was a little jealous. You were just a little kid who smiled and danced all the time. But I can see it now.'

'How?' said Kalisa, momentarily sobered by his brother's words. 'That's not what my teachers said!'

Damascene took his brother's face in his hands.

'Our father, may he rest in eternal peace, taught you just to be you. To laugh and sing and dance. He felt the joy you gave our family, and he saw the smiles you brought to other people. I always thought my little brother was too light-hearted and frivolous, but our father could see you have a gift.'

'A gift?' said Kalisa.

'Yes, a gift to help people to smile, to relax, to stop being so serious and to leave their troubles behind them,' Damascene explained.

'Really, brother?' said Kalisa.

'You did it tonight,' said Damascene. 'You helped me and Patricia be friends. Many years ago, we were good friends, but in 1994, because of me, we became enemies. Tonight, you helped us to discover our friendship again.'

In a moment of shyness, Kalisa looked down, shook his head and then, smiling again, he patted his brother on the back tenderly.

'Thank you, Dammy,' he said.

As they walked down the street, now with his arm around his brother, Kalisa began singing in his ear. Damascene reflected on the evening's encounter. He began to wonder, for the first time, if life really could be worth living again.

Chapter Forty-Three

'He's funny!' said Patricia.

'Oh, I know!' replied Ferdinand.

It was a few weeks since Patricia had welcomed Damascene and Kalisa into her home. Ferdinand and Patricia were standing in front of the reception desk at Fame Construction.

'I had forgotten all about his crazy singing and dancing and that silly laugh,' said Patricia.

'I know Kalisa well,' said Ferdinand. 'I could tell you many stories! Any time I get mad at him at work, he ends up just making me laugh. I'm just about to yell at him and he says something hilarious and I can no longer keep a straight face.'

'He was like that when he was a little boy too,' said Patricia. 'He used to look after my chickens, and no matter how naughty he was, I could never stay angry at him.'

'Of course, his brother is another matter,' said Ferdinand. 'He seems to carry the troubles of the world on his shoulders.'

Patricia nodded.

'Kalisa told me you forgave him,' said Ferdinand. 'I admire you, Patricia. I'm not sure I could forgive.'

'It's not easy but it's a choice,' said Patricia. 'Forgive and start to live again, or hate and die with a bitter heart.'

'Wise words, Uwera Patricia,' said Ferdinand. 'You are more than just the smartest legal secretary from Gisenyi. I think the whole world could learn from you!'

Patricia blushed and laughed. She had not been in a relationship with a man since Bernard died. She assumed she would never find love again and she would live out her days alone. However, as her heart warmed, she was rediscovering her flirtatious nature. When she engaged in a little flirting with tall, handsome Ferdinand it made her feel young, free and hopeful. Of course, she wasn't interested in Ferdinand in that way and he was too young for her, she thought, but she enjoyed the flirting anyway.

As Patricia and Ferdinand continued to chat, the receptionist observed everything.

'That woman has changed so much since she first started working here,' she whispered to the secretary at the next desk.

'What happened to her?' asked the secretary.

'I don't know, but thank God she has changed,' said the receptionist. 'She was always so serious. I was afraid to go anywhere near her.'

'She used to wear the same dark clothes every day,' whispered the secretary, 'but look at her now – new hairstyle, bright clothes and red lipstick.'

'It must be love!' said the secretary, nodding towards Ferdinand.

The receptionist nodded and winked.

'A little bit of loving can bring a smile to the sourest of faces!' she said.

'He looks like he could give her some good loving,' said the secretary.

The women giggled as Ferdinand picked up his documents and bade farewell to Patricia, who made her way to the office, greeting colleagues on the way.

Those gossips think I'm deaf, she thought, smiling and enjoying the fact that she was being talked about.

Her days at Fame Construction were long and busy and sometimes she took the bus to Kigali so she could sleep on the way home to Gisenyi in the evenings. Patricia didn't mind because she was enjoying the work and meeting new people. She was simply happy being normal. As the weeks and months passed by, Patricia felt a new purpose and enjoyment in her life. The hours of counselling over the years had helped her a lot.

'I've had more counsellors than chickens!' she joked to Doctor Louise during one of their weekly chats at the park.

Patricia noticed the parts of her heart that had been full of sorrow and anger were slowly being filled with hope and reason. A deep residue of pain persisted, but Patricia was surprised by her experience of happy days and unexpected moments of joy. Some evenings as she travelled home on the bus, she gazed out of the window at the beautiful hills as far as the eye could see, and felt a sense of peace and contentment that she had not known for nearly two decades. Alone in her home at night, as she watched romantic movies on the television, or if she listened to love songs on the radio, she began to wonder if it was possible that she could find love again. Patricia had no doubt this is what Bernard would have wanted. Sometimes, in the mornings, she awoke in the afterglow of a romantic dream, where she had been held in the arms of a man who loved her, cared for her and protected her. They weren't dreams of longing for Bernard. The man in her dreams was different. At first, she felt guilty, as if the desire was unfaithful, but as the months went by, she began to entertain this dream in her waking hours.

'Do you think I will ever find love again?' she asked Louise.

'I have no doubt,' said Louise. 'When you are least expecting it, when you are not even looking for it, I believe love will find you.'

Chapter Forty-Four

By the following April, Patricia was still single. Several dates and a few nights with Ferdinand had been fun but did not lead to a serious romance. At least the receptionist at Fame Construction felt her gossip was vindicated. Patricia was relieved to discover it was possible to be intimate with a man once again. She concluded that even though Ferdinand was a good man and a generous lover, she didn't love him, not in the way she had loved Bernard. She had no desire to get to know him in a deeper way, and Ferdinand was a closed book regarding his past anyway. Patricia began to wonder if a person only deserved one true love in life. Perhaps she was destined to be alone. She spent most of her days working hard, either in the office or around her home and garden. She never discovered which men in the church had rebuilt her outhouse, but she bought some chickens and the shed was once again full of fresh eggs and magnificent avocados. She employed Nana, a teenage girl who lived nearby, to help with the garden and to sell her produce at the market on Saturday mornings, to raise money to help orphans in the village. Today, Nana had just returned from this weekly expedition with a purse full of profit and Patricia was singing as she fed the chickens.

'Keep those eggs coming, my little friends!' she said.

'Everyone in the village wants to buy Miss Patricia's avocados!' said Nana, as Patricia paid her and bade her farewell for another week.

'Thanks Nana,' she said. 'This money will help to send some of those poor little orphans to school.'

As she sat down with a coffee to relax, Patricia heard a knock on the door. She was not expecting any visitors.

'Who is there?' she called.

'Damascene,' was the reply.

Patricia raised her eyebrows. She had spoken to Damascene in the canteen at Fame Construction on quite a few occasions over the past few months, but this was the first time he had returned to her home since the visit with Kalisa. It was as if everyone felt guilty about the enjoyable evening they shared and had agreed not to repeat it anytime soon. Opening the door, Patricia noticed the nervous look in Damascene's eyes, and felt a need to reassure him.

'Oh good! No dancing little brother this time,' she said. 'Come in, Damascene.'

'Thank you, madam,' he said.

He noticed this was the first time she had uttered his name since the genocide.

'I hope you are not busy. I came to ask if you need any help in the garden. It must be hard on your own, so I wanted to tell you I will help if there are heavy jobs you need done. Here, I brought you a small gift from the market.'

'Thank you,' said Patricia, accepting a little package containing a pot of *urusenda* oil. 'Come in, please. It's good of you to offer but I can cope okay. I have a girl from the village who helps me, and the men in the church rebuilt the shed. That was a blessing.'

'That was very kind of them,' said Damascene.

He was glad to hear of the fruits of his secret penance but underneath a calm exterior, his mind was in turmoil. So many thoughts and questions were spinning around in his head.

You don't deserve to be here!

How dare you come back to Bernard's house!

All that drinking and laughing the last time was a disgrace!

Such thoughts swirled around in his head, day and night, and it was exhausting.

What will neighbours think if they see you visiting her alone?

Leave her alone! You've done enough damage!

It's all a trick! No one could truly forgive what you did!

'Sit down, I have fresh coffee,' said Patricia.

Damascene looked uncomfortable.

'I promise I will not poison you!' said Patricia. 'I'm glad to see you look well and your wrist has healed.'

'Oh yes, thank you,' said Damascene.

The pair made small talk for a few minutes about the market, the garden and the latest gossip at Fame Construction until Patricia decided she wanted to have a deeper conversation.

'Damascene, do you believe me that I have forgiven you?' she asked.

Damascene was taken aback at the directness of the question, but he realised this was typical of Patricia.

'I do believe you, madam,' he said, 'but I do not understand how you can forgive. You are a stronger person than me. Did you get this from church?'

'A little,' said Patricia. 'My friend Grace takes me to her church sometimes and they preach about forgiveness. But many years ago, I learnt to live without the help of God. When I was abandoned by God, I learnt to find my own strength within me. And that includes the strength to forgive.'

'I thought all such miracles must come from above,' said Damascene. 'God helped me to confess.'

'No,' said Patricia. 'Whatever we do in this world, we must take our own time to think, to use our minds, to decide what is right and what is wrong. I alone decide what I must do. It was the hardest decision in my life, but I have no regrets.'

Damascene nodded.

'You always knew exactly what you wanted,' he said. 'I remember the day you told me that Bernard would be your husband. We were only twelve years old!'

As soon as he said these unguarded words, Damascene felt a deep sense of shame.

How dare you speak his name in this place!

However, Patricia was unfazed.

'Damascene, when I make a decision, I stick to it,' she said. 'The only person in this world who can change my mind is my friend Louise.'

'The doctor, from Kigali?'

'Yes. Louise is my angel. Did I tell you how I still meet with her every week?'

As Patricia shared the story of meeting up with Doctor Louise, the lilt of her voice reminded Damascene of the times when they were teenagers, cooking fish on a campfire at Lake Kivu. With Bernard, Amina and the others, they chatted about life, music and football, for hours on end until the sun went down.

'Do you remember all the crazy things we did growing up?' asked Patricia. 'We were so young and the world seemed so harmless.'

'I was thinking the other day about the time your sister, Amina, fell out of the tree,' said Damascene.

'Oh yes!' said Patricia. 'I haven't heard that story for years. Tell me again.'

Damascene laughed and began to recount the story.

'Once upon a time, there was a girl called Amina,' he said, 'who liked climbing trees that were ten times her own height…'

Patricia enjoyed the revival of a familiar old tale. The story was bittersweet because Amina, like so many others, was gone, but somehow the retelling of an innocent tale of youth blessed the memory of the lost ones. As Patricia listened to Damascene, she saw, behind the harrowed face of a weary middle-aged man, the remnants of a boy who was once like a brother to her. In fact, he was always kinder to her than Albert. This was why the betrayal had been so brutal. Albert was a jealous sibling, sniping at their parents' alleged favouritism towards Patricia, even though she was certain her parents gave him no good reason for such feelings.

243

When Damascene had completed the story, Patricia sighed.

'The past lives with us today – the bad and the good,' she said.

Damascene felt a sudden pang of shame.

You have gone too far, you fool! he thought.

'Anyway, I must go now,' said Damascene, always wondering if every minute was a moment too long to impose his presence on Patricia.

'I just wanted to let you know I'm here for you if you need an extra pair of hands around the house or in the garden.'

'Thanks for the story and the chilli oil,' said Patricia.

Then, naturally, and without thinking, she hugged Damascene. At first, he stiffened. How could this woman look at him or talk to him, never mind touch him? Noticing the awkwardness, Patricia let go.

'One more thing,' said Damascene.

'Yes?' said Patricia.

'Next Thursday is the Walk to Remember,' he said.

'Yes, I know,' said Patricia. 'Grace told me about it.'

'May I walk with you, madam?' asked Damascene.

Patricia looked at him intently for a few moments. The boldness of this request impressed her.

'Yes, Damascene,' she replied. 'You may walk with me.'

CHAPTER FORTY-FIVE

Damascene did not sleep well. Several times during the night, he stirred from a dream where he was late for the Walk to Remember. He dreamed of missing the bus, getting lost in the city and no matter how fast he ran, he could not catch up with the crowd. He skipped breakfast and left home early to catch the bus to Kigali. Even though the sun was shining, he wore a dark jacket over his white t-shirt. This was his first time at a Walk to Remember. Every April, it seemed the genocide memorial events became more and more significant to his friends and neighbours of all backgrounds and generations. However, until today, Damascene felt too ashamed to take part. He understood the annual memorial events were for everyone, not just survivors, but he believed he would never be truly welcome. Sometimes, he caught the coverage on television and it reminded him of his personal sins. Until this year, the 7th of April was a day to forget and hide from the past. He needed Patricia's permission before he dared to show his face at a Walk to Remember. Today, however, as he walked alone towards the bus station, Damascene felt like he was walking into sunlight for the first time.

Patricia did not sleep well and rose early. She washed and dressed quickly, putting on her white t-shirt, before realising she had more than enough time to drive to Kigali, park the car and arrive for the start of the event. Instead of leaving immediately, she spent an hour walking around her own home. She started outside and ambled around the garden, stopping for a chat with the chickens. Feeling the warmth of the sun on her cheeks, she felt glad to be alive. Then she entered each room of the house, stopping and remembering at the front door, in the living room and the kitchen. This was her personal walk to remember. Finally, she visited each photograph of Bernard, Alice and Innocent, touching the frames and the glass, as if trying to touch their faces. She noticed her pain was just as deep but not as intense as it used to be. She felt a twinge in her back at the scar from the long-healed machete wound. Patricia wept quietly then on checking the clock, decided it was time to leave. She stopped at a garage to fill up the car with petrol to make the journey to Kigali. She had never attended a genocide memorial event before. The public readings of the familiar names of the lost and the appeals for more information on hidden burial sites were too much for her to bear. Doctor Louise had invited her to the event in Kigali many times before, but Patricia had always declined.

'I do not wish to remember,' she had said. 'I wish to forget.'

Last year, seeing the change in Patricia, Grace had asked her to join her at the annual church memorial in

Gisenyi, but Patricia had politely declined. She had not been ready. However, this year was different. Having decided to forgive Damascene, she felt released to commit to this public declaration of remembering and reconciliation. Damascene's request to walk with her confirmed in her mind that this year she must walk to remember. She chose not to tell Louise or Grace. Patricia wanted to take these steps alone and the only person she arranged to meet was Damascene himself, at the starting point of the walk.

Arriving in Kigali by different modes of transport, Damascene and Patricia approached the starting point at the Ministry of Justice from different directions. Both noticed how the normally bustling city streets were empty of cars and motorcycles. People of all ages emerged from side streets, all dressed in the same white t-shirts. The crowd converged on the main road to prepare to make their way to the memorial ceremony at the Amahoro National Stadium. As Damascene and Patricia arrived on the main road, they noticed the silence of the gathering. Many people were holding candles to light at the stadium in memory of the victims. The atmosphere was a strange mix of sadness and hope.

'Welcome, Rwandans!' began an official with a microphone, addressing the assembly from the front of the crowd.

'We are one people here today,' he said.

Damascene spotted Patricia at the front of the crowd.

'Before we begin our Walk to Remember, there is just one thing I want to say,' he continued. 'Remembering is everyone's responsibility.'

Patricia noticed Damascene walking towards her. She had wondered if he would show up. Perhaps he would not have the inner strength to be part of an event of this kind. She felt strangely proud of this broken man.

'All of us must remember,' said the speaker, 'and we must teach our children and our grandchildren to remember, to make sure this tragedy can never happen again in this country or anywhere else in the world.'

As Damascene approached, Patricia smiled and held out her hand. Damascene removed his coat to reveal a white t-shirt emblazoned with the words *Never Again*, the same as the words on the t-shirt worn by Patricia and every other person in the crowd. Patricia took Damascene's hand and they walked together through the streets of Kigali with hundreds of neighbours, young and old, Tutsi and Hutu, perpetrators and survivors, walking to remember. They walked silently with the crowd to the stadium. Today was not a day for speaking.

As darkness fell, Patricia and Damascene sat together in the stadium, along with thousands of others, holding candles in memory of the victims as many of their names were read out. As they listened, they were amazed at the dignity of the survivors and the powerful messages of reconciliation. There was complete silence in the packed stadium as a middle-aged Tutsi woman shared her survivor's story. Damascene looked around as many women of the same age broke down in tears as she described the day she saw her husband alive for the last time. Patricia began to weep. At first, Damascene did not know what to do. His natural urge was to try to comfort her but he hesitated. He feared rejection of the offer of support from a perpetrator. He knew there were many perpetrators here who were forgiven by survivors, but even the rising tide of hopefulness of reconciliation surrounding him was not enough for Damascene to try to reach beyond his guilt.

I'm the last person who should comfort her, he thought, tears of shame now streaming down his face.

He turned his head away in case Patricia saw the tears. He felt he had no right to cry. Only those who suffered had a right to weep. He did not want his tears to be a selfish distraction from the grief of survivors. Hoping Patricia had not noticed, once he had composed himself, he did what he felt was the right thing to do. He took Patricia's hand. She accepted his offer of compassion and it seemed that in this moment there was a deeper healing in both of their hearts.

'Thank you for coming,' said Patricia.

'It is my responsibility,' said Damascene. 'I will always do the same. As long as you want me to, I will walk to remember every year now. I will walk with you to remember until the day I die.'

Patricia gripped Damascene's hand. Everything about this day seemed right to her. She felt peace about coming here for the first time. She was certain that to attend with Damascene was the only way forward. She knew the killers of her family had been dead for many years now. She used to hope they were burning in hell, but today, even this bitterness was dissipated. Damascene was the final link to what had happened to her and she had chosen to forgive him. Once the choice was made, for Patricia, this was the outworking of forgiveness. As she looked around the stadium, she noticed how many young people present had not yet been born in 1994. She imagined Alice and Innocent standing among the teenagers, holding candles, bright young faces, sincere in their desire for reconciliation. Patricia knew in her heart that her children would be proud of their mother today. A young man, introduced as a national youth leader, stood up on the stage to address the crowd.

'Here in Rwanda,' he said, 'we must choose what is right for us and what builds our nation. As young people, keep in mind that you're the future. My brothers and sisters, you must fight against any genocide ideology wherever you are, by using all means available, including new technology and social media. As we remember what happened, also keep in mind your responsibility in building the future.'

The young people in the crowd cheered.

'And, of course,' he continued, 'we are not just the future leaders of our country. We can lead by example, today, by living our lives in unity and reconciliation.'

'That's a message for the old ones like us, too,' whispered Patricia in Damascene's ear. 'We can lead by example to this new generation. If you and I can be reconciled, they will know it will never happen again.'

Damascene nodded, processing every word in his mind and feeling a softness in his guilt-filled heart. The grace, strength and determination of this woman overwhelmed him. He kept hold of Patricia's hand as a government minister rose to address the people in the stadium.

'Today, around the world,' he said, 'from Uganda to Tanzania, in Canada and the USA, from the UK to India, people are marking this day, to ensure that the world will never again see another genocide.'

The crowd applauded.

'Never again!' they chanted.

'Never again!' said the government minister.

Damascene turned to Patricia and looked into her eyes.

'Never again,' he said.

Chapter Forty-Six

'The food was delicious,' said Patricia.

'Thank you, sister,' said Grace.

'You are a very lucky man, Rwibutso,' said Patricia.

'Yes!' said Rwibutso.

He clapped his hands and kissed Grace on the cheek.

'Your new wife is smart, beautiful and a very good cook!' said Patricia.

'Not so smart!' laughed Grace. 'I do recall asking you to help me with a few horrible assignments a few years ago.'

'Oh yes!' said Patricia. 'You used to come to me in the library saying, "Please can you give me a little intellectual help, my friend?"'

'I got my degree because of you!' said Grace.

Patricia shook her head and laughed.

'Hold on!' said Rwibutso. 'When we were at high school together, I remember Grace coming to me in the classroom and saying, "Please can you give me a little intellectual help, my friend?"'

'You're lying!' said Grace. 'I'll tell your father you are bearing false witness against your own new wife! The pastor will be angry!'

'Please, no! Anything but that!' said Rwibutso.

'This shows us how smart Grace has always been,' said Patricia. 'You don't learn without asking for a little help.'

'I was always smarter than you at school, my husband, and don't you ever forget it!' said Grace.

'That's good advice!' said Patricia.

'Oh, now the ladies are ganging up on me!' said Rwibutso.

It was an evening of good food, conversation and laughter and a pleasant distraction for Patricia, who spent most of her time at work or in the garden. Even when she was young, she preferred to spend time with a few close friends rather than large social groups. Tonight was her first visit to the home of her newly married friend for the kind of social interaction she enjoyed. Without romance in her own life, she enjoyed the frisson of the newlyweds' love drama. The teasing between the young couple took her back to her teenage days with Bernard, Damascene, Isabelle and Felice. During those seemingly endless summers, the flirtations changed all the time. One day, Damascene had a crush on Isabelle and the next day Bernard had an infatuation with Patricia, of course. Then Felice and Isabelle fell out over their sudden enchantment with Bernard, and yes, at one stage, Patricia was convinced she was madly in love with the young, handsome Damascene. Patricia's heart was renewed by the intimacy and warmth of her recent brief relationship with Ferdinand. She had enjoyed being the object of his care and affection but there was little passion. Patricia concluded that Ferdinand deserved to be with a woman who adored him.

'Well, as my father would say, all we can do is to give thanks to God that any of us managed to graduate from university!' said Rwibutso.

'Well, as we all know, your good father has a lot to say about everything!' said Grace.

Just then, there was a knock on the door, which Grace answered.

'Who can that be at this time of night?' asked Rwibutso.

'It's Kanyarwanda, Grandpa!' said Grace, ushering in a smartly dressed elderly man.

'Welcome, wise old man!' said Rwibutso.

'Pleased to meet you,' said Patricia.

Kanyarwanda reminded her of her own grandfather.

'I was just passing on my way home and I suddenly remembered I had forgotten to tell you something,' said Kanyarwanda.

'What is it, Grandpa?' asked Grace, obviously used to his ways.

'Listen to this, my children,' he said, 'I have been thinking about our land, our beautiful Rwanda. I have lived through many different times in this place, good and bad, and I want you to know this. I have never seen a better time than today. So listen to an old man, please. I want to tell you this. You must not take it for granted. Hold on to this peace with every breath. Smile with every tooth and laugh until you are falling on the floor!'

Patricia was amazed at the casual wisdom of the old man.

'Thank you, wise owl,' said Grace. 'We are glad to have you with us. Will you stay for some food? There is chicken with tomatoes and your favourite beans and banana.'

'No,' said Kanyarwanda, 'I must go now! Your grandmother will think I have run off with a young woman!'

Grace smiled and hugged her grandfather. Her grandmother had died before Grace was born. Of course, Kanyarwanda did not leave for some time. When he departed, the chat and laughter continued until midnight, and Grace walked with Patricia to her car.

'It's hard to believe, Patricia,' said Grace, 'that Rwibutso is my husband now. When you first met him at church, he was just my boyfriend, and now look at us, married and in our new home together.'

'I am very happy for you,' said Patricia. 'He is a good man. And one day he will be the father of your children.'

Grace smiled at the image these words created in her mind.

'What about you, Patricia?' she asked. 'Do you have a boyfriend? You are still a very attractive woman. What happened with that guy from the construction company in Kigali?'

'Ferdinand is a nice man,' said Patricia. 'He made me feel like a desirable woman again.'

'Really?' said Grace, her eyes lighting up at the prospect of some gossip. 'Tell me more, please!'

'But, Grace, I do not love him,' said Patricia. 'I have known great love and great loss. I do not wish to be with a man that I do not love. And Ferdinand should be with a woman who worships him.'

'Patricia, he is a strong young man, the same age as me,' said Grace. 'Ferdinand would make a very good husband. He would look after you when you get old.'

'Stop!' said Patricia. 'I know what I want and what I do not want.'

Grace put her arm around Patricia's shoulder. She knew that once Patricia had spoken like this, there was no point in trying to argue.

'Well, I hope and pray you find love again,' she said. 'No one deserves peace more than you, my dear sister. I'm certain there is one man out there who will know your heart and love and respect you.'

Grace noticed a thought cross Patricia's mind, then a quiet laugh and a shake of her head.

'What is it?' asked Grace.

'Oh, nothing,' said Patricia, taken a little off guard.

It was clear to Grace that something important had just occurred to her friend. It looked like a golden penny had dropped.

'Come on, my sister,' said Grace, 'I see a spark in your eyes. What is it?'

Patricia shook her head, as if dismissing a thought. She paused for a few minutes and the two friends stood, looking up at the moon and the stars in the clear sky.

Then Patricia spoke. 'This must be a secret, sister.'

'Yes?' said Grace.

Patricia hesitated, took a breath and then continued.

'I've just realised that… I… I think there is someone I might have feelings for.'

CHAPTER FORTY-SEVEN

'How could she?' Albert shouted, ripping up the latest letter from his sister and flinging it into the fire.

'If I was there, I would allow him back into my home too. Yes, Mr Damascene would be most welcome. I would meet him at the front door. I would let him grovel and beg for forgiveness on his knees. Then, do you know what I would do? I would find a machete and cut his fucking throat!'

Rachel was used to Albert's rages by now. She knew the best way to deal with an outburst was to stay out of his way and then try to calm him down later. Ever since her sister Matusi had died of AIDS, Rachel alone had helped Albert to recruit younger girls to sell their bodies in the slum. Over the years, she had come to care for Albert, but more as a work colleague than a lover. She had given up hope of love a long time ago. Matusi had always been Albert's favourite and he was unable to speak her name since the day she died. Albert's anger and drug abuse had worsened over the years. He often boasted of the justice he meted out to Hutu killers in Congo, but he hid the terrible memories of women and children who were butchered in the jungle. The faces of the innocent haunted his nightmares, and the only way to wipe away these images was to drink and smoke some more until his conscience drifted away with his consciousness. As he watched younger men progress out of the slum and into legitimate businesses in Kampala, he became jealous and bitter. He felt left behind by progress, by so-called friends, and by life itself.

'Look at those thug boys with their smartphones, ridiculous white-man clothes, pretending they are businessmen now,' he said. 'I know all their secrets and I wonder what would happen if I spilled the beans!'

Julius, now a young man, no longer a street kid, entered the hut.

'Man, the smell of weed in here!' he said. 'Boss, you are smoking away our profits again!'

Albert hurled a jerry can at Julius, missing him but knocking over a pile of logs in the corner of the hut.

'Just you remember that I am still the boss here!' he shouted. 'If it wasn't for me, you would be dead in a ditch, you miserable little shit!'

'The police are clamping down. We can't move and some are refusing the bribes. It's bad for business, boss. It's the worst time I can remember. You need to be playing the game, not lying there on your bed, so high you don't care anymore!'

'Listen to me, kid,' said Albert, 'what would you know about bad times? You have no idea what the worst time would be like. If I took you—'

'Yes, I know,' Julius interrupted. 'If you took me to Rwanda in 1994, you would show me what bad times really looked like. I've heard it all before.'

'Don't you mock me, you little shit, or I will beat you like a snake! Do you know what those Hutu devils did? Do you know what I saw with my own eyes?' he snarled.

Julius did not back down.

'Maybe one of these days I will have taken enough of your crap and it will be you who is beaten like a snake,' he replied.

Albert lunged towards Julius.

'Are you threatening me? After all I have done for you? You ungrateful, slimy little toad. I have been like a father to you!'

'You have done nothing for me that wasn't about you!' said Julius.

He hurled a bag of money onto the table, spat on the ground and walked out of the hut.

'Get out and stay out! Fuck you!' screamed Albert.

'Fuck you!' shouted Julius, slamming the door behind him.

Rachel waited for twenty minutes until Albert caught his breath and appeared to calm down.

'What has upset you this time, Albert?' she asked.

'It's my idiot sister back home in Rwanda,' he said.

'What has happened to her? Is she okay?' asked Rachel.

'What has happened to her? You will not believe what has happened to her! She has only gone and forgiven the man who betrayed her and got her whole family killed! And to make matters worse, she has welcomed him back into her home. She has given him food and… become his fucking friend!'

'Oh my God!' said Rachel. 'How could she do that?'

'Because she is weak,' said Albert. 'She has gone to university and been brainwashed with stupid books! She listens to all the church and Rwanda government nonsense about forgiveness and unity. She has swallowed that drug and now she is blind to evil.'

'I don't understand it,' said Rachel, 'but I have watched programmes on TV about people in Rwanda who have forgiven. I watched the Walk to Remember in April. It seems to be happening more and more. It's not so unusual, Albert. Remember those stories of survivors' and perpetrators' family members who fall in love and get married?'

'Traitors!' yelled Albert. 'Everyone who forgives curses the memory of a Tutsi victim. They shame our ancestors!'

'Maybe if you returned home, it would be different,' said Rachel. 'You have talked many times about missing your home in Gisenyi. You have told me all those stories of growing up near a lake even more beautiful than Lake Victoria.'

Albert's countenance changed from anger to sadness, the way it often did.

'I will never return now,' he said, lighting a roll of marijuana. 'How could I live among such shame and betrayal, all around me every day? Even my only surviving family – my own sister!'

'It couldn't be any worse than life in this slum,' said Rachel. 'You always told me this lifestyle was just for a while, until we could afford to get out of here. But look at us, Albert. We are never getting out of here!'

Rachel began to cry.

'Then get out! Get out, woman!' shouted Albert. 'I don't want to listen to you, sitting there whimpering like a miserable bitch! Go and find some fat old man to fuck you and make us some money!'

Rachel swiftly departed before Albert got violent. She had scars to prove that this was a good time to escape. She would return in the morning to find him in a sleepy haze, with little memory of his rage. She knew this pattern so well by now. She had learnt how to survive it.

Albert sat at the fireside alone, looking at the ashes of Patricia's letter.

'My own sister,' he said. 'My own sister.'

CHAPTER FORTY-EIGHT

After several extensions, Patricia's work assignment at Fame Construction was finally coming to an end. She enjoyed being a part of the project team and Jacqueline, back in the office in Gisenyi, was very happy with her performance. In twelve months, Patricia had learnt as much about how to interact in society again as she had absorbed the legal complexities of a government-funded construction project. More importantly, fate had placed her in regular contact with Damascene, ironically in Kigali rather than in their hometown. This provided an opportunity and a safe distance for Patricia and Damascene to get to know each other again. Following their initial meetings at home, they sometimes had lunch together in the canteen at Fame Construction. This friendship caused no raised eyebrows around them, as no one in the office knew the full story of their tragic history. Ferdinand knew that Patricia had forgiven Damascene but he was unaware of the details, and he didn't ask any questions because he preferred to keep his own past locked away.

'Are you going for lunch?' asked Kalisa.

'Yes, I'm meeting Patricia,' said Damascene.

'Again!' said Kalisa. 'How many times do you need to ask her for forgiveness?'

'Come on, brother. That's not what we talk about nowadays,' said Damascene. 'Patricia forgave me a long time ago.'

Kalisa was happy when Patricia forgave Damascene because he thought it would clean up their lives and they could move on, but he was finding it increasingly difficult to hide his disapproval at the frequency of their interaction.

'So what do you talk about? Her dead family?' said Kalisa.

'Not funny, brother!' said Damascene. 'Don't be so cruel. We talk about ordinary things like football and music, like you. Except we talk about good music, not that crap you listen to. We talk about politics and our hopes for our country. And we reminisce about when we were kids and you were an annoying little boy dancing with her chickens!'

'Be careful, brother,' said Kalisa, 'you are walking a dangerous path. You know what it is like back home. If you continue this in Gisenyi, people will talk and you will have more trouble. And I don't know about you but I'm tired of trouble.'

'You know, little brother, I learnt a long time ago not to care about what other people think of me,' said Damascene. 'I have always enjoyed Patricia's company. We used to sit together for lunch when we were at school, you know. Today is her last day at Fame Construction and she asked me to join her for lunch. I won't see her much after this, so calm down. It's not a big deal.'

'Not for you,' said Kalisa. 'If some of the people in Gisenyi knew about this...'

'Stop worrying, brother,' said Damascene. 'Go and listen to your favourite song, *Don't Worry, Be Happy*!'

Patricia was waiting at the end of the table in the far corner of the canteen, the same place they had met for lunch many times over the past year.

'How do you feel about working back in Gisenyi five days a week?' asked Damascene.

'I will not miss the driving,' said Patricia, 'the traffic in Kigali at rush hour is crazy! But I will miss the people.'

Damascene looked across the canteen towards Ferdinand, who was heading in their direction.

'I think you will miss some people more than others!' he said, with a wink.

'Oh, Damascene. Stop teasing. That was just a little moment of fun. Ferdinand and I are just good friends now. He's too young for me.'

'Promise me you will keep in touch, beautiful lady,' interrupted Ferdinand.

'Of course,' said Patricia. 'You promised to visit me in Gisenyi and if you keep your promise, I will take you fishing on Lake Kivu.'

'It's a deal!' said Ferdinand, hugging Patricia, much to her embarrassment. 'I'll see you soon.'

Then, just as he was leaving, Ferdinand punched Damascene's arm and whispered in his ear, 'Looks like you're more her type, Papa!'

Damascene was taken aback by this suggestion and hoped Patricia had not overheard the comment over the clatter of cutlery in the canteen.

'I know he will never visit Gisenyi,' said Patricia, as Ferdinand marched off. 'He's a city boy. He thinks the world begins and ends in the city. Unless I visit his favourite cabaret in Kigali, I will never see him again. He will visit New York before he ever visits Lake Kivu!'

'I'm sure he will miss you. But, madam, you don't know how much I will miss you too,' said Damascene. 'When you are gone, I will have to eat lunch with Kalisa every day, so you must pray for me!'

The couple laughed and chatted for half an hour until it was time to return to work.

'Will you come to my home for dinner on Saturday?' said Patricia. 'It will be my way of saying thank you for being my lunchtime buddy in the big city.'

'Come on!' interrupted Kalisa, running past the table, 'we are leaving for the site in five minutes! See you around, Patricia!'

'Of course, I'll come over for dinner, thank you,' said Damascene, ignoring his brother, 'but you do not need to thank me for anything. I owe you so much. I could never do enough for you. If you ever need any work done around the house, I will help you.'

With every act of kindness from Patricia, Damascene felt a lightening of his burdens, but the more she lived out her forgiveness, the deeper were his feelings of shame for what he had done to her. He felt a confusing mix of relief and remorse.

'Okay,' said Patricia, 'I will see you at the weekend.'

Patricia enjoyed the rediscovery of their pre-1994 friendship. She felt it was important for her healing and she believed it was a powerful sign of the possibility of reconciliation. As Damascene followed Kalisa to the construction site, she remained sitting alone, smiling and using her fork to play with her food. The invitation to dinner was not an impulsive act. Patricia had been planning this occasion for weeks.

When Damascene arrived on Saturday evening, the first thing he noticed was some damage to the roof of Patricia's house caused by a recent rainstorm.

'I'll fix this while you are fixing the food,' he said.

He retrieved the ladder from the outhouse he had secretly constructed, checking and confirming that his work on the wooden building remained secure after the storm. As he worked on the roof, he recalled the day he built the outhouse. He still felt some pain in his wrist, and the large scar on his thigh was a reminder of his secret penance. Forty-five minutes later, the roof was mended and the food was served, a whole *tilapia* grilled and served with onions, celery, garlic and carrots.

'*Bon Appétit!*' said Patricia.

'Delicious!' said Damascene after his first mouthful of fish.

'Thank you, mister,' said Patricia. 'I remember how we used to cook this on a campfire on the lakeside when we were young.'

'This is much more sophisticated cuisine!' laughed Damascene. 'Thank you, Patricia.'

'How is your little brother? Is there any sign of a girlfriend?' asked Patricia.

'Ha ha! He says he's too young to settle down,' said Damascene. 'I can't imagine it!'

'And what about you?' asked Patricia. 'You never married. Are you happy on your own?'

Damascene tensed then took a sip of beer, before replying.

'There was someone a very long time ago,' he said, staring at the beer bottle, 'but she fell in love with someone else and since 1994, I have not deserved the love of any woman.'

'Really?' said Patricia. 'You have been with no one for seventeen years?'

'Well, apart from some drunken nights after too much *urwagwa* at the cabaret in the city,' he said, 'and that was nothing to be proud of.'

'I learnt a long time ago not to judge people,' said Patricia. 'Love is love, and everyone deserves love and happiness whenever they can find it. Life is too short.'

'You are a good woman, Patricia,' said Damascene. 'After all you have been through, you still have compassion,' then pausing and deciding to lighten the mood, 'even for my crazy little brother.'

'You know, Damascene,' she said, 'I asked you here this evening for a reason…'

'Yes,' said Damascene, 'how can I help you? I will do anything. I promise. Are there any other jobs around the house?'

'After the genocide, I was alone and I was no one,' Patricia began. 'I was nothing, barely alive, I was almost dead. I couldn't be happy in my life.'

'I am sorry, Patricia,' said Damascene, 'I will never be able—'

'Quiet!' said Patricia. 'You have apologised to me enough times. No more speeches. No more "sorry". It has to stop!'

'I'm sorry,' said Damascene.

Patricia shook her head and laughed a little.

'This is what I want to tell you,' she continued, 'I never felt human again until the day I forgave you. I do not fully understand it, Damascene, but I know in my heart it is true.'

'I am glad,' said Damascene.

'And then, to my surprise, in these last few months, as I got to know you again, you brought some happiness to me.'

'Thank you, sister,' said Damascene. 'This is all I want for you, to be safe and well and to be happy.'

'I cannot believe it,' she said, 'but you have taken away my nightmares. There was a time when you were a part of my nightmares, but now my dreams are peaceful.'

'Thank God,' said Damascene. 'I must die with my nightmares but I pray that your nightmares are gone forever.'

Damascene stopped eating. He was not expecting the conversation to become so intense.

'Damascene,' said Patricia, 'there is something else I want to tell you.'

'Yes?' said Damascene.

'In these past few months, as we have spent more time together, I have realised that I have feelings for you,' said Patricia.

'What?' said Damascene.

He was taken aback and confused.

'What do you mean?'

'I think…' said Patricia, taking both of Damascene's hands in her hands, across the table, 'I think I am falling in love with you.'

The words hit Damascene like his hammer on a nail piercing wood.

'No!' said Damascene.

He fell back into his chair, shaking his head in disbelief.

'No, no, no!' he cried.

He looked across at Patricia like a wounded animal, as if she had just struck him.

'It's true,' said Patricia.

'Don't play games with me, sister,' he said.

'It's not a game, Damascene, believe me. Do I ever play games?'

'This is madness, madam,' said Damascene. 'I know I deserve your cruelty but this is too much. You invite me to this house, after what happened here, knowing it was all my fault, and you mock me with your words. I know I deserve your disdain but it is too cruel to punish me in this place!'

Patricia was surprised at the strength of Damascene's reaction.

'I'm not mocking you,' said Patricia. 'You know I have forgiven you.'

Patricia had gone over the expected progression of this conversation in her mind for weeks. Once she was certain about her feelings, she was compelled to share them with Damascene. However, this was not how she expected it to go.

'How could YOU love ME,' he said, 'after what I did?'

'If it was not for the genocide, I know you would have killed no one, Damascene,' said Patricia. 'I have known your heart since we were children.'

'I killed many,' said Damascene.

'I love you, Damascene, and I think about you all the time,' said Patricia.

Damascene got up from the table and paced across the floor with his hands across his eyes.

'No, no, no… I don't deserve this… You are unwell in your mind. Don't do this to me! No, no…'

'Yes,' said Patricia, standing up.

'I betrayed you and Bernie. I was weak. I stood by and did nothing. I could have refused. I could have had the courage of a good, decent man. I could have said "No!" It would have been better to die with courage than to live with this shame.'

'But, Damascene, you faced justice and you paid the price in prison,' said Patricia. 'You confessed and I forgave you. It was not easy for me. For many years, I hated you more than anyone else in the world. I wanted revenge. I wished you dead. But since those days when I read and re-read your confession, I recognised the heart of my old friend again. I chose to forgive you, to forgive you completely.'

'If only it was so simple. I will never forgive myself,' cried Damascene.

He fell to his knees.

'I betrayed you, in this very place. I watched as my friend was murdered. I stood by as they killed your… oh my God… your beautiful children!'

Damascene fell to the floor, sobbing. Patricia was crying too now, but her tears were of pity for the man suffering before her eyes.

'If I had refused to help them, they would have killed me too. I was a coward. I should have sacrificed myself to save my friends. It would have been better to die saving my friends in 1994 than to live this life of shame. To survive hell, just to live in this hell, before I finally die and burn in Hell!'

Patricia knelt down to comfort Damascene, but he recoiled at her touch.

'This is too much, Patricia,' he said, stumbling to his feet. 'You cannot love me. I am a devil. I deserve your hatred, not your love. Do not torture me with love!'

'Damascene, this cruel world almost destroyed us both, but we can live and love again,' said Patricia.

Damascene ran from the house, leaving Patricia standing alone in the middle of the living room. She looked up at the framed picture of Bernard and nodded. Patricia felt that Bernard nodded back.

Chapter Forty-Nine

Damascene sat on a rock near the top of Mount Kigali, protected from the searing midday sun by the shade of a eucalyptus tree. He looked out across the city, towards the hills on the other side, and squinted his eyes to behold a hazy ribbon of mountains in the distance. It was quiet here, apart from the crickets and the faint sound of children laughing in the school playground in a nearby village. Damascene was amazed at how peaceful it was up here, only one hour from the city centre, where he was supposed to be at work. The smell of eucalyptus was intoxicating and the view over the city was stunning, but in spite of the peace and beauty, he was unable to escape his tortured thoughts. Since the shocking encounter with Patricia, he had not slept. In his mind, he repeated the conversation over and over again. Every time he replayed Patricia's words, he tried to block them from entering his heart. This morning, he travelled to work as usual but, without thinking, he left Kalisa at the front gate of Fame Construction and turned to the hills. He could not face people today. The old familiar turmoil in his mind was back in full force – the guilt, the shame and the pain that seemed to tear him apart from within. Dressed in his typical work clothes of jeans and a t-shirt, Damascene remained sitting on the rock all day long. He picked up a jagged stone and juggled it from hand to hand. So much of his working life was focused on fashioning buildings from the roughness of stone. He spent his days creating shelter from coarse materials. As he felt the harsh, cold texture of stone beneath him and in his hands, he longed for warmth and love. He pondered the words of Patricia and cried until the sun went down.

It was after midnight when he finally arrived back home in Gisenyi. As soon as he opened the door of the house, Kalisa came running from his bedroom.

'What happened to you, brother? Where did you go? I've been worried about you all day.'

'I'm okay,' said Damascene. 'Don't worry about me.'

'Don't worry about you? You disappeared! I thought you were dead in a ditch! Don't tell me not to worry about you!'

'I climbed Mount Kigali,' said Damascene.

'What?'

'I've been there all day.'

'On a Monday morning when you were supposed to be at work, you went for a hike up a hill!' said Kalisa.

He pushed Damascene on one shoulder.

'I'm sorry,' said Damascene, 'I needed some time to myself.'

'Well, we all need a little time to ourselves sometimes, but we don't have to climb up a fucking mountain!' said Kalisa.

'I needed space,' said Damascene.

'Why didn't you come back to work?' said Kalisa. 'Why didn't you let anyone know where you were?'

'I did not want to,' said Damascene.

'Oh God! You did not want to! Now you sound like Uwera Patricia! "I do not wish to!"'

Damascene was surprised at this remark and wondered if his brother knew what was on his mind.

'I'm sorry, little bro,' he said, sitting down with his head in his hands. 'My head is full of so much junk. I thought it was going to burst.'

Kalisa sat down beside his brother.

'Look, Dammy,' he said, 'this is your first job since being in prison. It's Fame Construction, for God's sake. Don't throw it away! I lied for you because you need this job. I told them you were sick.'

'I am sick,' said Damascene. 'My mind is sick.'

'What's the matter, Dammy?'

'You are my brother, okay?'

'Always,' said Kalisa.

'I can tell you anything. Right?' said Damascene.

'Of course, what have you done?'

Damascene shook his head and laughed.

'I haven't done anything.'

'Well, what is it then?' asked Kalisa.

Damascene paused, took a breath and shared his burden.

'Patricia told me she loves me.'

Kalisa's eyes opened wide and his whole face stretched with incredulity.

'She loves you?'

274

'Yes, she told me on Saturday night. She told me she loves me.'

'What are you saying?' said Kalisa, clearly having difficulty processing this information.

'Every day, I thank God that Madame Patricia forgave me,' said Damascene. 'She rescued me from the darkness. After all the great wrong I did to her. She helped me to start to live again, but this is too much. I just want to tell her—'

'That woman is crazy!' interrupted Kalisa. 'She's always been as stubborn as an ox, but now she has gone completely mad!'

'I believe her,' said Damascene. 'Why would she lie to me?'

'She knows how to torture you,' said Kalisa. 'I knew it! All this forgiveness shit is a big act! She is playing with you, like a cat torturing a pathetic little mouse before she kills it!'

Damascene stood up, angry now.

'Are you calling me pathetic?' he shouted.

'You got her husband killed! You stood with the killers and cheered with a club in your hand! How can you believe her?'

'You're the pathetic one!' shouted Damascene. 'You have no idea what I have suffered. You were lucky to be too young in 1994. All you ever have to worry about is the latest dance move, you selfish little shit!'

Kalisa stood up and stomped his feet in anger.

'I was old enough to notice you fancied her before she fell for Bernard. Were you planning this when you betrayed your best friend? Eh?' he snarled. 'Get rid of him and then she'll fall in love with you? Eh?'

275

Damascene's nostrils flared with anger. The brothers knew exactly what would hurt the other most.

'Well, why don't you grow up and get a woman? Or is that not your thing?' snapped Damascene.

The two brothers squared up to each other, eye to eye, nose to nose, staring and shaking with anger. A fight was seconds away. Kalisa had never had a physical fight with Damascene. He knew it would be like hitting a father, and so he took a breath and stepped back.

'Dammy, don't believe her, please,' he said, now standing back and speaking more softly. 'I'm sorry, I didn't mean all that stuff about Bernard, may he rest in eternal peace. But, please, brother, look at what this woman is doing to you. Just stay away from her and get on with your life.'

'I can't stay away from Patricia,' said Damascene.

'Why not?' said Kalisa. 'You don't have to see her at work anymore. You are becoming obsessed with this woman! Just leave her alone with her avocados and her fucking chickens.'

'I can't,' said Damascene, 'I owe her a great debt.'

'I know, brother,' sighed Kalisa. 'You confessed your crimes and you asked for forgiveness. You even rebuilt her outhouse. You have a broken wrist and scar on your leg to prove it! Let her go, brother. You don't need to torture yourself forever.'

'I know,' said Damascene, 'I hear your words, but there's something else.'

'What else?' said Kalisa.

Damascene sat down and turned away from his brother's face.

'I think… I'm in love with her too.'

CHAPTER FIFTY

'Hello, Patricia, it's Jacqueline. I'm just calling to ask how you are feeling.'

'I am unwell, Madame Jacqueline, but I want to return to work tomorrow,' said Patricia.

'Only return if you are feeling better,' said Jacqueline. 'We can cope for a few more days without you. We just want you to be well. Have you been to see a doctor?'

'I wish to return tomorrow,' said Patricia, ignoring the question. 'I'm sorry for my absence, madam. I promise you I will catch up with my work.'

'Okay. Take care and get well soon, Patricia,' said Jacqueline, hanging up the phone.

Patricia was suffering only from a lack of sleep, but her insomnia was not due to the nightmares of old. Since Damascene's sudden departure on Saturday evening, she had struggled to comprehend all that was going on in his head. She felt she had misread him. She thought she knew him well by now, but obviously she was missing something. Perhaps it was the depth of his brokenness, she thought. By Monday morning, feeling exhausted and distraught, she could not face work, hence the call with Jacqueline.

Instead of going to the office, she walked to the shore of Lake Kivu. While Damascene was sitting on a rock on Mount Kigali contemplating their relationship, Patricia found herself once again barefoot on the lakeside. As she looked across the lake towards the volcanos in the distance, suddenly her thoughts were interrupted.

'How are you, beautiful woman?' a voice said. 'It's you, isn't it?'

Patricia looked up and saw a handsome young fisherman preparing his rods and nets for the night's toil ahead. He had stopped working and was staring at her in amazement.

'Do I know you?' asked Patricia.

'I recognise you,' he said. 'Your head was shaved the last time I saw you, but I will never forget your face. You are Uwera Patricia.'

'Did I meet you at one of the Unity and Reconciliation meetings?' asked Patricia.

'No, madam. My name is Hassan Karasira. I found you in the water here many years ago. I was just a teenager. You were like a ghost in the water. I thought you were dead. My brothers rescued you and we took you to the hospital.'

'You are one of the fishermen who saved me?' said Patricia, in astonishment.

'Yes, I was the one who saw you in the lake and I found your message in the bottle,' said Hassan. 'That's how I know your name. You signed your note at the bottom.

I have never forgotten your name, Patricia Uwera, the beautiful woman in white from the lake.'

The young man looked down, embarrassed, remembering the intense emotions of the contents of the message in a bottle. Patricia was familiar with the story Doctor Louise told of how three brothers, fishermen on the lake, saved her life by plucking her from the stormy waters, but until this moment she did not know the identity of the men. Sometimes, she even wondered if these enigmatic saviours had been real. In her dreams, they were mysterious angels who arrived from the mists of the lake and disappeared into the night. Doctor Louise told her the story of how the youngest brother found the bottle containing her suicide note.

'Thank you, Hassan,' said Patricia, walking towards him. 'You were a gift to me then and you are a gift today.'

Patricia hugged Hassan and they sat down together on the side of his boat.

'How are you, madam?' asked Hassan.

'You saved my life and it is better now,' said Patricia. 'I do not wish to die. Today, I want to live. Now I want to be happy.'

'I used to dream about you,' said Hassan, 'the beautiful lady in white in the lake. I kept the bottle to remind me of you. When I was a boy, during the genocide, I saw many dead bodies floating in this lake. For years, I had terrible nightmares. But the bad dreams stopped the night we saved you. Instead, I had new dreams of a lady in white, standing on the shore, her hair fully grown, like yours, waving at me in the boat and smiling. I am going to be a father soon for the first time and I will tell my children the story of the lady in the lake. I will tell them that even in the darkest of times there is always hope.'

'Hassan Karasira, you are a very wise young fisherman,' said Patricia, 'wiser than all of my professors at university.'

'You went to university? Wow!' said Hassan. 'I will tell my brothers tonight. They will be so happy. At first, they won't believe me, of course. They heard you had gone to Kigali and died of a broken heart.'

'Please thank your brothers from me,' said Patricia. 'I almost died of a broken heart, but Doctor Louise saved me.'

'Oh yes,' said Hassan, 'I remember that doctor. The kind woman at the hospital. She was determined to save you.'

'She is my best friend to this day,' said Patricia.

'Tell me this,' said Hassan, deciding to go further than seemed appropriate for this first encounter, 'you know I read your note. I remember what you said about Hutus. Did you ever get justice for the devils who killed your family? I have read many books about the genocide. My brothers think I am crazy to be reading so much when I am not fishing.'

'Maybe you could go to university like me,' said Patricia.

Hassan shook his head, smiled, and continued.

'Did you go to a *gacaca* court? Did you go to Unity and Reconciliation meetings?'

Patricia smiled. Writing the suicide note seemed so long ago, when she was a different person, or barely a person at all.

'I did get justice,' she said. 'The killers are dead and gone and the traitor of my husband went to prison.'

'Madam, I don't see any bitterness in you,' said Hassan. 'May I ask you, are you one of those survivors who has forgiven?'

'Yes, I am,' she replied. 'I forgave the one who wronged me most, my husband's best friend who betrayed him, and you will not believe this but now...'

She hesitated. She had only just met this young man but there was a sage softness in his spirit that she trusted.

'And now what?' asked Hassan.

'And now I have fallen in love with him.'

Hassan's eyes widened.

'Wow, beautiful woman!' he said. 'In real life, you are even more special than in my dreams.'

'Really?' said Patricia, surprised by the encouraging response.

'You give me hope for Rwanda. Hope for my children. You are the true heart of Rwanda, not the *genocidaires* of the twentieth century. Not those who hold their hatred and never forgive. You are the future.'

'But there is one problem, brother,' said Patricia. 'This man cannot accept my love.'

Patricia looked around on the sand and picked up a twig of driftwood. She broke the stick into two pieces.

'I was broken like this,' she said, 'but I have been able to put the pieces back together.'

She lifted a piece of string from the boat and tied the twig back together again.

'I will never be the same. There will always be this break,' she said, pointing to the fracture in the wood, 'but I can be whole again.'

Hassan smiled.

'And what about him?' he asked.

Patricia untied the string holding the twig together and it fell apart.

'As for him,' she said, 'I fear he will be broken forever.'

Hassan picked up another twig, snapped it in two and tied it together with the two pieces of the other twig.

'Two broken twigs healing together will be stronger,' he said.

'So young and yet so wise,' said Patricia, ruffling his hair affectionately, 'but I fear it is too late for him and that means it is too late for us together.'

As she got up to go, Hassan took Patricia by the hand and said, 'Come back and see me again, please, madam. I want you to meet my brothers.'

'I will,' said Patricia. 'I want to thank your brothers in person and I will bring you a gift of the best avocados in Rwanda!'

Hassan laughed.

'I cannot believe this has happened,' he said.

'It was meant to be, and on this day,' said Patricia, turning to go. 'Goodbye, wise fisherman!'

'Goodbye, beautiful woman,' said Hassan, 'and one more thing, Madame Patricia.'

'Yes?' she said.

'Sometimes, the nets on the lake are fullest after the biggest storm.'

Returning home, Patricia marvelled at the encounter with the young fisherman. When she went to bed, she pondered the wise words of Hassan late into the night until she fell asleep.

She was awakened by a knock on the door. It was very early, so early the cock had not yet crowed. In fact, it was too early to safely open the door.

'Who's there?' she called.

'It's me,' said Damascene.

Patricia opened the door. The two souls stood apart, hearts racing, looking into each other's eyes. Finally, Damascene broke the silence.

'I love you too.'

CHAPTER FIFTY-ONE

'It's too hot!' cried Ngabo, blowing on the steaming food on his plate.

'Look at him, Mama!' said Kevin. 'The little kid still needs help with his food!'

'Leave your little brother alone,' said Doctor Louise. 'Everyone needs a little help from their mama now and then. Even big boys like you!'

Louise joined Ngabo in blowing cooler air over his hot food.

'Let him do it himself,' said Jean Pierre. 'We will come to the rescue if it goes on fire!'

Jean Pierre and Kevin started to blow over their food, mimicking Ngabo in an exaggerated way.

'Now there is a big storm at our dinner table!' said Ngabo.

The family stopped puffing and started laughing.

'Okay, eat, my son,' said Louise. 'Do not listen to them. Okay?'

'Yes, Mama,' said Ngabo.

He stuck out his tongue at Kevin, who responded with his own tongue full of half-eaten food.

'Now,' said Louise, holding up her glass, 'I want us to drink to my special friend, Patricia's birthday.'

Jean Pierre and Ngabo raised their glasses but Kevin was confused.

'But, Mama,' he said, 'why are we celebrating? Why is she special?'

Louise set down her glass and leaned forward. Kevin and Ngabo knew this meant their mother was going to share a story.

'Patricia is my friend,' said Louise. 'Do you remember her coming to stay here once when you were little?'

'He's still little!' said Kevin, pointing at his brother.

'Mama!' said Ngabo.

'Enough,' said Jean Pierre.

'I meet Patricia in the park every month because she is a very special woman.'

'But why?' asked Kevin.

'Sometimes, God makes miracles in this world,' said Louise, 'and the day I met Patricia, it was a miracle. Some fishermen found her in the lake. They rescued her from the water and brought her to the hospital. Some very bad things happened to her in the genocide.'

'In 1994?' asked Ngabo.

'Yes, remember what you learnt in school? Patricia was heartbroken because of what a big enemy had done to her.'

'What did her enemy do to her?' asked Ngabo.

'They took away her husband and children,' said Jean Pierre, trying to avoid the brutal details.

'You mean they killed them with machetes!' said Kevin.

Jean Pierre and Louise looked at each other in surprise. Their children were growing up fast and it was only a matter of time before they knew the full horror of the genocide.

'Patricia had lost the desire to live,' said Louise. 'So, I took care of her. I helped her to get better and after a while Patricia's heart began to heal.'

'Was she very sad?' asked Ngabo.

'Yes.'

'And very angry?' asked Kevin.

'Yes. But, you know when you cut your knee when you fall over?'

'Yes, Mama, Kevin pushes me over all the time!' said Ngabo.

'Well, you know how it takes a while for the pain to stop and you are left with a scar on your knee?'

'Yes.'

'Good. My boys, Patricia's heart was like that. She needed time to heal. And then she did something amazing.'

'What's that?' said Kevin. 'Did she find the enemy and kill them like Papa did in 1994?'

This comment brought silence to the table. Jean Pierre never talked about his actions during the conflict, not even to Louise. However, his sons were old enough now to understand that their father had fought in the army, and they often speculated about the enemies he might have killed heroically. Jean Pierre froze.

'No, no, no!' said Louise, moving the conversation away from the obvious. 'Patricia did something very difficult and courageous. She forgave her enemy. Like what you learnt at Sunday school. Remember? "Love your enemies. Do good to those who hate you." She forgave the man who betrayed her family.'

'And is she still sad and angry?' asked Ngabo.

'She will always be sad for her family,' said Louise, 'but she has let go of her anger.'

'Does she still want to live?' asked Ngabo.

'Oh yes!' said Louise. 'She has peace now. She went to university and got a good job and works hard, just like we want you boys to do. So that is the story of my special friend, Patricia.'

'But how can you forgive someone who has killed your family?' asked Kevin. 'It's impossible!'

'It might seem impossible,' said Jean Pierre, 'but I see it every day in my work. Many survivors eventually forgive the perpetrators I arrest and bring to justice.'

'Would you forgive a bad man who killed us?' asked Ngabo.

'I don't know,' said Jean Pierre.

'It's a good question, my son,' said Louise. 'I don't know either. But what I do know is that when Patricia forgave the man who betrayed her, when she let go of the hatred and bitterness, she began to come alive again.'

'I feel sorry for Patricia,' said Ngabo. 'Can you ask her to visit us again and we can make her a cake?'

Louise smiled.

'You don't need to worry about Patricia. She is a strong woman and after years of pain, she is okay. I'm going to call her now to wish her happy birthday and I want all of you to sing when she answers the phone. Okay?'

287

'Yes!' cried the boys in unison, jumping up and gathering around their mother.

'Hello!' said Louise. 'Yes. We have something to share with you, Patricia!'

The family sang *Happy Birthday* to Patricia.

Then Jean Pierre and the boys began to clear the table while Louise continued chatting to Patricia.

'You are welcome, my dear sister… Yes, I've put the men to work with the dishes now! That sounds interesting… a big secret, really? Okay, you know you can trust me… Okay, go ahead, I'm listening… No, I won't judge you, I promise. You know me, sister… What's the big secret?'

As the call continued, Louise furrowed her brow in confusion and then took a sharp intake of breath.

'Oh wow! Patricia! In love? I can't believe it! I'm so happy for you. No one deserves love as much as you… Yes, I know… I'm thrilled. And who is the lucky man?'

Suddenly Louise's eyes widened, her mouth fell open and she almost dropped the phone.

'Oh my goodness, Patricia… are you sure? Yes. It's okay. It's just a bit of a surprise… And does he feel the same way? Really? God bless him, I'm not surprised he found it hard to hear. He is a decent man… I know, yes, I know. From everything you have told me, he has changed completely… Listen, Patricia, you do not have to justify your love to me. If you feel this way and both of you are in the same spirit, I am happy for you. I have always stood with you, Patricia, and I will stand with you on this too… May God bless you both. It's a big surprise, sister, but you are a strong woman and I believe that God is with you… Yes, okay, we will talk next week in the park. I want to hear all the details! Happy birthday! Bye-bye!'

Louise ended the call and sat down on the sofa, still in a state of disbelief.

'What's up?' asked Jean Pierre. 'How is Patricia?'

'You are not going to believe this, Jean Pierre,' said Louise, 'but Patricia is in love.'

'Oh, that's good news. I'm happy for her,' said Jean Pierre, 'but why are you so shocked? It's not the first time. She was seeing that young guy at Fame Construction, was she not?'

'No, it's not Ferdinand,' said Louise. 'You will never guess who she is in love with.'

'Who?' asked Jean Pierre.

'Damascene.'

Jean Pierre could not hide his disbelief.

'You mean, that Damascene?'

'Yes, that Damascene.'

'Oh my God!' said Jean Pierre. 'First, she hated him, then she tried to kill him with my gun, then she forgave him and now she loves him?'

'They have known each other since they were kids,' said Louise, 'but, still, he's the last person I thought she would fall in love with.'

Jean Pierre sat down beside Louise and the boys returned from the kitchen, curious about the conversation with the special woman.

'I remember when I arrested him,' said Jean Pierre, 'and every night before I left the police station I took a look at him. He was angry then and in denial of his crimes. But later when I saw him at the *gacaca* court and then at the Unity and Reconciliation meeting, he had changed. He had the courage and strength to confess his crimes. But he is such a sad man. He carries so much pain. I don't know how he could cope with a relationship. I hope it works out for them. He must never break her heart again.'

'Are you talking about Patricia and her enemy?' asked Kevin.

'Yes, son,' said Jean Pierre.

'Is it possible that they are really in love?' asked Kevin.

'Yes, it is possible,' said Louise.

'Survivors and perpetrators can be reconciled. I've seen their children fall in love. It's very unusual, but it is possible,' said Jean Pierre.

'Wow! That's amazing,' said Kevin. 'Rwandans are awesome people!'

'Are they going to get married?' asked Ngabo.

Jean Pierre shook his head.

'No, my son. That's never happened before. Some things are possible but for Patricia and Damascene to get married, that is impossible.'

Chapter Fifty-Two

"Imana imana
Mana y'irwanda nsingize imana se bagenzi
Imana niyo nkuru
Imana itera amapfa burya."

The women raised their voices in harmony to sing a song of hope and peace. *"My children, never worry, all mothers are together with you..."*

"Ni nayo itanga aho bahahira
Nyabusa bana banjye nimuhumure
Impumbya zababyeyi turi kumwe
Mbafatiye iry'uburyo
Kandi umusibo nejo
Ejo bundi nzakabya inzozi yehe."

Patricia and Grace were holding hands in a circle and singing *Inzozi* along with other members of their local Survivors' Club.

'"*Izo narose
Izo narose se bajyenzi.*"'

'Tomorrow, our dreams will come true,' said Grace, quoting the song and squeezing Patricia's hand as the group sat down. Madame Charlotte stood in the middle of the circle to begin the meeting.

'Thank you very much for the zeal you show here every time we meet,' she said. 'This week, I would like to invite one of our regular members, Uwera Patricia, to come into the middle of the circle to share her story with the whole group for the first time. Our sister wants to tell you about her experience of forgiving the perpetrator who betrayed her family.'

Patricia stood up slowly and stepped forward into the middle of the circle of survivors. Grace felt nervous and proud at the same time. Patricia had come such a long way since she first came along to one of these meetings. Grace remembered the first time it was her turn to stand in the centre of the group to share how she had forgiven the man who killed her mother.

'Thank you for offering me this time to share my story,' began Patricia. 'It is not long since I started to come here to these meetings. I want to thank Madame Charlotte for encouraging me to join this club. I promise you, I was not easy to persuade. I can be a very strong-willed person!'

Grace gave an exaggerated nod and a ripple of laughter danced around the circle.

'But since the first day I came here and listened to Madame Charlotte, and then heard all of your stories, I have changed my life,' Patricia continued. 'I couldn't be

292

who I am today if I had never come to this group. I want to thank my dear friend Grace, who brought me here for the first time.'

The other survivors turned to Grace and gave her a gentle round of applause. Grace raised her hand over her mouth to cover a shy smile.

'I want to thank all of you here in this club for sharing your stories, and especially you, Madame Charlotte,' said Patricia. 'You are a strong Rwandan woman, a good leader and a great inspiration to me.'

Charlotte nodded in appreciation of the kind acknowledgement and as the group applauded her, she diverted their attention back to Patricia.

'Thank you, sister, now please continue with your story of hope,' she said.

'After many years of hatred and bitterness,' said Patricia, 'all I wanted was revenge against the man who betrayed my husband. I hated Hutus so much. Even when the murderers of my family died, I had no peace. The men with the guns and machetes were gone, but I was still full of hatred towards the childhood friend who led the killers to our house in 1994. He fled to hide and escape justice and I hated him so much. But I hated my life even more. And, I'm sorry to tell you, my sisters, that I did not wish to live. However, as I listened to the testimonies of so many other survivors here and as I heard the confessions of perpetrators at other reconciliation events, in the end, my heart told me to forgive this man called Damascene. When he confessed his crimes and begged for my forgiveness, at first I refused to even listen to him. But then one day I made a choice. It was not an easy choice, but it was the right choice for me and the best choice for Rwanda. I know in my heart it is what my husband would have wanted, because it allowed me to find peace and to want to live again. I chose to forgive Damascene, the man who betrayed his best friend, my dear husband, Bernard.'

'God bless you, Madame Patricia,' said one of the other members of the club as the others nodded and added a mixture of 'Yes!' and 'Amen!'

'And now,' continued Patricia, 'I can love myself again. I love Hutus and Tutsis, but I don't even see those differences anymore. Ethnic differences mean nothing to me now. I am happy that these days we are all Rwandans.'

Grace and the others in the Survivors' Club smiled and nodded encouragingly at Patricia's testimony, as she continued.

'And today I want to tell all of you something new and amazing that has happened to me over the past few years. You might find this hard to believe, but I love Damascene. In fact, I am in love with him. We have fallen in love with each other.'

Grace gasped. Charlotte sat forward. The mood in the room shifted in an instant. Stories of forgiveness and reconciliation were often heard here, but a survivor falling in love with a perpetrator was new territory. As Patricia continued to tell the story of how her heart had transformed from hating Damascene to falling in love with him, many of the other survivors shifted in their chairs and stared at Patricia in disbelief. No one more so than Grace, who was most disturbed by this sudden revelation. When Patricia's speech came to an end, she sat down again in the circle. There was no applause. Some of the members murmured to the person sitting beside them; two of the women whistled and shook their heads and most of the others just stared. Patricia, seemingly unaware of the change in reaction, went to take Grace's hand, but Grace pulled it away. Charlotte stood up.

'Thank you, Patricia,' she said. 'Now, come along, sisters. I see that some of you are surprised at Patricia's relationship with Damascene. Every story is different. We all choose our own best path. Let's all clap for Patricia.'

The group put their hands together in a polite round of applause, but Grace did not join in.

'I have to say this to you, Patricia,' continued Charlotte. 'Thank you for sharing this with us. You did not have to open up to us in this way. Others like you have kept such relationships secret. But you have opened your heart to us and we are here for you,' and then addressing the whole group, 'Patricia is happy. And that is all that matters.'

'Thank you,' said Patricia.

She appreciated Charlotte's support but she was genuinely surprised at the less-than-enthusiastic response, especially from Grace.

'There are other, similar stories in this town,' continued Charlotte. 'Remember Doctor Peter's story? As you know, his wife died while the whole family were fleeing from the genocide. But Doctor Peter forgave the perpetrator many years ago and last year, to everyone's amazement, their children got married. This reconciled survivor and perpetrator now share a grandchild. My dear friends, it is possible for love to grow where hatred once dwelt. We have accepted these others as a symbol of hope for the future, so why not Patricia and her forgiven perpetrator?'

Then Charlotte touched the shoulder of the oldest woman in the circle.

'May I share, Madame Elizabeth?' she asked.

The woman nodded.

'As many of you here know, Elizabeth's husband and two of her sons were slaughtered by Jean de Dieu. Like many courageous survivors, she managed to forgive him. She created hope and out of that new hope grew love in the families of former enemies. Today, Elizabeth's only surviving son, Esau, the best mechanic in town, is married to the daughter of Jean de Dieu and they share three beautiful grandsons.'

The members of the group nodded and affirmed Elizabeth, who dabbed some tears from the corner of her eyes with a white handkerchief.

Charlotte's words warmed the hearts of the women in the circle, apart from Grace. As soon as the meeting ended, she got up to leave. Patricia followed her, catching her up in the street outside.

'Grace, what is wrong?' asked Patricia. 'You told me to share what was in my heart, and that is exactly what I did.'

'But I did not know that you had been cooking some craziness of being in love with Damascene in your heart,' said Grace, still walking on. 'The one who took your children and husband away from you is the one in your heart!'

'But I have forgiven him, and you were the first person who told me I must forgive!' said Patricia.

'Think twice and think thrice, Patricia. Think about what you are doing,' said Grace.

She pulled away from Patricia.

'Even if you forgave him, he is still the one that betrayed you. I don't trust him. He is just using you and he will discard you and you will be heartbroken once more! How can you be in love with such a man? And you didn't even tell me!'

'What is wrong with you, Grace?' said Patricia, grabbing hold of Grace's arm. 'You told me to forgive. You are the one who brought me to the church and told me that God wanted me to forgive Damascene. And you told me how you forgave your mother's killer.'

'That is different! You have gone too far, Patricia,' snapped Grace, once again pulling away and walking on.

'What has happened to you today? Are you the Grace of 1994?' asked Patricia.

This accusation hurt Grace and she stopped, turned around and spoke again.

'Don't play with your life, Patricia,' she said. 'Do you know where this relationship is going? Is he just playing games with you? It is wrong. It's a sin! A relationship is sacred and leads to marriage. And we know very well that you and Damascene can never be husband and wife!'

Patricia looked directly into Grace's eyes and, before walking off in the opposite direction, spoke in a low, slow and clear voice.

'Listen to me, sister, and listen well. I love Damascene and I will do what I want.'

Chapter Fifty-Three

Kalisa removed his safety helmet as he arrived at the Fame Construction office, whistling a happy tune, as usual. Ferdinand was examining the master plan for the latest building they were in the process of constructing in the city centre.

'Excuse me, boss?' said Kalisa.

'Yes, what's up?' replied Ferdinand.

'We need a C clamp, boss. We have to strengthen the—'

'Close the door and have a seat, please, my friend,' said Ferdinand.

The engineer was glad of the opportunity to speak privately with Kalisa. It had been an exhausting day on the building site and Kalisa, feeling tired, yawned and eyed the coffee pot in the corner of the office.

'Hmm... May I?' he asked.

'Yeah, serve yourself. I've been wanting to talk to you all day about something.'

As Kalisa poured coffee, he was unprepared for the intensity of the ensuing topic of conversation.

'So are the office gossip headlines true?' asked Ferdinand.

'What?' said Kalisa. 'It's not like you to want to talk about gossip, boss. Football, always, even when Arsenal lose! Music, sometimes. But gossip, never!'

'The headline I've heard is that a woman is in love with a man who betrayed her and got her husband and children killed!' said Ferdinand.

'Oh, I see,' said Kalisa, setting down his coffee cup.

He felt embarrassed that the news had reached Fame Construction. The relationship between Damascene and Patricia had been the talk of Gisenyi for the past few weeks. Patricia had been telling everyone, while Damascene was keeping his head down.

'News travels fast!' said Kalisa, trying to keep a light tone.

'Very few people here knew anything about their past connection before this,' said Ferdinand. 'I knew more than most, because Patricia shared a little of her story when we were—'

'Sleeping together?'

Ferdinand ignored the question.

'We were close, for a while,' he continued.

'So that's a yes, then,' said Kalisa with a smirk.

He hoped to avoid the conversation becoming any more serious.

'You kept this whole big love story a secret from people here,' said Ferdinand, 'all three of you – the victim, the perpetrator and the fun-loving little brother!'

'I'm sorry, boss,' said Kalisa, 'I don't know what to say. It was good to be working in a place where no one knew all that history. It's a big burden for them. Damascene doesn't share much with anyone.'

'What is he thinking?' asked Ferdinand.

'I don't understand,' said Kalisa. 'It was good that she forgave him but this is too much. I warned him not to get involved with Patricia in that way, but my crazy brother has packed love in his ears!'

'Was he interested in Patricia while they were working together here?' asked Ferdinand.

He thought of the good times he had shared with Patricia.

'I don't think so. It all seemed to happen so quickly,' said Kalisa, determined to defend his own reputation. 'Honestly, Ferdinand, I have no idea. If love is blind then my brother has no eyes to see!'

Ferdinand got up and walked to the window. He looked out at all the workmen, coming and going to the construction sites, and wondered about all of the secrets and untold stories of the genocide in the hearts of these men, and in his own heart too.

'Perhaps he is not blind,' he said. 'Perhaps he is not as foolish as you like to think.'

'Really?' said Kalisa.

He was surprised at Ferdinand's lack of hostility to the relationship. He assumed Ferdinand might still be interested in Patricia, but he seemed more upset at finding out through the grapevine than about the relationship itself.

'Look, it will never last. Damascene doesn't know what he's doing,' said Kalisa. 'Patricia is the most stubborn woman I know, and my poor brother will do anything she says because he feels so guilty.'

'Don't speak of Patricia like that!' said Ferdinand, sharply. 'She is a good woman. She is attractive and smart and many men would be happy to be with her. Perhaps your brother is a hero and you are the foolish one for not supporting his chance at happiness!'

This response was the opposite of what Kalisa had expected. He thought he might lose his job over this shameful revelation. He was glad Patricia had forgiven Damascene, but he could not understand how she could fall in love with him. Kalisa felt he needed to protect his vulnerable older brother because he knew better than anyone the depth of his guilt and shame. He thought people in Rwanda said all the right things about reconciliation, but he assumed this would be a step too far for many people, who secretly harboured resentment regarding the hurts of the past. However, it was becoming clear that Ferdinand was not this type of person.

'Listen,' said Ferdinand, 'we all have our story of this place. I suppose we all have our secrets. I never talk about it here, but my father is still in prison. He was a soldier in Habyarimana's national army. He trained thugs in the Interahamwe. Unlike Damascene, my father never confessed.'

'Really?' said Kalisa. 'I had no idea.'

'Why would you?' said Ferdinand. 'I don't talk about it, because it is the shameful past. I have left my father and the whole twentieth century in history.'

'I wish I could do that,' said Kalisa, 'but the past will not let me go.'

'If Damascene is able to do what no one else can do, maybe you are the foolish one for insulting your brother,' said Ferdinand.

301

Kalisa was taken aback.

'So if your sister came to my house with a machete and killed my wife, do you think I would fall in love with her?' asked Kalisa.

'But you don't have a wife, do you?' said Ferdinand. 'And that's an interesting story too, I believe. So, let's face it, you don't know what you're talking about!'

'I just don't know what that woman is up to, but I do know she's not good for my brother,' said Kalisa.

'And what would you know about love?' said Ferdinand. 'The only one you love is yourself! Any man would be lucky to be loved by Uwera Patricia.'

Suddenly both men became aware of another presence in the room. They looked up and noticed Damascene standing in the doorway. In the intensity of the exchange, they had not noticed the subject of the conversation entering the room. Damascene had heard everything. He was glaring at Kalisa.

'Follow me!' he barked. 'Thanks and see you later, boss.'

Ferdinand nodded and shrugged his shoulders. Kalisa escaped the embarrassment of the argument with Ferdinand by obeying his brother's command. Outside, the building site was noisy and the two men had to shout at each other to be heard over the clamour of machinery. Standing behind a pile of concrete slabs, they spoke freely.

'So that's how you really feel! You little snake!' Damascene shouted.

'Well, there's no point in trying to argue with you,' said Kalisa. 'I'm glad you heard it. I meant what I said to Ferdinand. Love is blind and in your case love is also stupid!'

Damascene grabbed his brother by the collar and clenched his fist.

'What the fuck are you talking about?' yelled Damascene. 'Can't you see that at long last I might be happy?'

'I'm sorry, brother,' said Kalisa, cowering below the expected punches. 'I'm just worried about you. You can't trust her!'

Damascene grabbed Kalisa by the shoulders and shook him, as if by doing so his brother would accept his words.

'I trust her with my whole heart!' he shouted.

'Please, Dammy, I am your brother,' said Kalisa. 'I love you and I want to protect you. She will never treat you like a king after you helped to kill her king! Even if she has truly forgiven, you know in your heart that you betrayed her.'

'I know,' said Damascene, 'but I was a different man then. I must do what my heart tells me today. If you loved your brother, you would not try to stop me.'

'I bet she fears every day that if there is another genocide you will kill her too!' said Kalisa.

'Are you out of your fucking mind?' said Damascene.

'She is tricking you, Dammy. She has trapped you in a spider's web. This is not love. It's a game of revenge!'

These words were too much for Damascene to bear. He punched Kalisa in the face and his brother fell to the ground with a bloodied lip.

'Genocide will never happen again and I am a changed man!' he shouted. 'No more violence!'

'Really?' said Kalisa.

He spat blood from his mouth onto his hand and held it in Damascene's face. Immediately, Damascene regretted striking his brother, snapped out of his rage and sat down beside him.

'I'm sorry, little brother. You have watched too many stupid American movies!' he said.

Kalisa recoiled and tried to move away as Damascene put his arm around him.

'Listen to me, little brother,' he said, 'you do not need to worry about me. I know Patricia's heart and the hatred is all gone. In the past, I was weak and I did shameful things, but today I am stronger because I accepted her forgiveness and love. If you can't trust her then please trust me. This is my last chance at happiness. I need you to give me this chance. Look at both of us. Neither is married and we have no children to pass on our family name. We are shaming our ancestors!'

'Huh!' said Kalisa. 'It's too late for Patricia to help you with that problem!'

The two brothers sat in silence for a few minutes, both exhausted by the events of the afternoon.

'I'm sorry, brother,' said Kalisa, finally.

'I'm sorry too, Kalisa. Just trust your big brother.'

'I do trust you,' said Kalisa, 'but I am against this madness. I will stop it if I can, and I am telling you now, I will be watching her every move.'

CHAPTER FIFTY-FOUR

'Everyone knows now,' said Damascene. 'We are the talk of the cabarets of Gisenyi!'

'Good!' said Patricia, lying in his arms on the couch. 'It's been more than three months and I do not wish our love to be a secret. But maybe some people think you are just helping to repair my roof!'

'It would have to be a very leaky roof!' said Damascene.

'I want everyone to know about our love,' said Patricia. 'It gives our children hope for the future.'

'There are other couples like us who dare not reveal the truth. They meet in secret but I come here to your house every evening,' said Damascene.

'I know,' said Patricia. 'That is their choice, but we must live our truth.'

The couple smiled, clinked their bottles of beer together and kissed before sipping.

'Some people don't want us to be together,' said Damascene. 'They fear our love. Look at Grace and Kalisa. They really think they know us so well. They are certain it will never last.'

'You are such a worrier, my love,' said Patricia.

She kissed Damascene on the cheek.

'Maybe it's because they know I don't deserve you,' began Damascene.

'Shhh...'

Patricia put her finger to Damascene's lips to stop his fretting.

'I am blessed by you. The only thing that matters is that I love you and you love me,' she said. 'We can't be the captives of the past. We all need courage to change, to make our new world. I love you, Damascene.'

Patricia leant in to kiss Damascene. He set down his beer and returned a passionate kiss. Patricia held the nape of his neck as Damascene caressed her face.

'Damascene,' said Patricia.

'Yes, my love?' replied Damascene, instinctively knowing what Patricia was about to say.

'Do you want to stay tonight?'

'I want to stay every night, beautiful woman, but only when you are ready.'

Neither had felt love and intimacy for a long time. Damascene's fleeting sexual encounters had been impersonal and forgettable, and Patricia's affair with Ferdinand had lacked the depth of love she craved.

'I am ready,' said Patricia. 'Please stay with me tonight.'

'Are you sure?'

'I always know what I want and tonight I want you. All of you.'

Patricia led Damascene to the bedroom. In the dark, they slowly undressed each other. They kissed and caressed each other's bodies and moved onto the bed. They held each other's naked bodies so close and eventually they became as one. As they made love for the first time, they shared an overwhelming sensation of freedom and passion. When Patricia cried out, the feeling of letting go was overpowering. Then Patricia and Damascene kissed and wept and fell asleep in each other's arms.

The next morning, Damascene woke first and wondered if this was what happiness felt like. Patricia's eyes were closed and her breasts were exposed to the morning light. He lay on the bed admiring the sensual curves of his lover's body and began to trace his finger along the side of Patricia's back. As the sheets fell away, he saw, for the first time, the scar on her lower back. He froze, suddenly remembering Patricia's account of the attack in 1994. In this moment, he felt he had intruded on her body and he jumped up to put his clothes on.

What sort of a man are you? he thought.

As he stood up, he noticed the picture of Bernard on the bedroom wall and felt another flash of shame.

What sort of devil sleeps with the wife of the friend he hunted to kill?

The sudden movement woke Patricia and she looked up at Damascene, seeing him completely naked for the first time. She remembered his lean torso from their teenage days swimming at the lake, and she noticed how he had gained little weight and still had the well-defined body of a younger man. Then she noticed the large scar on his thigh.

'What happened to your leg?' she asked.

Damascene was startled, unaware that Patricia had opened her eyes, and he quickly grabbed a sheet to cover the scar.

'It's nothing,' he said, unguarded. 'It was just an accident I had the day I built the outhouse…'

'What?' said Patricia.

Immediately, Damascene realised he had revealed the secret. Patricia pulled the sheet away to expose the scar.

'It was you!' she said. 'You were my secret helper and you suffered this injury to help me. And your broken wrist too?'

Damascene nodded.

'It was nothing and I didn't want you ever to know it was me,' said Damascene, angry at himself for letting it slip.

'It's a sign of your good heart,' said Patricia.

'I'm sorry, Patricia,' he said, looking again at the fading old photograph of Bernard, 'maybe this was a mistake. Maybe I should go.'

Patricia sat up and pulled Damascene back onto the bed and before he could utter another word she began to kiss and caress the scar on his thigh. The intimacy and pleasure overwhelmed his doubts like a crashing wave and instinctively, Damascene reached around Patricia's body and began to kiss the scar on her back.

'We all have our scars,' said Patricia.

They lay together kissing and caressing their scars until they could do nothing else but make love again.

'What time is it?' said Damascene, eventually waking again in Patricia's arms.

'What day is it?' laughed Patricia.

'Patricia, my love,' said Damascene, 'I promise you I will never be the same again. I will always be who you want me to be.'

'I know,' said Patricia, 'and I have decided who I want you to be.'

'What do you mean?' asked Damascene.

Patricia sat up in bed and took both of Damascene's hands in her hands. She looked through his eyes and deep into his soul and spoke words that Damascene had never dreamed he would hear.

'I want you to be my husband.'

Chapter Fifty-Five

'She's not coming,' said Kalisa.

He set his teacup down on the restaurant table.

'I knew this would be a waste of time.'

Louise realised this was not going to be easy. Kalisa arrived at the restaurant straight after work, but there was no sign of Grace and she wasn't answering her phone.

'Let's wait ten more minutes,' said Doctor Louise.

'I'm grateful that you are trying to help, Doctor, but I fear my brother and Patricia are beyond saving. I spoke to Grace on the phone last week and she agrees with me. Why would she travel the whole way to Kigali for us to discuss a lost cause?'

'Look!' said Louise, as Grace entered the restaurant.

Louise felt butterflies in her stomach, as if she was scheduled for carrying out major surgery. Feeling a great sense of relief, she quickly got up from the table to give Grace a warm welcome.

'Good evening, Doctor. Hello, Kalisa,' said Grace, shaking their hands and getting straight to the point.

'Thank you for meeting us,' she continued. 'This problem with Patricia has become serious. I was happy that they became friends, but a relationship is a bridge too far for most people. I don't know what she sees in that shadow of a man, and it's simply wrong for them to be in a relationship. How are we going to stop them?'

'Hold on a minute,' said Kalisa, 'I'm as much against this as you, but there's no need to insult my brother. Patricia is the crazy one!'

'Please have a seat,' said Louise, intervening to prevent an argument before they had even started. 'I have news. I think you will need to be sitting down. Here is some coffee.'

'What is it now?' asked Grace.

'What is going on?' asked Kalisa. 'Why did you call us? Have you heard about the anonymous threats?'

'Are they in danger?' asked Grace.

'Is she pregnant?' asked Kalisa.

'Oh my God! She can't be pregnant!' said Grace. 'Please tell me they have seen sense and decided to end this foolish relationship, for all our sakes!'

Louise took a deep breath.

'I called you here today because I am asking for help with something,' she said, 'and your support will be very important.'

Kalisa and Grace leant forward across the table with a look of confusion and anticipation.

'How can we help?' asked Kalisa. 'I'll do anything.'

'I will do what I can to stop this nonsense,' said Grace. 'I mean, I'm all for forgiveness and reconciliation, but this is going too far. People are offended!'

Louise took another deeper breath.

'I need your help with plans for a wedding,' she said.

Louise sat back in preparation for the reaction.

'A wedding?' said Kalisa.

There was a moment of silence as the penny dropped.

'Oh no!' said Grace, standing up again. 'You're kidding me!'

Kalisa and Grace turned to each other with a look of horror on their faces.

'Please tell me this is a joke, madam!' said Kalisa.

'Oh my God, they have gone completely mad!' said Grace.

'Damascene and Patricia are getting married,' said Louise.

'Married?' said Kalisa.

'Dear God, have mercy on us!' said Grace.

Kalisa stood up and began to pace around the table in the restaurant.

'He's going to get himself killed!' he said.

'He's going to get her killed!' said Grace.

'Why is it always his fault?' said Kalisa.

'Well, he has always been the one who is at fault,' said Grace.

'You speak of my brother as if he is a piece of garbage,' said Kalisa.

'They're going to get us all killed,' said Grace.

'Please,' said Louise, 'this is helping no one. No one will be killed. Please just sit down and take a breath before you say anything else.'

Kalisa and Grace sat down and said nothing for five minutes as they absorbed the initial shock. Grace sipped her coffee while shaking her head and Kalisa ordered a beer. When she thought the time was right, Louise continued as calmly as possible.

'The wedding will be in Gisenyi in December and they want all of their close friends and family to be there and to support them.'

After the initial anger, Grace and Kalisa seemed to withdraw into sadness.

'Please, Doctor,' said Grace, 'I know you are a kind and intelligent woman, but let me tell you the truth before you start talking about plans for the wedding and whatnot. I have no interest in hearing about a wedding. I love that girl, I mean, that woman, but she has no idea about what she really needs. She loves creating too much drama in her life. The facts are that she is a widow, and the man who helped to make her a widow is the very one she is going to marry! She forgave him. Yes – good! But now she must move on with her life. Has she lost her mind?'

Louise did not reply. She wasn't going to argue.

'You are wasting your time calling me to this meeting,' said Kalisa, standing up to leave. 'My brother is the most stubborn and foolish man in Rwanda! His mind has been sick since 1994. I can't do anything for him as long as he is making stupid decisions like this. Who knows? Maybe it's a trick for revenge from her and her brother in Uganda. Maybe she wants to lure him in and then break his heart and kill him softly!'

'Oh, don't be ridiculous!' said Grace, standing up.

She was offended by the suggestion that Patricia was seeking revenge.

'You are almost as crazy as your brother!' she said.

'And you sound almost as stubborn as your foolish friend!' retorted Kalisa.

Doctor Louise stood up too.

'Please listen, before you go,' she said. 'Damascene and Patricia share a history – a terrible history – but both of them want their shared future to be better. They have been courageous in confessing and forgiving. Grace, I believe in my heart that Damascene wants nothing more than to heal Patricia's wounds, and, Kalisa, you know Patricia. She left hatred and revenge behind years ago. Yes, she is strong-willed, but if she wants to marry your brother, she will be committing her whole heart to him, I know it.'

'This is too much!' said Grace.

'Crazy, crazy!' said Kalisa.

Louise was not going to back down and spoke again, firmly.

'I believe Patricia and Damascene are heroes of reconciliation,' she said. 'They are a symbol of hope for Rwanda, and for the whole world. I know you love them and want the best for them. I do too. So why not trust them, and give them a chance to be happy? They deserve to have peace.'

Grace and Kalisa did not reply. Louise picked up her handbag, shook the hands of both and walked out, leaving the unhappy duo standing, staring at one another in the middle of the restaurant.

'Oh. My. God,' they said.

CHAPTER FIFTY-SIX

Apollinaire Muhire had two goals in life: to enjoy the company of others and to take as much of their money as possible. These priorities had combined to make him the most successful cabaret owner in Gisenyi. He opened the bar in 1985 and, apart from a temporary closure in the dark years after 1994, Muhire's cabaret was the most popular place to meet for a drink with friends, to watch a football match on the ancient television, to celebrate a birthday or to sup alone to forget your troubles. Now in his late sixties, Apollinaire had been a constant presence behind the bar for decades, serving his regular customers oceans of *amarwa*[17], *urwagwa* and Primus beer and, more recently, exotic whiskies from Scotland and Ireland. He listened to the secrets of most of the local men, spilled out after one drink too many, and he was usually the first to hear and spread the latest gossip. Muhire was skilled

---

17   A beer made with fermented bananas.

in conflict resolution, preventing and de-escalating tensions and fights between inebriated customers with the simple aim of maintaining a happy, safe and profitable environment. There was no place for political fights or family feuding in this place. Muhire understood that the happier his customers, the more money he made, and so he ensured that his bar remained convivial no matter what was going on in the world outside. Tonight, in the bustling cabaret, he was serving beer and listening in on the conversation of some local fishermen, three brothers who were regular customers who worked hard, looked after their families and came here to unwind.

'I'm telling you! I saw her one day at the lake,' said Hassan. 'It was about three months ago. At first, I thought I was dreaming!'

'You were dreaming, little brother. You are always dreaming,' said Migambi.

'She told me her name – Uwera Patricia. I didn't imagine it,' said Hassan. 'I remember her name from the note I found. How could I forget it? She survived and she went to university and now she lives and works in Gisenyi again.'

'And is this the same woman everyone is talking about?' said Eugene.

'Yes,' Apollinaire interrupted, 'she is the survivor who is getting married to Hakizimana Damascene, the builder who brought the Interahamwe to her door in 1994. The hairdresser's daughter, Nana, works in her garden. The lady told the girl everything and she told her mother and now everyone who comes to the hairdresser's hears the whole story.'

'Oh yes, I heard about this couple,' said Eugene. 'So are you saying the crazy woman who is marrying a perpetrator is our beautiful lady in the white robe from the lake?'

'Yes,' said Hassan. 'She told me she had forgiven him. She said she loves him. Patricia is not crazy. It's the world that is crazy.'

'My little brother, the philosopher!' said Migambi, before swallowing the final drops of a bottle of Primus.

'Did Damascene's wife abandon him when he was in prison, like so many others?' asked Eugene.

'No,' said Apollinaire, 'neither he nor his little brother, Kalisa, ever got married. I've heard they might be strange that way. The little brother dances, you know!'

Apollinaire tapped his nose and winked.

'You are such an old gossip, Muhire!' said Migambi. 'Like an old woman! You're pretty strange too!'

The brothers laughed.

'Careful, or I'll put up the prices!' said Apollinaire. 'Damascene was lucky he was not married when he went to prison. Many wives had to go back to the fields while their husbands were in prison, and some found it easier to find another man instead.'

'That's true,' said Eugene. 'I remember release from prison was not a happy time for many men around here.'

'At least those men confessed to their crimes,' said Hassan. 'They decided to do the right thing in the end.'

'Or maybe they pretended to be sorry,' said Migambi. 'Do you think this guy Damascene told the whole truth at his *gacaca*? I know many men who didn't!'

'Believe me,' said Apollinaire, 'for some of those guys, it's safer to forget than to remember.'

'And what about those guys who never went to prison? They got away with murder!' said Migambi.

Hassan was growing impatient with his brother's cynicism. It always got worse after a drink or two.

'What made you so cynical, my brother?' he said. 'Why is it so hard for you to accept that they might be in love? Is this not a good story of reconciliation for our country?'

'Listen to me, Nelson Mandela!' said Migambi. 'This is not about unity and reconciliation. It's all about economics.'

'It's always about money,' said Apollinaire, looking towards his cash till with a smile.

'The reason the prisoners had to be released was to save the fallow fields,' said Migambi. 'If all those men had stayed in prison, many people would have died of hunger. Even the best fishermen like us could not feed a whole country!'

'So, this couple is getting married?' said Eugene. 'I've never heard of that before.'

Apollinaire tapped his nose again.

'There are secret relationships between families of survivors and perpetrators. The only difference is these two have decided to do it in public. God save the poor souls.'

'Well, I think they are an example to all of us,' said Hassan. 'We can survive the worst of times and be happy again.'

'What they are trying to do is impossible,' said Migambi. 'We can live together again as we are expected by the government, but we cannot be friends, we can't truly trust again and we certainly can't marry.'

'I've heard whispers that some people will try to stop them,' said Apollinaire.

'What do you mean?' said Hassan.

'Secret thoughts of revenge remain in the hearts of some people,' said Apollinaire. 'I hear about it when they have too much to drink. This couple could find themselves in danger with this public declaration of love. Already some threats have been whispered.'

'No!' said Hassan.

'They wouldn't, would they?' said Eugene.

'They need to be very careful,' said Migambi. 'Those who seek vengeance can find themselves avenged by the same government that says "no more revenge"!'

'Is Patricia in danger?' said Hassan.

'She's a danger to herself,' said Migambi, shrugging his shoulders and finishing another beer.

Apollinaire collected the empty glasses and bottles from the brothers' table.

'No one knows the darkness and secret plans conjured up in the human heart,' he said, 'so I think the finest fishermen on Lake Kivu need to buy another few rounds of drinks to discuss these important matters.'

CHAPTER FIFTY-SEVEN

News of the impending wedding of a perpetrator and survivor was travelling fast on the grapevine, from hairdresser's to cabarets, from fishing boats to markets, as well as rippling further afield to the offices of Kigali. The reaction was a mix of shock, inspiration and anger. On this Saturday morning at home, Damascene opened a letter from Pastor Gasongo, his spiritual advisor and counsellor from Prison Fellowship Rwanda.

When I first met you, Damascene, your heart was hard and you had no future. Today, because of your faith, humility, courage and love, you, sir, are making history. I am proud to have counselled you through all of these years. I know the depth of your shame but I want you to know the depth of my admiration for the man you have become. I pray you will finally let go of the hatred of yourself and find a way to forgive and love yourself, the same way that Patricia has forgiven and loves you, and the same way that God has forgiven and has always loved you.

Damascene wept. He wrote back immediately, asking Pastor Gasongo to conduct the wedding ceremony. The date was set for 27th December and rather than risk a public wedding in a church, the couple chose to get married in the garden of one of the shoreline hotels beside Lake Kivu. Damascene and Patricia agreed it was the perfect location for their Big Day. It would be a small gathering of close friends and surviving family, although it was still unclear which invited guests would actually show up.

Kalisa had climbed onto the sheet metal roof of their home and was moving the television antenna in different directions. He had barely spoken to Damascene for weeks now. The day he returned from meeting Doctor Louise they had another blazing row which almost came to blows. The wedding had not been mentioned since, even though it was the main topic of conversation in every other household in Gisenyi.

'Is it okay now?' he shouted from the rooftop.

'No,' called Damascene from inside the house.

'Here?' asked Kalisa as he pointed the aerial in a different direction.

'No!'

'Here?'

As Kalisa stretched across the rooftop, careful not to lose his footing, his wallet fell from his trouser pocket, bounced off the roof and fell onto the ground below, spilling its contents everywhere.

'Careful, little brother! That could have been you!' Damascene shouted.

'It will be worth it!' called Kalisa, shifting the antenna a little further.

'That's better! Just a little more!' called Damascene.

'Like this?'

'Yes! Right there, right there,' called Damascene. 'That's a good picture now.'

'Okay, brother,' said Kalisa, climbing down the ladder from the roof, 'now can we forget about your crazy wedding talk and just watch Manchester United beat Arsenal this afternoon?'

Damascene laughed and helped Kalisa to pick up the contents of his wallet.

'The other billions must have blown away!' he joked.

As Kalisa stuffed his money and ID card back into his wallet, he found a battered old photograph of the two brothers, taken in 1992, both wearing Manchester United shirts. Kalisa was only six years old and Damascene was carrying him on his shoulders like a champion. Looking at the image, Kalisa felt a mix of guilt and sadness. Damascene noticed tears in his brother's eyes.

'What's wrong?' he asked. 'Did you hurt yourself on the roof?'

'No, I'm okay, Dammy,' he said. 'I just want you to be okay too. I'm worried about the gossip. I'm afraid of what might happen next.'

'Primus?' said Damascene.

Kalisa shook his head.

'I'm off to play football to clear my head.'

In the afternoon, Madame Charlotte from the Survivors' Club visited the house.

'I just want to thank you personally for the courage and love you are showing to this community, and to the whole world,' she said.

'We are nothing special,' said Damascene. 'We are just two people in love.'

'I cannot think of anything in the world more special than two people in love,' replied Charlotte. 'You and Patricia are a living example of how our hearts can be healed through reconciliation. After your wedding, I want you to come to the Survivors' Club and tell us your story.'

'Thank you, madam, but we just want to live quietly and at peace and, to be honest, I'm not sure if my heart will ever completely heal,' said Damascene.

Madame Charlotte did not argue but she stayed for coffee. She chatted to Damascene about his work in Kigali and his hopes for the future, only mentioning reconciliation once more in a prayer before she departed.

'May the god of peace and reconciliation bring complete healing to the heart of my brother,' she prayed.

'Amen!' said Damascene.

In the evening, Kalisa arrived home from his football match.

'Beer?' asked Damascene.

'No!' snapped Kalisa.

'Come on, little brother, give me a break,' said Damascene, opening a bottle. 'You can pick the best music for the wedding day. You will ensure we are all dancing!'

'Stop trying to make it better,' said Kalisa. 'Do you know what I heard yesterday?'

'I'm not interested in gossip. I've given this town enough gossip to keep them going for a whole year,' said Damascene.

'It's not just this town!' said Kalisa. 'It's at work too! One of the receptionists at Fame Construction asked me if Patricia was pregnant and if you are the father, and God knows how she heard about it in Kigali!'

'Patricia is not pregnant,' said Damascene, laughing. 'Our love might seem like a miracle, but a baby at our age would be a true miracle!'

'I would thank God for no more miracles!' said Kalisa.

'Some people have so little going on in their own lives that they create such imaginary drama in the lives of others,' said Damascene. 'Gossiping tongues will not stop us!'

'Well, what would stop you from going ahead with this madness?' asked Kalisa.

Rather than proceed into another well-worn argument with his brother tonight, Damascene paused, took a drink of beer and said, 'There is one thing.'

'Really?' said Kalisa.

'I love her and I know she loves me, but every time I see her smile, I cannot help but remember the pain I caused her. I know she has forgiven me and it lightens the burden of my guilt, but Kalisa... I have told no one else this, not even Patricia.'

'What is it, brother?' said Kalisa.

Refraining from further hostility, Kalisa placed a supportive arm around his big brother's shoulder.

'I cannot forgive myself. Patricia has forgiven me and I know that God can forgive all of my sins, but I will never forgive myself for what I did. I just can't do it. What kind of man was I… am I?'

'I know your heart, my brother. You have been like a father to me. You did bad things but you are not a bad man.'

'Only a deeply wicked man could do what I did,' said Damascene.

'Oh, my brother,' said Kalisa, 'why can't you let go of this guilt, let go of this wedding, let go of Patricia and move on with your life?'

Suddenly there was a sharp bang on the front door of the house, causing the brothers to jump to their feet.

'What the fuck was that?' said Kalisa.

Damascene dashed to the front door and opened it to see what had caused the sudden noise. A note was impaled in the wood of the door with a machete.

Abandon her or you both die!

Damascene ran outside to see who had delivered the threat, but the culprit had disappeared into the darkness.

'Cowards!' he shouted. 'Hiding in the shadows! Come out and say it to my face!'

'Oh my God, Dammy,' said Kalisa, 'get inside before they return!'

Damascene stared into the shadows before slowly walking back towards the door. He seized the handle of the machete, extracted it from the door and threw it into the bushes. He spat on the threatening note, tore it into pieces and chucked them into the fire.

'Now this is what I feared was going to happen. That is what I call a death threat! Now will you change your mind, brother?' said Kalisa.

325

'No! That's made up my mind for me!' said Damascene, grabbing his coat. 'Do you really think that some fucking coward is going to stop me? Come with me to Patricia's house. I want to make sure she is okay.'

Chapter Fifty-Eight

'What's the matter, honey?' asked Rwibutso, as Grace tossed and turned in bed.

'The wedding invitation came today,' said Grace.

'And are we going?' asked Rwibutso. 'Patricia came to our wedding last year.'

'I can't stop thinking about it,' said Grace. 'Last week, Kalisa told me about a threat to Damascene, delivered with a machete. I am worried sick. I fear that Patricia is in great danger.'

Since hearing about the threatening note, Grace had found it hard to sleep at night. In the aftermath of the meeting with Doctor Louise, she had avoided Patricia and remained steadfastly opposed to the marriage. However, tonight, she was surprised by the response of her husband.

'I'm not so sure about that, my love,' said Rwibutso. 'How many empty threats have we heard since 1994? And how many were actually followed through? I've lost count of the threats my father got over the years. Anonymous threats in the darkness are a sign of cowardice, not of danger.'

'But I think my friend is making the biggest mistake

327

of her life, and she has suffered more than enough,' said Grace. 'What do you think?'

Rwibutso turned around and put his arm around his wife.

'If they love each other, and only love could make them do something so shocking, then why not?'

'But he is not right for her,' said Grace. 'There is too much history. He will break her heart again and it will be even worse than the first time. I cannot go to a wedding I do not support.'

'Listen, my love,' said Rwibutso, 'they are only human. They were childhood friends. Damascene committed awful deeds but Patricia forgave him. You understand this. You believe in forgiveness. You are a survivor too and look at how your own family has forgiven. Your grandpa thinks this wedding is a blessing! Human beings can change, and it's clear that Patricia and Damascene don't care what anybody else thinks. If Patricia really forgave him and truly loves him, then why not just let the love flow between their hearts?'

'You are such a romantic man,' said Grace, turning towards her husband and caressing his face with the back of her hand. 'You only see the good in people.'

As Rwibutso dozed off, Grace remained awake, eyes open, staring at the ceiling. Finally, just as the first light of day began to peek through the bedroom curtains, she smiled, nodded to herself and fell asleep.

As the countdown to the wedding day continued, Patricia was at the shop buying some treats for Christmas, when a stranger approached her and spat at her feet.

'So you are the traitor who is marrying one of the Hutu killers!' said the woman. 'The same Hutus who called me a cockroach and raped me. God forgive you, you disgusting whore!'

The other customers looked on and said nothing and Patricia felt completely alone. She was shocked and embarrassed to be attacked in public in this way, but nothing could shake her resolve.

Many miles away in the Kisenyi slum in Kampala, Albert lay slumped in the mud in an alley behind the shops, when Rachel arrived with Pastor Samuel.

'He's been drinking all weekend,' said Rachel. 'He beat Julius like a snake and almost broke his legs. I've been hiding because it's my turn next.'

Pastor Samuel bent down to speak to Albert.

'What has happened to you, brother? If you keep on along this path, you are going to die.'

'He's been getting worse for months now, Pastor,' said Rachel. 'He listens to no one. Please help him, Pastor.'

'Leave me alone,' said Albert.

Pastor Samuel noticed a scrunched-up piece of paper in Albert's hand.

'Is that the letter from your sister in Rwanda I gave you last week?' he asked.

'It's not a letter,' growled Albert. 'It's a fucking wedding invitation!'

'Albert, don't speak to the pastor like that,' said Rachel.

'Is that not good news?' asked Pastor Samuel.

'Yes, Albert,' said Rachel, bending down and stroking Albert's forehead. 'Maybe this is a good time to go back to

Rwanda for the wedding and to start a new life back home. You can get out of this slum and leave all the drugs and alcohol and debt behind you.'

'That's a good idea, brother,' said Pastor Samuel. 'Are you going to go to your sister's wedding?'

Albert staggered to his feet.

'Oh yes,' he said, 'I'm going to go back to Gisenyi for the wedding of my demented sister to the Hutu devil who betrayed her husband. I wouldn't miss it!'

Rachel and Pastor Samuel looked at each other in surprise.

'Is this the guy your sister says she forgave?' asked Pastor Samuel.

'Yes,' said Rachel. 'Albert says that guy always wanted to have his sister, and he used the excuse of the genocide to get rid of her husband.'

'But, Albert,' said Pastor Samuel, 'this is a wonderful story of forgiveness and love! It's a miracle! Praise the Lord!'

'Oh yes,' said Albert, 'it is a wonderful story, but every story needs a good ending. I've already asked one of my old friends back home to send a message to the door of my sister's fucking fiancé.'

'Don't curse in front of the pastor,' said Rachel.

'Says the sinless prostitute!' hissed Albert.

'Brother Albert, please,' said Pastor Samuel.

'The only problem is no one has the guts to follow through on what needs to be done,' said Albert. 'I'm telling you, if no one else is going to give them the ending they deserve, then I will!'

'Stop spitting hatred, Albert,' said Rachel. 'Are you going to the wedding or not?'

'Oh yes,' said Albert, 'I will be there. I wouldn't miss it. But I am not going alone.'

'Who is going with you?' asked Rachel.

'She invited my wife, Matusi, and my son, Julius,' he said, throwing the letter into the mud.

'You told her they were your family?' asked Rachel.

'Years ago,' said Albert, spitting on the ground.

'So who is going with you?' asked Pastor Samuel.

'I will go with you, if you wish,' said Rachel.

'No!' cried Albert, shaking his head.

He pushed his face so close to Pastor Samuel's face that the clergyman was overwhelmed by the smell of alcohol on Albert's breath.

'Going with me, to the wedding of the year, is the one thing those two devils deserve most!' he shouted.

'What's that?' asked Pastor Samuel.

Albert lowered his voice and hissed, 'A fucking machete!'

CHAPTER FIFTY-NINE

'Hello,' said Patricia, answering her mobile phone.

She was on the way to the shop for a final fitting of her wedding dress.

'Congratulations!' said a familiar voice.

'Who's this?' said Patricia.

'I just hope the wedding reception is not on the top floor of a hotel. I don't want to have to stop the bride from jumping off!'

'Faustin!' said Patricia.

'Yes!' he replied. 'I am so happy for you. You are a changed woman.'

'When I first met you,' she said, 'I thought my future had been swallowed up by all the pain I lived through. But thanks to friends like Louise and with support from people like you, I have learnt to live again and I am blessed to love again.'

'You are an inspiration, madam,' said Faustin.

'You must come to the wedding,' said Patricia. 'We will get married beside Lake Kivu. It's a beautiful place that is close to my heart.'

'I know,' said Faustin, 'but no swimming this time!'

'You are so funny, Faustin,' said Patricia.

'Of course I will be there,' he said. 'This is one wedding I cannot miss.'

In the shop, Patricia gazed at herself in the mirror in her white wedding dress. The sadness of Grace's refusal to accompany her for this final dress fitting was compensated by feelings of elation about the forthcoming wedding day. As she looked in the mirror, Patricia thought for a while about her first wedding day with Bernard. Then a fleeting memory flickered of six years ago when she walked into the waters of Lake Kivu in a long white robe and with a shaven head. This reminded her to ask Nana to arrange for her mother, the hairdresser, to come to the house to prepare her hair for the wedding day. Following the recent threat, Patricia did not want to risk prying eyes and information-seeking questions at the hairdresser's. However, as she walked home from the shop, in the midst of all the excitement buzzing in her head, she became aware of a nagging issue that had been at the back of her mind for some time. She resolved to deal with it that night. It was a risk she was prepared to take.

'Everyone has confirmed,' she said.

Damascene was tidying up the kitchen after dinner at his house.

'Apart from my so-called best friend and your little brother!' said Patricia.

'Maybe they love us too much!' said Damascene.

'Maybe those two are more stubborn than the betrothed couple they accuse of being the King and Queen of Stubborn!' said Patricia.

'I haven't given up on them,' said Damascene. 'I'm sure they will be there on the day.'

The couple sat down on the sofa for a relaxing night together chatting and watching television. On the news was a recording of Paul Kagame, the President of Rwanda, giving a speech on Rwanda Day during a visit to Belgium.

'What type of Rwanda do we need? A Rwanda of Rwandans. Not for Hutu, Tutsi or Twa. Not for foreigners. It's Rwanda for Rwandans. For Rwandans, I repeat.'

Damascene and Patricia held hands.

'But what I mean is this,' said the President, 'for those who usually say we are proud to call ourselves Hutu or Tutsi. It's up to you if you are proud, but you must know the value of being a Rwandan.'

'Amen!' said Damascene.

'Even my brother, Albert, is coming to the wedding, all the way from Uganda!' said Patricia. 'And I had given up hope of ever seeing him again. He wrote back to tell me he is coming with his wife and son. I hope and pray they decide to stay in Rwanda.'

'That's good news,' said Damascene. 'You deserve the perfect wedding, my love.'

'And so do you!' said Patricia.

Damascene shook his head.

'I am blessed by your love, but I deserve nothing,' he said.

Damascene attempted to put his arms around Patricia's waist, but she stiffened and moved away from him. She felt this was her last chance to face her doubts head-on.

'Damascene, I am tired of you saying that you deserve nothing.'

'But you know this is how I feel,' he said.

'Well, I do not wish to be married to a man who thinks he deserves nothing!'

Damascene was taken aback. Patricia stepped away and folded her arms.

'Are you serious?' he said.

'I love you, Damascene, and I want to be with you, but I do not wish to be married to a man I have forgiven who cannot forgive himself.'

Patricia was shocked at the sharpness of her own ultimatum. Damascene was more shocked and he sat down on the sofa with his head in his hands.

'What you are asking is impossible,' he said. 'I have found some peace and happiness with you, but I cannot let go of my shame. I just can't do it.'

'Well, I want to be married to the strong man that you once were, not a shell of a man with his head in his hands!'

Damascene looked up at Patricia in disbelief.

'So, are you saying the wedding is off?' he asked.

'It's up to you!' said Patricia, crying now. 'I want to be your wife more than anything else in the world.'

'So what is the problem?' asked Damascene.

'If you cannot let go of your guilt, I do not wish to marry you,' said Patricia.

Damascene and Patricia sat together in silence. With just days to go to the wedding, it seemed that Kalisa and Grace may have been right all along. Damascene was in shock and Patricia could not believe she may have ended the relationship so close to the wedding day.

'I will say one last thing,' she said. 'Unless you kill the devil of shame within your heart, I do not want you to show up on our wedding day.'

CHAPTER SIXTY

She had found peace. No more pain. No more hatred. An end to the despair. She gazed across the tranquil waters of Lake Kivu. The bright midday sunlight danced across the waves that gently lapped along the shore. She remembered standing on this very spot watching her father fish. She recalled walking barefoot with Bernard here. She remembered a perfect family day with a picnic on the shore and little Alice asking questions about the baby growing in her tummy. This was her place of peace. Her long white wedding dress fluttered in the breeze, framing her mature elegance. In one hand, she held three red roses she had taken from her wedding bouquet, and one by one she cast them into the lake, one for Bernard, one for Alice and one for Innocent. As each rose floated out into the lake, she affirmed her eternal love for the family she had lost. In her other hand, Patricia held a faded, water-stained piece of paper. It was the note she had written eight years ago and placed in a bottle, on this very spot, on the day she chose to give up on life. At the time, Doctor Louise gave her the note in the hospital and advised her to destroy it. Patricia could never do it, but today was the day. She took the suicide note, tore it into tiny pieces and cast them towards the lake. The faded fragments of paper fluttered in the light breeze like the first confetti of the day and drifted out into the vast expanse of water.

Patricia turned back to the hotel for the final preparations for the wedding. She smiled as she looked up at the clear blue sky and then across the garden to a neat arrangement of tables, chairs, flowers and ribbons on the lakeside. She breathed in the scent of garden flowers and freshly cut grass. Today would be a small wedding, with no dowry, few surviving relatives and only those friends who did not disapprove of such a marriage. In one hour from now, she would marry Damascene. Her ultimatum still stood but she believed in Damascene and was certain he would arrive at the altar with a heart liberated from the past. Inside the hotel, Doctor Louise was waiting to continue to assist Patricia with the final preparations, before the guests began to arrive.

'Oh, there you are!' said Louise. 'I thought you'd changed your mind!'

'That only happens to me when you're around!' laughed Patricia. 'I just had something I wanted to do alone today.'

'You look so beautiful in your silk *mushanana*,' said Louise.

She fixed the sash across Patricia's shoulder and helped the bride to accessorise her gown with hair jewellery, earrings, bracelets and armlets.

'Damascene is a very lucky man,' said Louise.

337

'Thank you, Doctor Louise,' said Patricia. 'You are my family today. You are my mother, my father and my sister.'

'It is truly an honour,' said Louise.

Jean Pierre and the boys, in smart matching white suits, were the first guests to take their seats beside the lake. Kevin and Ngabo played a game of spotting monkeys on the trees on the nearest island. Then Faustin arrived, sat beside the boys and joined in the game. Next, Pastor Gasongo arrived to prepare to conduct the wedding ceremony, welcomed by Madame Charlotte and a few of the older women from the Survivors' Club. The next group to arrive was Jacqueline and some of Patricia's colleagues from work, all dressed in colourful *pagnes*. As the seats began to fill, the cheerful wedding guests chatted in the sunshine. It was almost as if this was a normal wedding.

'I didn't expect to see you here,' said Grace.

She had just arrived with Rwibutso, Pastor Robert and her grandfather.

'I didn't expect to see you here either!' replied Kalisa.

He was seated in the front row, waiting for his brother to arrive.

'Well, who else would be his best man?' he said.

'In the end, I had to come,' said Grace. 'After all, she is my best friend.'

'And he is my only brother,' said Kalisa.

'I'll be watching him,' said Grace.

'And I'll be watching her!' replied Kalisa.

Kalisa and Grace smiled at each other.

'That's a lot of watching!' said Rwibutso.

Ferdinand arrived with his new girlfriend, prompting a discussion among Patricia's colleagues about who would be next to be married. Finally, Damascene emerged from the hotel, wearing a black, tailored knee-length shirt and pants and traditional white gloves. He stood at the front of the gathering, awaiting his bride. As he looked across the lake shore, he remembered the long summer days he spent here in his youth, with Patricia and Bernard and so many others who had not survived the genocide. He wondered if this missing generation were somehow present today for this ultimate act of reconciliation.

'Pastor Gasongo,' said Damascene, 'please pray for me to be strong today, for Patricia and our family and friends.'

'You are a stronger man than you know,' replied Pastor Gasongo.

Damascene noticed the nails through the hands of Christ on the crucifix the pastor wore around his neck. He remembered his club of nails from 1994 and prayed once more for the mercy of God.

Doctor Louise, wearing a colourful *pagne*, led Patricia towards the front of the gathering in a slow and dignified wedding procession. Turning to catch the first glimpse of his bride in her elegant long wrap skirt, beautiful bracelets and armlets, Damascene could hardly believe his life had come to this. He was entranced by the beauty of his bride. He was about to marry an elegant woman, a strong woman, the most remarkable woman he had ever known. The only woman he ever loved. He felt a sense of joy he had not thought possible. The small congregation stood up together as the handsome groom greeted his beautiful bride.

'I finally made the choice last night,' whispered Damascene. 'I killed the devil within. I finally let go of my shame. I stand here today as an unbroken man, committed to you for the rest of my life.'

Patricia smiled. She never doubted that Damascene could forgive himself. He just needed a little firm persuasion. Today, she would marry a man who was whole again.

Pastor Gasongo asked the guests to stand for a prayer, but just as the wedding ceremony was about to begin, suddenly there was a disturbance at the back of the congregation. It seemed a latecomer had just arrived. Patricia turned around to see if it was the person she hoped for. It was indeed her brother, Albert. He was straight off the overnight bus from Kampala and still carrying his bag.

'Albert! You came!' she called towards him.

Albert's presence made her wedding complete. She jumped up and down with delight, waving her flowers in her brother's direction. Albert failed to reply and nodded awkwardly as all heads turned in his direction. There was no look of delight on Albert's face.

Pastor Gasongo asked the congregation to be seated.

'You are here today to witness the joining in holy matrimony of Damascene and Patricia…'

Albert could not comprehend the scene in front of him. He was completely sober but his head was spinning with exhaustion and anger. The last time he was in this place there were bloated bodies floating on the lake, Tutsi neighbours murdered by Hutu devils.

'If any person present knows of any lawful impediment to this marriage, he or she should declare it now,' said Pastor Gasongo.

He looked up and smiled for a second, about to continue.

'I do!' shouted Albert, standing up at the back.

Everyone turned around to look in his direction.

'Albert!' cried Patricia.

'What?' said Pastor Gasongo.

He was shocked that someone had actually responded to this question, the first time in his thirty years as a pastor.

'What's wrong with you, Albert?' said Patricia. 'You are my brother. The only family I have left!'

'You cannot marry a Hutu devil! After what he did!' Albert yelled.

'No!' cried Pastor Robert. 'We don't want that sort of dirty talk here.'

'Be quiet, Albert!' said Jacqueline.

Various people in the congregation tried to intervene.

'Calm down!' said Kalisa.

'Sit down!' said Ferdinand.

'Sssshhhh!' said Grace.

'Please,' said Jean Pierre, standing up, 'I understand you are angry but please, brother, do not ruin your sister's attempt at happiness. Sit down and we will talk later.'

Albert did not sit down. Instead, he unzipped his bag and produced a large machete from within. Raising it above his head, he walked forward, towards Damascene and Patricia. There were gasps and screams in the congregation. Jean Pierre stepped forward, while Doctor Louise grabbed her children and pulled them onto the ground.

'Is this going to be another genocide?' cried Ngabo.

'No, young brother, you will be safe,' whispered Faustin.

Grace screamed and ran towards Patricia, taking her hand and staring at Albert. Kalisa also ran forward and

341

stood in front of Damascene, who had frozen on the spot. *Perhaps this is how it is meant to end*, thought Damascene, prepared to accept his fate.

'Stop, brother,' said Pastor Gasongo. 'We can sit down and talk about this. There is no need for violence.'

'That's not what he thought in 1994!' yelled Albert.

'Please, Albert!' cried Patricia, holding on to Damascene. 'This is madness!'

'You are the mad one, my sister, getting married to one of the Hutu devils that slaughtered our family! You are as bad as him. I didn't come here to celebrate this fucking insult of a wedding. I came here to kill the devil and the traitor. I came here to cut you both!'

These words produced more gasps and shrieks in the crowd, and the guests in the back rows dashed for the safety of the hotel. Albert lunged forward with the machete and the front rows scattered. Swiftly, Jean Pierre took a gun from the holster concealed under his suit jacket.

'Freeze!' he called, pointing the gun at Albert's head.

Albert was now within striking distance of Patricia and Damascene. He looked at the gun and stopped short, the machete still raised above his head. Jean Pierre prepared to pull the trigger. It was a very long time since Jean Pierre had killed a man, but today he knew he was prepared to end a life once more.

'Please, Albert,' cried Patricia, 'I don't want to lose you too! You are all I have left and I love you, my brother. Do not shoot him, Jean Pierre!'

Jean Pierre did not flinch.

'No!' cried Damascene.

He walked forward towards Albert.

'I deserve this, not your sister! No one here deserves to die but me! Strike me but spare Patricia.'

This was not the reaction Albert had expected from the monster he came here to kill. He was expecting a fight to the death.

'Noooo!' screamed Patricia.

She fell to her knees.

'Kill me, Albert, I beg you, my brother, but do not kill the man I have forgiven, the man who loves me.'

Albert held the machete over Damascene's head. Jean Pierre aimed the gun at Albert. Then Doctor Louise got up from the ground, where she was crouching with Kevin and Ngabo. Faustin held on to the boys, cowering beneath their chairs, as Louise walked forward.

'No one here needs to die!' she cried.

Albert looked into his sister's eyes. He didn't care about the gun pointing at his head. He didn't care whether he lived or died but he was confused. No one here seemed to hate him as much as he hated himself.

'I forgave him and it changed my life, Albert,' said Patricia. 'If you forgive, you can start to live again.'

Just then, to everyone's surprise, Grace's grandfather shuffled forward.

'Grandpa!' cried Grace. 'What are you doing?'

With the machete and the gun still frozen, on the verge of inflicting death, the old man spoke to Albert.

'Young Albert,' he said, 'what has happened to you?'

'Kanyarwanda?' said Albert, suddenly distracted by the old man.

'You were always a good boy in Sunday school. A kind boy with big dreams. What has happened to you?'

Suddenly Albert appeared child-like. He remembered the kind face of the man who had encouraged and mentored him in his youth.

'Genocide happened. Life happened,' he said.

'I have been blessed to see a longer life than any of you here today,' said Kanyarwanda, 'but I know I can die at peace now because I have seen forgiveness and reconciliation with these young people. Look, Albert, see beyond your hatred. See the forgiveness in your sister's heart. Look at the joy and happiness they have created today!'

'How could you forgive him, Patricia?' asked Albert.

'I forgave him for me. I forgave him for you. I forgave him for all of us,' said Patricia.

Albert looked around at the faces of the people surrounding him – familiar faces from a distant past gathered here today in hope and reconciliation. He had never experienced love like this before. It was smothering his hatred. He felt an unexpected longing for more of this kind of love in his own heart.

Louise stepped forward and touched her husband's arm and Jean Pierre lowered his gun. Albert turned around and threw the machete into the lake. The sharp blade sank into the murky depths of the waters. The splash on the lake released a huge collective sigh of relief, and Patricia rushed forward to embrace her weeping brother, who collapsed on the grass.

'You can start again here, my dear brother,' she said. 'A new life here in Gisenyi.'

'I'm sorry,' said Albert, now sobbing uncontrollably, as if letting go of eighteen years of pain. 'I am so ashamed, my sister...'

'It's okay, Albert, you are home now,' said Patricia.

'But all the other men died, Patricia. I am the only man who survived, because I fled. I am so ashamed. I ran away like a coward and I've been running away every day since.'

'You did what you had to do to survive, my brother,' said Patricia. 'Do not be ashamed. I am blessed that you are alive.'

'But I was hiding in a slum and robbing with drugs and whores,' he confessed. 'I have no wife. No kids. I lied to you. I have nothing.'

'Albert, you have a sister who loves you and a community here who will help you to rebuild your life,' said Patricia. 'We are all one Rwanda now.'

Kalisa approached and introduced Ferdinand.

'Listen, Albert, this is my boss,' said Kalisa. 'If you want a job in construction, this is the man to speak to.'

Ferdinand shook Albert's hand.

'Call me when you are settled,' said Ferdinand.

'I can also help you to get a house and a job,' said Faustin.

'Thank you, sir,' said Albert.

'You see, brother, you are not alone here,' said Patricia.

Feeling overwhelmed by the support, Albert got up and approached Damascene.

'I'm sorry for ruining your wedding, brother,' he said. 'I will repay you somehow if I can.'

Damascene put his arm around Albert.

'Just do one thing for me,' said Damascene, 'let go of the hatred. Do what Patricia did. She showed me the way. Kill the devil inside, and I promise you will be free to live again.'

Thirty minutes later, the guests reassembled and collected themselves from the drama. Pastor Gasongo recommenced the wedding ceremony, almost as if there had been no tragic interruption.

'You were a hero, Papa!' said Kevin.

'Patricia is the hero,' said Jean Pierre, 'and she has never used a weapon in her life.'

'Brothers and sisters,' said Pastor Gasongo, 'you are witnesses to a miracle today. The miracle of the healing of wounds. Remember, good people, a wound can be a place of pain and darkness. But a wound can also be a place where the light can enter your soul.'

The congregation stood as Patricia and Damascene made their vows.

'I, Hakizimana Damascene, take you, Uwera Patricia, to be my wife, to have and to hold from this day forward, for better, for worse, for richer, for poorer, in sickness and in health, to love and to cherish, till death us do part, according to God's holy law.'

'Amen!' said Pastor Gasongo.

'Amen!' cried Kanyarwanda.

'I, Uwera Patricia, take you, Hakizimana Damascene, to be my husband, to have and to hold from this day forward, for better, for worse, for richer, for poorer, in sickness and in health, to love and to cherish, till death us do part, according to God's holy law.'

Patricia and Damascene stood together, hand in hand, on the shore of Lake Kivu. Pastor Gasongo pronounced them husband and wife.

'Now you may kiss the bride!' he said.

Patricia and Damascene kissed and the crowd applauded.

346

'You have healed my scars,' said Patricia.

'You are the hope of my life,' said Damascene.

Grace and Louise threw confetti as the newlyweds began to walk together towards the hotel for the beginning of three days of celebrations. Suddenly the couple stopped as they heard the unexpected sound of music emerging from the lake. Turning around, Patricia recognised Hassan the fisherman, smiling, waving and accompanied by his brothers on their fishing boat on the lake. Doctor Louise cheered and waved at the fishermen.

'Congratulations, beautiful woman!' called Hassan, holding up a glass of *urwagwa*.

The fishermen who saved Patricia's life stood on their boat, near the shore and sang.

"'Uh'umuhisha aba bombi n'amahoro adashira!
Bazabyare bazaheke bayobowe n'umwuka wawe.'"

It was a song of hope for Patricia and Damascene, to wish them many blessings and endless peace. Damascene put his arm around his new wife's waist, his hand resting where, beneath her wedding attire, a scar remained. Patricia felt no pain.

'Everyone, sing with the fishermen!' cried Kanyarwanda. 'Sing it for Patricia and Damascene. Sing it for all the survivors and perpetrators of the genocide. *"Uh'umugisha aba bombi n'amahoro adashira!"* Sing it for all Rwandans! Blessings and endless peace! Sing it, sing it, my friends! Sing it for the world!'

As the guests sang the song, the fishermen rowed out into the lake. Hassan took an old object from his pocket.

It was the bottle he had found containing Patricia's suicide note all those years ago. He threw it as far as he could over the side of the boat, and the old bottle floated out into the expanse of Lake Kivu. Within it was a note, handwritten by Hassan Karasira, with the words:

Harakabaho Urukundo – Love Always Survives